WHITEHAVENS

WHITEHAVENS

Parker Bilal

**SEVERN
HOUSE**

First world edition published in Great Britain and the USA in 2021
by Severn House, an imprint of Canongate Books Ltd,
14 High Street, Edinburgh EH1 1TE.

Trade paperback edition first published in Great Britain and the USA in 2022
by Severn House, an imprint of Canongate Books Ltd.

severnhouse.com

British Library Cataloguing-in-Publication Data
A CIP catalogue record for this title is available from the British Library.

ISBN-13: 978-0-7278-5039-3 (cased)
ISBN-13: 978-1-78029-802-3 (trade paper)
ISBN-13: 978-1-4483-0523-0 (e-book)

All Severn House titles are printed on acid-free paper.

Typeset by Palimpsest Book Production Ltd.,
Falkirk, Stirlingshire, Scotland.
Printed and bound in Great Britain by
TJ Books Limited, Padstow, Cornwall.

'When we are near, we must make the enemy believe
we are far away;
When far away, we must make him believe we are near.'

Sun Tzu

ONE

The rain had been pelting down all morning. It played a merry tune on the tar paper roof over our heads. Outside, a ray of bright light cut through the cloud cover. Blue sparks glinted in the oily pools dotting the muddy, broken ground in front of the caff. Inside, a faint smell of burnt toast filled the air, which was thick and sluggish, like the tea. At that hour on a weekday morning the place was almost empty. People were driving. Through the grimy, bare trees, out beyond the row of parked vehicles, cars flew in both directions along the trunk road.

'There you go.'

The waitress was no more than about nineteen. A red-headed waif with nails painted black and bitten to the quick. The kid had commented the moment he set eyes on her. One of those stupid, thoughtless things that men say around other men to make themselves look tough. I ignored it, just as I ignored most of what he said.

I looked down at my plate and wondered what I had ordered and why. The daily special. There were eggs in there and sausages, along with a rather sad mound of beans perched on a raft of toast. I picked up my knife and fork and started to eat. Driving always made me hungry. For a few minutes I let my mind go blank, content with nothing but the business of eating. The clink of cutlery against porcelain, the taste of the margarine they'd smeared the toast with.

'Not bad, eh?' Zef said as he came back. I looked up. He'd had another go at rearranging his hair. It was a full-time occupation, doing his hair. He couldn't help it. The same with talking. He couldn't help that either. He just wouldn't stop.

'What's that?' he asked, nodding at my plate.

'Food. You should try it.'

'Right,' he sniggered. 'If you're looking for an early grave, that is.' He was fingering his pack of cigarettes, flicking his cheap plastic lighter. I could have pointed out the irony, but that would only set him off. I didn't care enough about him, and besides, it wasn't going to do any good. Each man to his poison.

'I'd do her,' he said.

'What are we talking about here?'

He nodded towards the counter. 'Her. Something slutty about a waitress.' He rubbed a nicotine-stained finger across his lips. 'I'd do her right here on this table, I would. With everyone watching.'

'Right.' I reached for my tea. It hadn't improved with time. I had a bad feeling this was going to be a very long trip. I dug my fork into a sausage and started sawing. 'Where'd you get a name like that, anyway?'

'Zephyr?' He gave a shrug like he'd heard the question a million times. 'People always ask that. Like, why was you named after a car?' He rolled his eyes. 'Original.'

'Understandable.'

'Right. Only it's not a fucking car, is it? It's a god.'

'A god?' I stopped chewing the piece of gristle in my mouth.

'Greek god of wind.'

'A wind god?' I managed not to smile. 'You mean like flatulence?'

'Like what?' he frowned. He wasn't sure if he was being wound up, but he didn't like it either way. I waved the question aside.

'Forget I asked.'

'OK, so this woman.' He lowered his voice as he hunched forward over the table.

'What about her?'

'Well, I mean, what does she look like?'

I looked him in the eye. 'You've seen the same pictures I have.'

'I mean, you know, the rest of her.'

I pushed my plate aside. I'd gone as far as I could with that.

'You can sit this one out, you know, kid.'

'No chance.' He sat back in his chair, jaws chomping up and down on a wad of purple gum. 'I'm looking forward to it.'

There was something about the leery cockiness of him that

invited you to slap him around, which, to be honest, I might have done if his uncle hadn't been my boss. He was small in build and maybe that had something to do with the insecurity. He told me he'd been working out recently, trying to change that flabby teenage boy's body into a man's.

'Well, just remember,' I said. 'It's strictly business. We go up there. We do the job and we come back again. We don't mess around, so don't go getting any ideas.'

'All right, grandpa. Keep your hair on. I've got it. I know what I'm doing.'

Which I doubted. I still couldn't work out why Donny wanted me to take his nephew along, but I'd stopped trying to figure out the whys and wherefores when it came to the Apostolis family.

'The thing is,' I said, leaning over the table towards him, 'I'm not that much into this whole apprenticeship deal. I'm going to do my job. As far as I'm concerned, you're just here for the ride. Donny asked me to bring you along and that's what I'm doing. But don't get in my way.'

'Or what?' He was grinning again, leaning back in his chair. 'You gonna do me an' all?'

I sucked my teeth. A piece of meat was stuck in there somewhere and I could feel it rotting already, I could smell it.

'You're here because your uncle asked me nicely. Don't think for a minute that he would question my judgement if I decided to leave you by the side of the road.'

He pushed a hand through the hair as he mulled this over. 'You and him go back a long way, don't ya?'

I wasn't interested in giving him a history lesson. I looked at my watch.

'We should get moving.'

On the way out he leaned over the counter to tug at the waitress's skirt. When she rounded on him, he laughed it off, backing towards the door, wide grin in place, pointing at her like he was Tom Cruise or something.

'You and me, darling. I'll be back.'

Outside, I waited until we were behind the car before turning and grabbing the lapels of his fancy leather jacket, slamming him up against the side.

'Hey, what you doin'?'

'Do something like that again and you'll be walking home.'

'All right. All right.' He made to brush me off, but I pushed back and held him there.

'We're not here to draw attention to ourselves.'

'OK, OK, Jesus!' He brushed the front of the jacket. 'This is quality.'

I held out my hand for the keys. 'I'm driving,' I said.

TWO

The rain eased off as we headed north. Zephyr, or Zef as he liked to be known, was keeping quiet for once. He chewed gum. He fiddled with his phone, listened to music on his headphones, and slept. I was glad of the break, happy to have a chance to be able to think.

The car was an old Jaguar XJ6. One of Donny's fleet of vehicles that he never used. It was a nice machine. Silver and sleek. Walnut steering wheel to match the fittings. The kind of vehicle that made driving a real pleasure. It had style and precision and I respected that. The professionalism of it. I needed some of that right now. The kid was all over the place. An unknown quantity. I didn't like that. So for a time, while he slept, I allowed myself to relax, getting lost in the smooth, reassuring power of the car as I steered. It took my mind off the fact that it was a while since I had done something like this.

This woman, as the kid put it, was Karima Coogan, an accountant. Early forties. Divorced. No kids. And, as the kid would have it, not bad looking at all. For six years she had cooked the books for Donny and the rest of the Apostolis family. They were what you might call a modern-day dynasty. An extended family built around the core of five brothers and sisters. Originally Greek, most of them had grown up in this country. Adonis, or Donny as he was generally known, wasn't the eldest, but he was the leader. He was the smartest, meanest one of them all. Zef's father was Donny's older brother Stavros, the most senior male and therefore the official head of the family, though in practice he was happy to leave the running of things to Donny.

Stavros had married Gina Ziyade, and therein lay something of a conundrum. Her brother Sal Ziyade was the leader of a sizeable crime family of his own, and one of Donny's rivals. The marriage should have made them allies, the way monarchies used to deal with such things of old, and maybe that's what Stavros had in mind. Take a peek under the surface of any royal family in Europe and you realize what a mixed bunch of bastards they all are. In those days it was to keep the peace. In Stavros's case, not so much. He was just smitten. Gina Ziyade, for her part, had something of a reputation. Stavros ignored this, just as he ignored the advice of his family, including Donny. But, hey, it's love, right, so what can you do? Now the Apostolis brothers were in an uneasy alliance with a rival syndicate. Call me a pessimist, but such arrangements rarely end well.

Like all crime dynasties, the Apostolis family had a legitimate side to their enterprise. They brought in furniture from the Far East, fuelling the decimation of Indonesia's hardwood forests in order to stock garden centres and furniture warehouses with crappy tables and wobbly benches. The designs were knock-off copies of items you see in classy magazines. But like everything they touched, these were rough and ready. In that difficult equation of value for money versus quality, the bottom line always won out. And as for the environment, nobody lost any sleep over that. Their other legit businesses included kebab bars, chip shops, cafés, hotels, fitness centres and table-dancing clubs. On the dark side there were a lot of drugs, construction scams, protection rackets and trafficking of illegals. As I understood it, Karima's job had been to put a nice sheen on the whole thing, to make sure that the sofas and dining tables covered other sources of income and that everything could be accounted for on the books.

The legit side of the Ziyades' operation was limited to fancy pizzerias and trattorias along with a couple of high-class restaurants in Knightsbridge that catered to the well-heeled

Middle Eastern crowd. There was a general agreement not to stir too much in each other's pots, which was fine in theory. According to Donny, the Ziyades were getting greedy, trying to edge them out of certain sectors, muscle in on Apostolis territory.

Donny was of the belief that Sal Ziyade had persuaded Karima to cooperate with an organized crime investigation. In other words, Sal was planning to sell Donny down the river in order to expand his own little empire and get the law off his back. Karima had stopped working for Donny a couple of years ago, but she knew, as they say, where the bodies were buried. Donny had no real evidence that Karima was planning to betray him, but he never allowed logic to get in the way of a plan. When he made up his mind about something, nobody could talk him out of it. And besides, he wasn't the kind of person who took chances.

The kid was still asleep when we came off the M1 and headed west into Derbyshire. We left the grey motorway behind us and found ourselves winding along lush green valleys out of which there rose rocky escarpments covered in windswept heather and glowering gritstone bluffs. The rain had eased off and water dripped from slick limestone walls towering over us as we twisted round narrow corners. The winding roads must have woken Zef because he sat up and yawned, rubbing his eyes.

'We there yet?'

'Almost.'

It took another hour to find the house. It was off a small lane behind a little village of rough, sandy walls, quaint tea shops and country pubs. We drove slowly through, then up the lane for about five hundred metres and kept going. The road ended in a small car park for ramblers. It was deserted on a weekday morning. Tall oaks and maple trees stirred densely overhead. Heavy drops splashed through the leafy canopy, drumming off the roof of the car. The kid came back from taking a piss and flipped open the boot. He fished out the fancy rucksack he'd brought along and zipped it open to pull out a stubby little submachine gun.

'What are you planning to do with that?'

'Sweet, huh?' He turned the thing over from side to side. 'This, my friend, is an Uzi Pro 9mm semi-automatic pistol.'

Whatever it was, it was an ugly piece of work, and as such perfectly suited to the person who was holding it. He unfolded the little stock and held it to his shoulder to sight along the short barrel.

'You could hurt yourself with one of those.'

He grinned. 'No fear, mate. Thirty-two rounds in a clip. You don't want to mess with one of these.'

'We're not here to take on Al-Qaida. It's one solitary lady.'

'Never underestimate the enemy.' He wagged the gun care-lessly in my general direction and I pushed it gently to one side. Those things had hair triggers and could go off without much warning, unloading a clip that would stitch you from head to tail in less time than it took to spit. 'What have you brought?'

I showed him the Browning. It was a simple work machine. Arguably, the most reliable 9mm ever produced. Up until recently it had been standard issue for most of the armed forces in the world. I had stripped this particular model down countless times and had probably replaced all its moving parts over the years. I still liked the feel of the walnut grips, the smooth mechanism, but I could dump it in a heartbeat if I had to. At the end of the day it was a tool. No point getting sentimental about it.

There was an old stile and a path that led across an open field. We walked in silence, the wet grass turning my boots and trousers damp. The air was clearing and the cloud lifting. Up ahead, the ground rose towards a slight hill. At the top of this a small copse of trees stood out against the sky. The branches, heavy with leaves, swayed back and forth in the light wind. I was sweating lightly as I came up the last stretch. The kid had bounded on ahead and now lay resting against a sandstone boulder the size of a car. He had the gun on a lanyard hanging underneath his jacket. I could see the short barrel sticking out.

I threw the shovel at his feet. 'This is where you start to earn your keep.'

He pulled a face. 'Why do I have to do it?'

'Hey, I didn't ask you to come along, so don't start whining to me. Take it up with your uncle.'

He wasn't happy, but to his credit he hopped down and took off his jacket. Setting the Uzi carefully down on top of it, he started to dig. The ground was sandy, but hard in places. There was a soft spot just behind the boulder that was perfect. I watched him hollow out a trench parallel with the rock.

'You have any idea why Donny sent you along?'

'Why?' He straightened up and leaned on the shovel, casting a doubtful look at me. 'I've been pestering him for years to let me in on the action.'

I shook my head. 'I suppose that's the bit I don't get. You're part of the family. Dirty work is not your job. You have people to do that for you. People like me.'

'Sure,' he said, pausing to light a cigarette. 'And who's going to respect me, ever, if they know I've never got my hands dirty?'

It was a fair point, but it gave me cause for concern. It suggested that underneath that youthful ambition there was a certain amount of resentment. He wasn't happy being just the son and heir of his dad's corner of the Apostolis empire, he was thinking about moving up. It wasn't a good combination. A young man with an automatic weapon and a chip on his shoulder. Not so much a dependable companion as an explosive device that could go off at any moment.

I took over the digging and after another half an hour or so we'd managed to scrape out a fairly decent hole in the ground. It sloped down under the boulder and would hold nicely for a few weeks or so. We were just off the walking path. Eventually, of course, someone's dog would come nosing around. By then, hopefully, it wouldn't matter.

'We should move,' I said. The sun was high in the sky which meant we still had plenty of daylight ahead of us. We started down the hillside and had gone no more than twenty paces when the kid called out.

'Hey, is that a llama?'

I stopped and turned. Someone had fenced a couple of them into a field. They peered at us curiously, uncomprehending, as the kid waved his gun at them.

'That would be a first. You ever bagged a llama?' He was already unhooking his gun.

'It's a defenceless creature,' I pointed out.

'Call yourself a button man. It's a dumb animal. What difference does it make?'

He was still laughing when I pushed the barrel of the Browning under his chin. 'I need you,' I said slowly, 'to stay focussed. You understand what I'm saying?'

'Lighten up, dude. Seriously. And don't forget who I am. How's it going to look if you waste the boss's son?'

I didn't move. I didn't say anything. We remained like that for a long moment, then I stepped back and lowered the automatic.

'Don't make me do that again,' I said. Then I turned my back and walked on. I could hear him swearing under his breath, but that was a lot better than the sound of the Uzi being cocked.

It was a nice house. Pretty. An old farmhouse that fitted so perfectly into its surroundings it could have been a natural feature. As though it had just sprung up out of the landscape. The slate roof had a slight dip in it. The walls were buried in thick layers of ivy and rosebushes that would soon be budding. It must have been quite a sight in the summer.

There were no other buildings around, which made it perfect for us. I signalled to the kid and we circled around the house on either side to meet up again at the kitchen door. I eased it open, stepped inside and looked around.

Everything was neatly in place. A teapot covered in a cosy stood in the middle of the round table in the centre of the room. I touched a hand to it and found it cold. A cardboard box behind the door was filled with empty wine bottles. I moved out into a short hallway that ran through the house towards the front door. I walked down this past the staircase where I stopped to listen. The whole house was silent. Behind me I could hear the kid's jaws chomping up and down on his wad of gum. The walls breathed easily. The tick of the silver carriage clock on the mantelpiece in the living room sounded like a drum solo.

I stepped inside. The room was cluttered with thick carpeting, little side tables, a standing lamp, an armchair and a short sofa covered in paisley motifs. There was a dark bookcase laden with books that had been carefully placed there by someone who cared for them. It looked like the house of a much older person than the one we had come for. On the other hand, it looked as though the person who lived here didn't really use these things. The bookcase and the carriage clock seemed to belong to another era.

Curious, I climbed the stairs looking for more information. I peeked into each of the rooms up there. A small bedroom that was filled with boxes still sealed with thick packing tape. There were no suitcases ready to leave and no signs of a hasty departure. Everything was in its place. The bedroom was probably the messiest of all. There were piles of books, this time more modern titles. I saw novels and books on the Iraq war, the Enron scandal and the financial crisis. I stood in the middle of the room and looked around me. I still had no idea who Karima Coogan really was. All I knew was that she lived alone and she didn't much like it. Either she was very smart or she had no idea what was about to happen.

A scream from below brought me down the stairs and back to the kitchen in a hurry.

THREE

K arima Coogan was wearing gardening gloves, jeans, a baggy cardigan and a red cagoule. The kid had an arm around her neck and a long carving knife held to her throat. Her long dark hair had fallen across one eye. The look on her face told me she was clearly terrified.

'Let her go, Zef,' I said quietly.

It was the first time I had used his name. I was hoping that might increase his sense that we were a team, that we were in this together, but the truth is I had no idea how he would react. It took a moment, but then he let the arm drop and propelled her away from him. I caught her and tried to help her into a chair. She wrenched herself free and stood somewhere between us, her eyes darting back and forth.

'Who are you? What do you want?'

'It's OK,' I said. 'We're here to help.'

'Help?' Her face twisted into a frown. 'To help me?'

'You shouldn't have used my name, man.' This from Zephyr, who had perched himself on the kitchen counter and was now playing with the carving knife as if trying to decide what to stick it into. Karima Coogan's eyes were fixed on him.

'I'm calling the police,' she said, reaching into her pocket.

'There's no need for that,' I said quietly. 'Like I said, we're here to help.'

'He doesn't look like he's here to help,' she said, glancing at Zef.

'You startled him,' I said, trying to sound reasonable. 'You walked in without warning.'

She laughed bitterly. 'I live here. I have a right to walk in. You, on the other hand, have no right to be in my house.'

She had the phone out now and was tapping the screen.

'You're making a mistake,' I said.

'We'll let the police decide that,' Karima said.

I could see Zef was getting ready to reach for his little toy. I shook my head at him, not sure he would pay any attention to me.

'Donny sent us.'

'Donny?' Karima folded her arms and addressed me. 'Why don't we back up a little here? You could start by telling me who you are and what you're doing here.'

'Like I said, Donny sent us. This is his nephew.'

She looked at the kid. She didn't look convinced. I had hoped this would reassure her somehow, the fact that Donny would send his nephew. Though I could see that the idea of the kid inspiring confidence in anything was a little unlikely. She certainly didn't look too reassured.

'Am I in some kind of danger?' she asked.

'Donny just wanted us to make sure you were OK.'

Her eyes searched mine. 'Why wouldn't I be OK?'

I felt a little out of my depth here. This wasn't what I had been expecting. She was a good-looking woman, smart and confident with it. The kind of woman who didn't have a lot of time to waste on a couple of losers who showed up in her kitchen.

'There's a . . . situation, with a rival firm,' I said.

'What kind of situation. Are you saying I'm in some kind of danger?'

'Donny just felt it would be better to play it safe.'

That didn't entirely convince her.

'All right, so now you're here. What happens next?'

'Nothing. We sit tight and wait for him to call.'

She said nothing, but I could see she wasn't happy.

'Why don't we just call him?' She held up her phone.

'You know how Donny is. He likes to do things his own way.'

Karima took a deep breath. She didn't like the situation, but was prepared to go along with it, for the time being.

My main concern was with the kid. We hadn't really rehearsed this part, largely because I didn't trust him to keep an idea in his head for long. Somewhere I read that humans have shorter attention spans than goldfish. Looking at Zef, I could believe that. Every thirty seconds or so his mind turned back to his favourite subject. Even now I could see him eyeing her up. I'd told him to just play along. Keep quiet and follow my lead, I'd said. We'd already seen how that could work out. I didn't want her spooked. We needed her to cooperate until we could get her out of the house. It was too risky doing it here. As soon as she was reported missing the cops would be all over this place with a forensics team. It was better that she just disappeared, with no sign of a struggle. Just an empty house.

'Nice place you have here,' I said. She looked at me as if I was taking the piss, then moved across the room to wash her hands at the sink, ignoring Zef, who went to stand in the corner by the back door.

'It belonged to an aunt of mine,' she said.

Which explained the knick-knacks and the dinky furniture. Zef was staring at her ass as she leaned over the sink.

'There's nobody else living here, right?'

She glanced over her shoulder at me, hesitated, then gave a short nod.

'There's no need to be alarmed.' I tried to smile. 'Like I said, we're here for your safety. We came in because I thought it was better to wait inside than out there where everyone could see us.'

'Right. Because it gets so busy out there.' She looked at the garden and the deserted country lane beyond. 'I didn't see your car.'

Karima Coogan was a smart woman. Certainly she was smart enough to see right through us.

'We decided to stretch our legs, so we left it up the road in the car park.'

She didn't respond. She picked up the teapot and realized it was cold.

'I'll make some more,' she said.

'Do you have any coffee?' I asked. I'd had enough tea for one day.

She stood there looking at me before setting down the pot.

'I can make coffee.'

I was intrigued. It takes balls to stay cool in a situation like this. Two strange men break into your home and hold a knife to your throat and she was carrying on like it was the most normal thing in the world.

'Do I know you?' She was still staring, trying to place me.

'No.' I had never seen her before. I was pretty sure of that.

'Your face looks familiar.'

I didn't like that. The idea that she might know me made it personal in a way that I wasn't comfortable with. She switched to the kid.

'So you're Stavros's son, right?'

The kid nodded, suddenly shy. The barrel of his gun was nosing out of the side of his jacket.

'Maybe take a walk round the building,' I suggested to him.

'Sure, but first I need to take a crap,' he said. He looked at her. 'If that's all right?'

She didn't blink. 'Help yourself. It's at the top of the stairs.'

He glared at me as I stepped aside for him.

'You have to excuse his behaviour,' I said when we were alone. 'He's new to this.'

She held my gaze steadily. 'He could have killed me.'

'He's a little jumpy. You took him by surprise.'

'I took him by surprise?' Her eyes widened in disbelief for a moment, then narrowed. 'I'm in some kind of danger, right? Who from?'

'Person or persons unknown.' I shrugged, trying to play it down. 'People on the outside.'

She stopped pouring tea into the sink. 'What kind of people?'

'The kind who want to hurt the family.' I could see she needed more. 'Look, I'm really not sure of all the details, but as I understand it you know a lot. Your work for Donny makes you a valuable asset. There are those who want to use that against us.'

'And that's why Donny sent you?'

'He cares about you.'

'Really?' She was looking at the table, her hand clawing softly at the cloth, like a cat trying to decide which way to jump. Karima Coogan was smart all right. Smart enough to believe she could still think her way out of this one. Right now she was trying to figure how far to go along with the fairy tale I was trying to spin.

'Like I said, Donny thinks these certain people have their own interests at heart. He's afraid they might try to hurt you to get at him.'

'So you're saying what, they might torture me?'

'We don't want to alarm you, Mrs Coogan.'

'It's Ms Coogan. I'm not married.'

'My apologies. May I?' I indicated the chair opposite her and waited for her nod of approval. It was still her house, after all. She had stopped clawing the tablecloth.

'Haringey, five years ago.' Close up she had small crow's feet in the corners of her eyes. Light, but they were there. They tightened when she studied me, and somehow it made her look more interesting. 'Donny's sister Maria. It was her daughter's wedding. There was a fight. You drove me home.'

It came back to me. She had been different then. Younger.

Thinner, too, as in skeletal. I remembered that she had been wearing a slinky black evening dress. Glamorous. Her hair had been shorter, or maybe pinned back close to her head.

'You got into a fight with someone?' I recalled.

'Michael.'

Another of Donny's nephews. A hothead usually off his nut on coke and whatever else he could find.

'He said something about my ex.' She ran a finger along the edge of the table. 'I was a mess. I remember it because that's around the time I began to start having doubts about what I was doing with my life.'

I didn't remember what the fight was about. I just remembered dragging Michael out of the way. He was always making an embarrassment of himself and the family. He had a temper and a tendency to pull a knife, even though he was a scrawny little bastard. Donny had told me to drive the woman home. I had forgotten.

'What's this I hear?' Zef asked as he came back into the room. 'You two know each other?'

'We've met,' I said, my eyes still on Karima. 'I didn't know you were an accountant back then.'

She shrugged as if it made no difference either way. I could remember thinking she was probably a dancer from one of the clubs, a hostess perhaps. Never make assumptions about anyone or anything. There was more to Karima Coogan than I had realized.

Zephyr was glaring at me. 'Can I have a word?'

'Don't go anywhere,' I said to Karima. 'We'll be right outside.'

She just looked at me without saying anything. It wasn't that I expected her to try and do a runner, I just wanted to establish some kind of an understanding between us. The kid didn't care. If she took off it would give him an excuse to use that pop gun he had slung under his jacket. We stepped outside and I closed the door behind us. We stood in the garden where we could see her through the window. She stood there staring into space.

'What's going on here?' Zef was snapping his lighter furiously until he got enough of a flame to light his cigarette. 'She knows you? That's fucked up.'

'It's fine. It was a long time ago.'

'Something's not right,' said Zef. He was puffing away and pacing. He spun round to jab a finger at me. 'She knew we were coming.'

'How do you work that out?'

'It's obvious, stands to reason. This was all supposed to go like clockwork. Now she knows who you are and she knows who I am.'

'What difference does it make?'

'What difference? How can you ask that?' He poked a finger at me, shoving his face into mine. 'Let's just do it. Right now. Get it over with and get out of here.'

'What's eating you?' I knew he was nervous, but I hadn't expected him to unravel so quickly.

A shudder went through him. He shook it off and glanced over his shoulder. 'This place gives me the creeps.'

'We're sticking to the plan.'

'No, no way, not now.' Zef was shaking his head. 'It's too risky. She knows something, I'm telling you.'

'Listen to me, Zef. You need to get your shit together.'

'This is no good. I have a bad feeling.'

'You sound like an old woman. I thought you wanted this.'

'I do, I just, you know. Why can't we do it here?'

'It has to be away from the house.' I stared at him. 'You understand that, right? We leave no traces here. She has to just disappear.'

'Why? I mean, somebody's going to find her.'

'You mean, eventually? Yes, somebody's going to find her. It's a matter of time.'

In a couple of weeks we would be out of the picture. Nobody would remember us, not even the waitress in the café. I wasn't sure he got it. I glanced back. Through the window I could see Karima looking right at us. Our voices were low and I was fairly sure she couldn't hear us, but there was something about the expression in her eyes that made me think she knew exactly what was going on. I took my phone out of my pocket and walked in a circle, pretending to be having a conversation. When I'd finished I came back to Zef.

'What was all that about?'

'That was the call we've been expecting. Just do as I say. We go back in. We drink our coffee and then we take her out for a walk.'

'Why would she go with us?'

I made an effort to speak slowly and calmly. 'We stick to our plan. We're here to take care of her. We're taking her somewhere safe.'

He was already shaking his head. 'She's never going to believe it.'

I carried on as if I hadn't heard him. 'We get her to walk back up the hill with us. We take care of things and then we go home.'

He clenched his teeth together so hard a vein bulged in the middle of his forehead. I wondered if Donny had been at all like this when he was young. I knew the answer. The Apostolis boys grew up on the streets. Their parents were poor. Donny and his siblings grew up without a lot of money, and they did what everyone does when they suddenly have a lot of it – they spoiled their children rotten. It wasn't Zephyr's fault that he was soft, it was his father's. That would have worked out fine if he'd gone into business, started running restaurants or holiday cruises, whatever. No matter how much money they had, though, they were still who they were, who they'd always been. They'd planted the seed, and now the kid thought the only thing in the world he wanted was to become a tough guy. It wasn't hard to see how that was going to work out.

'I need you to stick with me on this, kid. Just follow my lead and we'll get this done. Do what I say and don't talk.'

He wasn't happy, but he could see that he didn't have a choice.

'I made coffee,' said Karima as we came back inside. She'd also put out a plate of biscuits. Bourbons. Zef grabbed a handful and retreated into his corner. He munched away, staring at the floor. He looked like a caged animal.

'Do you have any milk?' I asked.

'Sorry,' she said. 'In the fridge.'

I went over to find it.

'Donny used to talk about you,' she said. 'I remember now.'

I sipped my coffee. It was good and strong and actually tasted of coffee. Every time she opened her mouth I was worried about what she was going to say.

'You know Donny,' I said with a smile. 'Half of what he says is crap, and the other half isn't worth remembering.'

I felt Zephyr shifting behind me. It probably wasn't the done thing, to talk of the boss in such disrespectful terms, but I needed to get her confidence, and besides, I'd been around Donny for long enough to have earned some privileges.

'He said you saved his life.'

'Not one of my most glorious moments. He was choking on a piece of steak. I performed the Heimlich manoeuvre.'

That brought a smile. 'So, a man of many talents.'

I didn't know what that meant. I couldn't see the kid's face but I could imagine the smirk. I looked at my watch.

'Maybe we should get moving.'

'Where are we going?' she asked.

'That was Donny on the phone, calling to confirm. We have a safe house a couple of hours away.'

'Where exactly?' She didn't like the idea.

'Place called Greystoke, up in the Eden Valley, near Penrith.'

'I don't know it,' she said, which was the idea. I'd never heard of it until I saw it on a map that morning. 'How long will I be gone? I'll need to pack a few things.'

'Just take the essentials,' I said. 'It's a very comfortable place. And if you need anything we can get it for you.'

When she had gone, Zephyr got to his feet and wandered out into the hall.

'She's up to something,' he said when he came back.

'Relax, will you.'

'One of us should have gone up there with her.'

'Why? Are you thinking of jumping her while she's packing her smalls?'

'That's not the point,' he hissed. He was fiddling with his gun.

'Relax. Why don't you make yourself useful and do the washing up?'

To my surprise, and with a good amount of grousing, he actually did. My phone rang. This time it really was Donny. I stepped outside and shut the door behind me.

'Where are you?'

'We're with her at the house.'

'Good. Good.' There was a long pause. I didn't like that.

'I told her we were taking her to a safe house.'

'Nice. I like that. And she's good with that?'

'Yeah, yeah. Once we get away from here we'll take care of business.'

'OK.' Another pause. Donny was getting ready to tell me something. Usually, that meant bad news. When it came to changing plans at the drop of a hat, Adonis Apostolis was king.

'I need you to listen to me very carefully,' he said.

Through the window I could see Zef at the sink, rinsing out the coffee pot. Maybe he wasn't such a bad person. Maybe he'd just suffered from having bad people around him all his life. Terrible parents who did nothing but throw money at him. Over his shoulder I saw Karima come into the room behind him. Donny was speaking again.

'I want you to take care of the kid.'

'Come again?' I thought I hadn't heard right. 'What did you say?'

'You heard me.' Another pause. 'I said take out the kid. Get rid of him.'

'Donny . . . What are you saying?'

'Listen to me, you need to do it quickly and painlessly. I don't want him to suffer. Don't give him a moment to realize what's happening. I don't want that on my conscience. Can you do that?'

'I don't get it, Donny. Are you sure about this? All due respect, but he's just a kid.'

I could see through the window that the two of them were talking. I wondered how they could have suddenly found so much to chat about.

'You work for me, remember? I don't have to explain why you have to do something. You just do it.'

'Sure, I get that. And most of the time I'm fine with it. This is different.'

'For fuck's sake, Brodie!' Donny exploded. 'I'm not debating this.' There was silence for a moment. The line was deathly still. When he came back on, Donny's voice was low and measured. 'You've been with me for a long time. We've seen things. So I'm going to tell you. The kid's a problem. I'm livid. He's been doing things, getting ideas above his station. Can you believe that? Well, there have to be limits. I mean, where would we be without that, right?'

'You can't spring something like this on me, Donny. He's family. He's Stavros's son. He's your nephew, for Christ's sake.'

'You know, every Easter, in Greece, we burn Judas. Like Guy Fawkes, you know?'

'An effigy.'

'Right, just what I said. He turned on his family. On me. There is nothing worse than betraying your own people. He's no longer one of us.'

The more I heard, the less I liked. The kid was looking out at me. I needed to get back in there before he said something he shouldn't.

'What about her?'

'Her?' Donny sounded offended. 'What about her? I'm beginning to wonder about you, Brodie. You getting soft in your old age?'

'So, you want me to do both of them?'

'Christ! Am I speaking in sign language here?'

'Donny . . .'

'Don't start whining, OK? I've had it up to here.' There was a long sigh. 'The kid went behind my back, cut himself a deal with the Ziyades. He's got some balls on him, I'll give him that.'

'The Ziyades? You're sure about this?'

Donny wasn't listening. 'He's confused,' he went on. 'Doesn't know where his loyalties lie. They offered to make him a king and in return the little shit has promised to give them my balls in a vice.'

'I thought the Ziyades were family? His mother.'

'Don't be ridiculous. They're fucking Arabs. My stupid brother was sucked in by that tart. They're our enemy. Believe me, they've been trying to get me for years. And now they've got one of their own on the inside.'

I realized there was no point protesting further. Right now, the smartest thing I could do was stay silent.

'I want him gone. I never want to think about this again.'

'If you're sure that's what you want.'

'Just do it, Brodie. I don't care which one of them you do first, right? Just get it done. I can feel a migraine coming on.' He fell quiet again. I could hear his heavy breathing. He was thinking about the consequences. 'One last thing. You can never mention this to anybody, right? As long as you live.'

'You know me.'

'You're the only one I can trust, Brodie. You understand that?'

'Sure, Donny.'

'Good. Let me know when it's done.'

He hung up. I stood there holding the phone. Through the kitchen window I could see them chatting. The kid had a dreamy look on his face, like a teenager talking to an older woman he fancied. It made him look ordinary, vulnerable. I almost felt sorry for him.

FOUR

B y the time we left the house the sun was sinking towards the stubby outcrops. I led the way up the narrow track. The llamas had vanished from sight, nowhere to be seen. Nobody said a word. We walked in single file with the kid bringing up the rear. He had Karima's overnight bag slung over his shoulder. My mind was distracted. I didn't like surprises and there was a lot that bothered me about what Donny had just asked me to do. It went against everything I knew about him, everything I knew about the Apostolis family. Worst of all, I couldn't see how this was going to play out.

The high, dark trees on the hilltop loomed over us like brooding sentinels. The wind was picking up and black clouds drifted in, hinting that it was going to start raining again any minute. I felt sick. I just wanted to get this over and done with. When we reached the top, the kid started moaning about needing a break.

'OK.' I waved him off and watched him lean against the

side of one of the giant boulders, dropping the bag on the floor and taking his cigarettes out. Karima wandered a few paces off in the opposite direction. I watched until she was close to the escarpment. Silhouetted against the sky, she had her hands in the pockets of her leather jacket as she gazed out over the open landscape. I wondered what kind of a life it might be to live here, in that house, at peace with the world, with nature, and have someone like her to share it with. I was worse than the kid when it came to getting sentimental.

'Not a bad place to live,' I called, trying to make conversation.

'You shouldn't have come here,' she said, turning to look back at me. I sensed danger.

'Now why would you say something like that?'

'Donny never trusts anyone completely.' The wind blew her hair around her face. She pushed it aside, holding it out of her eyes. 'That's why I left. Because there's always another story, and sooner or later, no matter how close you think you are, no matter how much you convince yourself that you're one of them, one of the family, the truth is that you never are, and never will be. There will always come a time when they will turn on you.'

'We're not here to hurt you,' I reminded her. 'Donny sent us here to help you.'

'It's OK.' She smiled. 'I know why you came.'

'No, you don't understand.' I took a step towards her. 'We're taking you to safety. You're not in danger.'

She was backing away from me, getting close to the edge. I had the feeling she was getting ready to jump.

'Wait.' I lifted my arm to stop her, afraid of what she might do, not realizing that she had already done it. The bullet punched into me like a screwdriver being stabbed into my left side. I felt it before I heard the shot. The force spun me round and I went down on one knee. The kid was standing there with his stupid popgun in his hand. He must have set it on single shot, which either meant he didn't want to kill me, or that he was planning to take his time. He stood there, a cigarette dangling from his mouth, like some cheap hood in a movie.

'Don't fuck with the Zephyr.' He grinned.

I pressed a hand to my side and it came away bloody. I felt faint, nauseous. If I passed out I would bleed out. It wasn't the first time I'd been shot. I knew I was going into shock. I tried to stand up but found I had no strength. I sank down again and this time went all the way, rolling on to my back. I lay there, unable to move. High above me the canopy of trees swayed back and forth as if caught in a heavy tide.

The kid stepped into view, blocking out the sky.

'She told me all about it,' he said, nodding over towards Karima. I tried to look at her, but couldn't turn my head far enough.

'Told you what?' I gasped.

'While you were on the phone outside. She told me about the money.'

'What money?'

'The half a million she took from my uncle. That's why he wants her dead.'

I started to laugh. I couldn't help it. The absurdity of it all. He didn't like that.

'What? What are you laughing about?'

'She's winding you up,' I gasped. 'Turning the tables.' I was having trouble breathing. I wondered if the bullet had punctured a lung. 'Think about it, kid,' I wheezed. 'Half a million? That's peanuts compared to what's waiting for you.'

'I get it.' He was trying to laugh now, managing only a strange hiccupping sound. 'I've seen you eyeing her up. Well, she chose me, old man, and we're going to take off, with the money.'

'Why? You don't need to even try. You've got it made. You understand, kid? You're the heir to a fortune.'

'You're not talking me out of it. I need to do this. For me. You know, like in the old days?'

'What old days? You're talking legends? King Arthur and the fucking grail?'

I didn't know why I was bothering. Somehow all of this tied into something that had been building up inside him for god knows how long, years maybe. That ship had sailed.

'Uncle Donny never liked me. Always saw me as soft. A spoilt little brat, never tough enough for him.'

'No,' I began, struggling to speak clearly. My tongue was slurring the words. 'You were the prodigal son, until you decided to try and cut a deal for yourself with the Ziyades.'

'What are you on about?' Zef was frowning at me. I wasn't surprised that he denied it. After this, shooting me, his game was up. It would be too dangerous to go back to London.

'She read you like a book, kid. She played you.'

'No,' he said, shaking his head. He came over and squatted down beside me. I tried to see where Karima was behind him. 'Tell me the truth, did Donny ask you to take care of me?'

'Come on, kid. He's your uncle.' I could feel my legs going numb. I felt cold. If I didn't get help quickly I would die on this hill.

'Exactly. He'd never forgive me.' He straightened up. 'Well, old man, too bad your lessons didn't pay off. No hard feelings.'

'Be smart, Zef. How far do you think you'll get? Donny has eyes and ears everywhere.'

'Half a million can buy a lot of space, and I intend to keep moving.'

'How long do you think she's going to stick by you? She's already played you once. She'll be gone before you know it. Hell, she's probably already long gone.'

That touched a raw spot. He looked round, over towards where Karima had been a moment ago, and I saw it in his face then. The loss, the failure, the betrayal. The utter conviction that life would never be fair to someone like him. The sense of disappointment all spoilt children carry with them. The knowledge that in the end, despite all the money and opportunities he'd inherited at birth, he would always be a loser. That's when I shot him through the heart.

I felt rather than saw him fall, and together we rolled the last few feet into the shallow grave we had dug earlier that afternoon. I wound up on my back with the kid lying across my legs.

I was gasping for breath. I could smell the dead leaves and taste the earth in my mouth. This was it. I stared up at the sky and the wonder of the trees swaying up there. There was something majestic and beautiful about the sight. Eternal. I felt at peace for the first time in a long, long time.

In the end it's the things we can't learn that do us in. The things it's impossible to pass on, to teach anyone. The understanding that takes a lifetime to acquire. It's as if the world is constantly trying to remind us that there are aspects to this vast complex universe that we will never grasp. And maybe that's what life is really about. The unknowable. The unteachable. The things we strive for but will never grasp. I felt the suffocating weight of the earth beneath me, drawing me in, ever closer.

FIVE

We spend our lives waiting for death, preparing for it, and most of all trying to avoid the inevitability of it. But it's there, coming steadily down the track to meet us, no matter how hard we try. Everything we do, every act, every breath, ushers us towards that final exit. When it comes, more often than not you're going to be unprepared. I've seen that look of astonishment a few times. The brief flash of enlightenment as it dawns that this is it. That what is about to happen is as real as it can ever get. No playbacks, no get-out-of-jail free card. Just the never-ending darkness closing in. The big sleep.

I knew what it was. I'd seen it coming for me enough times. I'd been shot before. In the army. In Afghanistan and later, when I was freelancing for an outfit in West Africa. But nothing, not even that, prepares you.

The pain came in waves. I could feel it digging through me, leaving me numb. I couldn't feel anything but pain. I wanted to tear it out, but I couldn't move. It was a shadow hovering just over me. A darkness that was outside me, trying to draw me in. And it was inside me, too, at the same time, churning up my guts.

I've been in the business of death for longer than I care to recollect. In places I had never heard of before I was there.

In most cases the person on the receiving end doesn't deserve it. But that's not the point. Nobody ever said life was meant to be fair. We didn't ask to come into this world. We were brought in. How or why is a matter for priests, or physicists who can explain how time bends, and distances grow shorter or longer. There are things in this world that we are never going to understand. You can try to get down to the nuts and bolts of it, how particles fit together and all that, but it's never going to change the facts. You have one life and when it ends, baby, you're done.

I wasn't. That was the first thought that went through my head when I opened my eyes and saw the light fluttering. This wasn't death. This was transition.

Religion has never really interested me. Although I will admit to having a certain superstitious inclination. Black cats and all that. Certain rituals that should never be neglected. How you dress. How you prepare. That's where it all comes from, in my humble opinion. Trying to cover the Not Knowing. That's what makes you avoid the cracks, or touch wood, or double check the locks, or take your gun apart three times before a job. Not twice, not four times. Why three? I can't explain that. It's just the nature of things.

That's what it comes down to. If I believe in anything at all, it is that we are born with a way of understanding the world that is hardwired into our systems. Two million years of evolution, most of that learning to survive with nothing but your wits. Learning to run, to hide. When to hunt, when to stay in your cave. All of this learning is stored inside us. Thanks to modern living we've just managed to forget a lot of it. That's why I believe in trusting your instincts. It's out of fashion, as everyone keeps telling me. Nowadays we can't take a piss without an app to tell us where and when.

The light came and went, dotting on and off intermittently. I thought I was imagining it, that this was a symptom of my mind closing down. I thought about my life and what it all added up to, but my thoughts were confused and the light went out again before I could reach any meaningful conclusions.

But the flashing light persisted and I wondered if perhaps I might be wrong. If this might be real. In which case it was not one light but many, a string of them skimming by overhead. There was something beautiful and mesmerizing about it. Hypnotic. Like flying saucers, or slow-moving stars shooting gently across a velvet sky. It was soothing.

My mind started leading me back to my childhood. I can't explain why. Perhaps it was that sense of feeling safe inside something that had purpose. I remembered that in primary school we would stand in the assembly hall every morning and recite the lines to the Lord's Prayer. In those days it was obligatory, none of that nonsense about all things being equal, or where your family came from. Black, white, brown, Hindu, Muslim, Sikh or Christian. It made no difference. We all spoke those words, not even understanding what they meant or who they were for. It was tradition, the way things were done. What you actually believed in was beside the point.

So I stood there and murmured along with the rest of them. I knew the words and as you spoke them you were drawn into the rhythm of that hall full of people all speaking in sync. I remembered feeling as though I was a part of something much bigger than me, something I could barely perceive the scale of, but it was there, all around me. I was inside it.

A part of me knew it was false, that the words we were saying were a lie, that we didn't really believe them, that this sense of belonging was just another way of making us feel small. I didn't like that. Even then. It didn't sit well with me.

I'm not so much a spiritual person as a lifelong sceptic. Let's face it, most people use religion to hide behind. If God exists, and I have my doubts about that, but if He has any power at all, then He should be able to see into your heart, no matter what colour you are, or what beliefs you profess. If the Almighty was up to scratch He'd be able to distinguish between the good and the bad when the time comes, rather than judging on how low you bow to Him.

I stared at the lights flicking by over my head. Everyone goes into shock when they are shot and don't let anyone tell you otherwise. No matter how many times it happens to you. It's the body going into survival mode. It's been attacked and needs all of its resources focussed on healing. I'd been here before and I recognized certain things.

I began to fade once more, falling into deep sleep, lulled by the comfortable motion of the car and the sense that, so long as we were moving, I was safe.

When I woke up again we were still moving and I was still alive. The pain had come back. The lights, I suddenly realized, were at intervals on a motorway. Lit up exit and entry ramps. I tried to work out which direction we were going and soon gave up. I couldn't see the stars. If I were to have hazarded a guess, I would have said south back to Donny, but I couldn't be sure. All I did know for certain was that I was lying in the back of the Jaguar. And that I was alive.

Sometime later I tried to speak. At first nothing came out but a faint croak. I swallowed with difficulty and tried again. Louder this time. What came out sounded nothing like me.

'What did you give me?'

There was a long pause. I could feel rather than see a shadow in the front on the driver's side. I recognized her when she turned to look back over her shoulder at me.

'I had some codeine tablets. I thought it would help with the pain.'

'The kid?'

She hesitated, then, 'He didn't make it.'

After that there was silence. The blackness swam in over me again like a tide and I faded out. I had other questions, but somehow none of them mattered any longer. I was on a journey in a strange land. I was far away. I saw the faces of people I hadn't thought about in years. My mother was there. Old mates from the army. Men I knew were dead. Men I had killed. I saw them all in the beads of light dripping across the sky above me.

I was flying through the dark air, floating on a current of water that was so light it kept me from sinking. We were in the Jaguar, heading along a motorway. The kid was dead. I was alive. I felt the ruts under the wheels, the unevenness of the road, the metronome beat of the wipers fighting rain, the hiss of wheels on wet tarmac. It was dark. She was driving. I was still alive. Zef was dead. Everything else would have to wait.

SIX

The room was dark save for the orange sodium light that streamed through the lace curtains on the window. I watched the rain shadows chase each other down the wall opposite. I'm not sure how long I stared at it. Maybe minutes. Maybe hours. How long had I been here? Hours, days, weeks? I wasn't sure where I was. It felt like a house. Old and silent. There wasn't a sound from the street, just the hiss of the rain against the glass and the soft moan of the wind.

I could remember only flashes of what had happened to me. Some of it had come back. Being dragged down the hillside to the car. How had she managed that? More importantly, why?

I felt pain in my arm and realized it was hard to move. With my other hand I explored slowly. A drip catheter had been inserted just above my wrist. A tube snaked up to a bag hanging from a stand. I had a slightly numb feeling all over and assumed that I was under the influence of a powerful sedative. I'd been given morphine in Fallujah when I caught a piece of shrapnel from a mortar in my thigh. It went in an inch away from my femoral artery, which would have been the end of my story right there. I moved my hand slowly around my body, trying to assess the damage. Zef's bullet had gone into my right side, low down. I could feel the bandage. It felt tight. Someone had done a professional job. I tried to sit up just to test if I could and discovered that I couldn't. I gave up trying and fell back again to stare at the ceiling. The soft patter of the rain seemed to fall through my thoughts, washing them away.

When I woke up again it was daylight. Afternoon, I imagined. The next day? Later? There was someone in the room with me. I could feel them moving around just out of sight. I turned my head and saw a woman I'd never met before. She was in her late thirties or early forties. Blonde, with a square set face and strong jaw. Her hair was cut in a practical rather than stylish manner. She wore trousers under her white coat. Realizing that I was awake, she came and stood over me, hands in her pockets.

'How are you feeling?'

My throat was dry and she handed me a water bottle with a straw and helped me to drink.

'Are you the one who patched me up?'

'That would be correct.'

'Looks like you did a good job, Doctor . . .?'

'Mallory. I'm not going to ask you your name. Karima told me it was better not to know.'

'Where is she?'

'She's around. I'll let her know you're awake.'

After that she carried on with her doctor's duties. She checked the feed on the drip, checked my dressings and asked if I felt any pain or increasing discomfort. She took my temperature and pulse. She listened to my chest. Through all of this I remained silent.

'Where are we?' I asked, when she had finished.

'Do you remember anything of how you got here?'

'Not much.'

It was coming back to me in dribs and drabs. I could recall lying in the back seat of the Jag. The rain coming down in sheets. We turned this way and that. We were in a city. A city that was vaguely familiar.

'The north?'

Doctor Mallory nodded. 'Very good.'

From my vantage point I could see gabled roofs and stone-walled houses on the other side of the street.

'I've been here before,' I remembered, thinking of the night we arrived. We'd slowed, turning off the main road and going round a roundabout to begin climbing a narrow street. The traffic grew distant. We pulled into the kerb and she switched off the engine. There was silence for a time. I remembered Karima getting out and coming round to the back. She opened the door and leaned in.

'Can you sit up?'

I stretched out my left hand and she helped pull me up. The codeine had worn off and the pain was like a handful of fishhooks being pulled from inside my guts. I gritted my teeth but other than that made no sound. I felt faint and closed my eyes for a moment, pressed my hand to my side. She had managed to dress the wound but the blood was seeping through. I tried not to think how much I might have lost.

'Can you stand?' she asked.

'I'm not sure,' I replied.

'It's only a few steps.'

The rain was still coming down. Now I remembered an arched entrance and a figure holding an umbrella. I knew I had to make it to that doorway, that if I stumbled and went down I would never get up again. The top of the car door was slippery with rain. I pulled myself up and Karima slipped under my other arm and put a hand around my waist. Her hair was already soaked through. I could feel it running down my face. Together we managed to stagger the few steps to the front door.

'Sheffield,' I said, coming back to the present.

'Very good,' said Doctor Mallory. 'It's a good sign that your memory is functioning.' She was standing there, twisting her hands in her pockets like there was something on her mind that she was trying to build up the courage to say.

'Karima saved your life.'

'I know that,' I said.

'If she hadn't applied a dressing and given you codeine you wouldn't have made it.'

'I take it you know each other well.'

'We've been friends for as long as I can remember.' Her tone hardened. 'I don't know exactly what this is all about, but my primary loyalty is to her, not you.'

'I hear you.'

I was dimly aware that she was holding a syringe up to the light. She connected it to the drip. I was suddenly tired again. I let myself fall back into the pillow as I heard her parting words.

'This will help you to sleep.'

I felt the darkness coming down over me like a warm fog. Like something you might encounter in some distant tropical sea. I fell under its spell, without a care in the world.

How many days passed like that, I can't say. I was in and out all the time. Sometimes I would be aware of people coming into the room. Other times I was alone for what felt like hours. I would wake up and have the sense that she, Karima, had been there. The shadows passed in front of me and disappeared again. I tried to speak but no words came.

That night was a restless one. I was already coming out of it. No longer in shock, eager to be moving. My body knew somehow it was going to make it. Survival now depended on staying one step ahead of Donny. The longer we stayed here, the more chance there was of him finding us. I was trying to get out of bed when Karima came in, carrying a tray.

'Where do you think you're going?'

'We have to move.'

She set down the tray and came around the side of the bed. She was wearing jeans and a navy blue cardigan. As she leaned over me, I could see a faint blue vein pulsing against the silver chain she wore around her neck. It was like watching a strange, wild creature up close.

'What?'

'What?'

'You were staring,' she said.

'I was thinking.'

'Right.' She straightened up and stepped back. I saw the distrust in her face.

'We have to trust each other if we're going to make it,' I said.

'You keep saying "we", as if we're on the same side.'

She had a point. I had no right to assume we were on the same page let alone that she saw things the way I did. I ate half a sandwich and some soup. Then I was asleep again.

When I opened my eyes the sun was shining directly into my face. I raised a hand to shield my eyes and saw her silhouette outlined against the window.

'Hello,' I said.

She turned slowly, setting down the mug she was holding. She took her time watching me as if not sure who or what she was looking at.

'How are you feeling?'

'Much better, thanks to Doctor Mallory.'

'Cressida is an old friend.'

'Cressida?'

She shrugged. 'Shakespeare. Her father was an officer in the army.'

I explored my body carefully, feeling dressings on my abdomen and shoulder. Already I could feel that it was healing up.

'She did a good job.'

'She's a good doctor.'

'And discreet.'

Our eyes met. I was curious. There were still gaps in my memory. I tried to speak, but my throat was dry. She came over and handed me the bottle from the bedside table. I sucked down the water it contained and she took it from me when I was finished. I managed to ask one of the questions that I'd had on my mind.

'Why didn't you leave me?'

She folded her arms, tugging the edges of the cardigan together. She stared down at the floor.

'I don't know, to be honest. I was so shocked by what happened. I couldn't believe it. My first instinct was to run.'

Her voice was a low whisper, hoarse and tense with emotion. I didn't speak. I was afraid I would cause her to break off. I just waited for her to go on.

'When I went over, I saw the boy was dead.' A hand came up to cover her mouth. 'I felt terrible, as though I had caused his death. I led him on, told him stories. I thought it would give me a chance to get away.'

'You knew why we were there.'

Her eyes found mine. 'You don't have to be a genius to work it out. The whole thing stank to me. Greystoke?'

'What about it?'

'Greystoke is Tarzan's real name. Did you expect me to believe you were taking me there?'

'It's a real place. I picked it off a map.'

'That doesn't make it believable.'

I felt I still needed to know. 'Why didn't you leave me there?' I repeated.

'I wanted to. I really did. My brain told me to run, but I had already crept forward and I could see the boy was dead. Then I saw you were still breathing.'

'If you'd left me I would have died.'

'Yes, but that's the thing. Then I would be responsible for taking another life, and I couldn't do that. I already felt bad about the boy.'

There was a long silence. I could hear a car going by up the hill.

'How did you manage to get me out of there and down to the car?'

She took a deep breath, wrapping her cardigan more tightly around her body. A shudder went through her as she recalled the scene on the hillside, then she seemed to shake it off.

'The hard part was getting you out of that hole in the ground.'

'It can't have been easy.'

'It wasn't. But after that it was all downhill. You were conscious for part of it, which helped. I went back to the house and found a first aid kit that had been lying there for years and had never been used. I gave you all the codeine I had.'

There was an old clock somewhere in the room. I couldn't see it, but I could hear its tick, measuring off the silence, the spaces between her words. Karima had been staring at a spot on the floor. When she looked up I saw the resentment in her eyes.

'I couldn't just leave you there to the crows.'

The bright light from the window behind her drew the outlines of her profile in stark contrast. She looked tired and worried, which was understandable. I realized that I had never really looked at her face properly. Some kind of instinct, I suppose. Not so long ago I had been preparing to kill her. In return she had saved my life. Funny how things work out.

I felt I should say something, to thank her in some way, though I sensed she wasn't too keen on hearing that from me, that she was still in doubt about whether she had done the right thing. Maybe she was thinking that with all this trouble it might have been better to leave me back there on that hill. In any case, whatever I might have said was cut short by the door opening as Doctor Mallory appeared, immediately altering the mood with her brisk, business-like manner.

'So, you're awake again?' She gave me the once-over as she examined the drip that was attached to my arm.

I looked up at her. 'How bad was it?' I asked.

Her eyes were busy with her work, adjusting the dosage, taking my blood pressure. 'You were very lucky. A few inches to the right and you wouldn't be here now. So, either luck, or whoever did this was a terrible shot.'

I thought about Zef. He had been reckless and impatient, never really paid much attention to what I tried to tell him. But he hadn't deserved to die. Then again, if he was big enough to carry a gun, he was big enough to know the consequences.

'The good news is that you're healing well. The important thing is to get some rest. And try to eat something.' She nodded at the tray on the bedside table that I had barely touched.

'We can't stay here,' I said. I was speaking to the doctor, but my eyes were on Karima.

'Well, I would advise against any unnecessary movement.' She finished checking my dressings and straightened up. 'This is not the first time you've been shot.'

I shook my head. 'Sangin, Helmand Province.'

'You were in the siege?'

'July 2006.' I knew I had seen something in her eyes. 'And you?'

'Camp Bastion. I was stationed in the field hospital.'

'That's where you learnt about bullet wounds.'

She said nothing. Her eyes were on the cannula that snaked into my forearm.

'Look, I don't know what kind of trouble you're in, but you're welcome to stay until you can move.'

She glanced at Karima as she headed for the door. They were outside for about five minutes. When she came back in, Karima went over to retrieve her mug from the windowsill. Still holding it in both hands, she turned to face me.

'They'll be looking for us, won't they?'

I nodded. 'We've already been here too long. They'll send someone to the house, then they'll find Zef. Then they'll put two and two together.' I let the air out of my lungs. 'They'll draw up a list of where we might have gone. They'll look for contacts, friends, yours and mine. How is it you know Doctor Mallory – Cressida?'

'We were at uni together.'

'Here?' I nodded at the window to indicate the city.

'I didn't last long,' she said. 'I dropped out in my second year and took up accounting.'

'She's a good person. She stuck her neck out for us. Most people would have turned away.'

Karima rested herself against the windowsill behind her.

'Cressida is one of the smartest and most compassionate people I've ever met.' She looked at me. 'They won't hurt her, will they?'

'Not if we're not here when they arrive. That's another reason we can't stay.'

'I wouldn't want her to be hurt.'

Neither of us wanted that. We were both silent for a moment.

'It doesn't matter how we see it. As far as Donny is concerned, we are together, and you're still alive. Once he has those two facts in front of him, things are going to move quickly.'

She folded her arms and turned to look out of the window. She spoke without looking back.

'This is crazy. You're asking me to trust a man who was sent to kill me.'

I managed to pull myself upright using the headboard. I stood there for a moment breathing heavily. At least I was standing. It felt like a victory of sorts. Karima stood and looked at me. She was shaking her head. Then she knelt down to help me get dressed.

'Just how far do you think you'll get alone?'

'However far it is, it's better than sitting here and waiting for them.'

'You're really afraid of them, aren't you?'

'I know them well enough to be sure they don't mess around.' I took a step forward and felt a sharp flash of pain. I gritted my teeth and took another. Karima didn't look impressed.

'You keep doing that you'll rip your stitches.'

'If I don't, the stitches won't matter.'

Karima sighed. 'You don't give up, do you?'

'I don't see that I have a choice.'

The smart move here was to go. Leave her behind and just walk out the door. No matter how bad I was, I stood a better chance on my own. Karima, after all, had been the hit. Whatever Donny's reasons were for wanting her dead, I had to assume they hadn't changed. As for me, on top of the fact that I had shot his nephew, I was a loose end and Donny didn't like loose ends.

It was raining outside and I made my way up the street slowly. I needed to find a safe place to rest, and quickly. I convinced myself that once I had got myself into the driving seat I would manage without too much trouble. I did reach the car, but bowed over it, unable to even open the door. I was considering my options when a voice behind me spoke.

'How far do you think you're going to get like that?' Karima said. I looked at her. She held out a hand and, after a moment, I took it and let her lead me back to the house.

'You need to do something,' I said, my voice a hoarse rasp. 'There's a spare set of plates in the boot. You'll need a screwdriver to change them. Do you think you can do that?'

'Use a screwdriver?' She looked at me. 'Yes, I think I can probably manage that.'

'I didn't mean . . .'

'I know what you meant.'

'Listen,' I said, when she had managed to get me back up the stairs to the room and into bed. 'I didn't get a chance to say it earlier.' She paused, her hand on the door. 'I wanted to say . . . I mean, thank you, for saving me. Your life would have been a lot easier if you'd left me behind.'

'Yes, but then I'd have had to live with it for the rest of my life. Some of us have one, you know.'

'What's that?'

'A conscience.'

SEVEN

We waited another twenty-four hours. The next morning I heard the sound of life coming back into the house as the business of the doctor's practice got underway. Doors opened and closed. Voices drifted up the stairwell from below. Mallory came up to see me in her lunch break. She was smartly dressed and business-like as she changed my dressings and gave me another dose of morphine for the pain. As she made to turn away I grabbed her wrist.

'Listen, I don't want to scare you, but I'm afraid you might be in danger.'

She pulled her hand free as her eyes searched mine. 'You mean the people who did this to you?'

'People connected to it, yes.'

'What kind of danger?'

'These are not good people.'

'I thought you were one of them.'

'I am . . . I was. But that's not the point.'

She considered that and gave a slight nod. 'What do you suggest?'

'Is there any place you can go, somewhere nobody would find you?'

That brought a crooked smile to her face. 'Are you serious? I have a job. People depend on me – patients, staff.'

'You must have a relief, someone who takes over from you when you're on holiday.'

'Of course.' She hesitated. 'Isn't that going to look suspicious? I mean, if they do come looking for you here, and I'm suddenly on holiday?'

'Better to be safe than sorry.'

'I've dealt with difficult situations before. I think it looks better if things are just as they normally are.'

'I'm just saying . . .'

'I appreciate your concern, but I'm not very good at running away.' She was standing there staring at me. 'Karima won't tell me what this is all about.'

'Makes sense. The less you know the better.'

'She's an old friend. I know she's been mixed up with the wrong kind of people, but she's over that and I don't want anything to happen to her.'

'She saved my life. I owe her.'

Mallory considered that for a moment. 'It's funny, you don't seem her type.'

'It's not like that.'

She looked at me as though she wasn't sure she believed me. 'You need to keep taking the antibiotics until you finish the course. And change the dressings every day. I'll make sure you have some to be going on with. And we can switch you to oral painkillers.'

'Thank you,' I said. 'I mean, for everything.'

'I'm not doing this for you. I'm doing it for her. Just make sure I never see you again.'

'It's a promise.'

I dozed on and off through the afternoon. It was still raining into the evening, and I lay there listening to it hitting the glass. It felt like the world was spitting out its wrath, daring me to come back to it. I wondered if Karima had managed to switch the plates, and how long we had before they came. I tried to work it out. Donny would have been trying to call me. I remembered telling Karima to get rid of our phones at some point. So Donny would have given it a day, not more, before wondering what was going on. He was resourceful and not exactly known to have an infinite amount of patience. It wouldn't take him long to realize that something had gone wrong. Then he would start running down the possibilities in his mind.

First course of action would be to send someone after us. They would have reached Karima's house to find it empty. No trace of her, and no trace of us. What happened next was key, but it was also hard to predict. It depended on who Donny sent. Whichever way you spun it, this was a tricky matter involving his nephew and a hit. My guess was that he would send his brightest and best. He'd want answers quickly and needed someone he could rely on to do what was necessary. My money would be on Shelby and Ramzan. Donny generally did not have much good to say about Arabs, Muslims, or anything from that general direction. His thoughts on the subject never evolved further than the level of obscenities, but for Naz Ramzan he was willing to make an exception. Ramzan was one of the most vicious characters I have ever had the unpleasant fortune to meet. Shelby was less distinguished, an old-school heavy who had worked his way up over the years from being a bouncer outside various clubs. He wasn't the brightest bulb in the arcade, but he got the job done.

Together, Shelby and Ramzan made a good team, sharp and mean. They would take one look at the empty house and wonder. If everything had gone according to plan, I should have been back in London. At the very least I would have called. They would have heard from me. I wondered how much Donny would have told them. Would they know that he had asked me to take out Zef? My guess was not. No reason for them to know, and this was sensitive information. You didn't want stuff like that floating around.

So they would be suspicious. Go up there and take a look around, feel it out and report back. I could hear Donny saying the words. Just have a poke around, see what's what. They would be looking for traces, anything that was out of place. The house was neat and tidy. No signs of a struggle. Three mugs on the draining board would confirm that we had been there. Which left the question of where we might have gone.

What would I do next in their place? Probably drive up to the car park and look around for tyre tracks, anything to show recent movement. We had seen a lot of rain but there was no guarantee it had been the same around Karima's house, or that it would have been enough to wash away our tracks. If nothing else, the car park would have led them to the track, and if they just followed that it would have brought them to the hill where Zef's body was lying.

This is where it would get interesting. Donny would hear that his nephew was lying in an open grave on a hillside. What would he do then? Scream and shout and demand vengeance, most likely. He would have to make his outrage look real. This led me back to the thing that had been bothering me ever since our phone call. How was he going to explain Zef being killed? What had he been planning to tell the world? That it had been an accident? That his hitman, me, whom everyone knew to be professional, had gone crazy and taken out his nephew? The more I thought about it, the less I liked it. Had Donny been planning to pin this on me all along? I could see how that might play out nicely for him.

He gets rid of his nephew and shakes off all responsibility on to one rogue employee. Easy. Throw me to the wolves and get rid of a family problem in one fell swoop. I'd always known that working for Donny came with a set of attached risks and no pension plan. No matter how much he told you he liked you, appreciated your work, you were always expendable. The second you forgot that, you put yourself in the firing line.

The more I thought about it, the more I was itching to get on the road. I had been locked inside a morphine-induced cloud for days. I should have worked this out faster. On the other hand, it made no difference. I was in no fit state to move. I needed time, and time was exactly what we didn't have.

I tried to sit up. My abdomen felt like a jagged blade had been dragged across it. It's amazing how much we rely on our stomach muscles, but that was out right now. I would just rip the stitches. Instead I put my hand out and, grabbing the side of the bed frame, used that to pull myself up. I gritted my teeth and made it to a sitting position. I stayed there for a full minute, gasping for breath. Not too bad. I felt exhausted already.

For some reason I remembered the look on Zef's face when I shot him. I hadn't really known him and I had never liked him, but still, he hadn't deserved it.

The door opened and Karima came in. She was carrying a tray with a bowl of soup and bread and butter on it. She was wearing jeans and a jumper I hadn't seen before.

'You changed your clothes.'

'I borrowed some things. I need to go shopping.'

'There'll be time for that later.' I winced as I tried to shift my position. 'We have to move.'

She set the tray down. 'We?'

The tone of her voice suggested that she still thought there were other options.

'You can't stay here. They'll be looking for both of us now.'

'I can manage by myself.'

'Not for long. These guys are professionals.'

'I can disappear.'

'They will already be drawing up a list of all your friends

and relatives. You'll endanger them just by going near them. They'll come here for sure, but Mallory should be all right so long as there's no trace of us when they arrive.'

She wasn't convinced. 'I'd still rather take my chances.'

'Your only chance is to trust me.'

'You're the one who was supposed to kill me, remember? Why should I trust you?'

'It's simple,' I said. 'You saved my life. Now it's my job to save yours.'

'That sounds very noble, but I'd rather not.'

In the silence that followed her words I could hear the sound of someone on the telephone downstairs. Mallory dealing with patients, or even better, making arrangements to go away.

'You need to stay clear of any place or person who's close to you. They'll start widening the circle.'

'What makes you think you can help me? You can hardly walk.'

'I can walk. I'm getting better, but we have to move.'

'And go where?' She was pulling at the cuffs of her sweater with her fingertips.

'We can talk about that. Right now we just need to get moving. How did you get on with the number plates?'

'I changed them. Just as you said.'

'Well done. OK. Well, that'll help for a while, but now we need to go.'

'You should try to eat something.'

She lifted up the spoon. I waved her off and took the spoon myself. I didn't spill as much as I feared and the soup was surprisingly good. I ate quickly, pausing only to stuff a slice of bread into my mouth. She watched me as I ate. I could feel a question coming.

'Go ahead and ask,' I said. 'Whatever's on your mind.'

'Something still bothers me.' She hesitated. 'Why did you kill the boy?'

'I didn't have a choice. He was going to kill me.'

'No, before that. You were planning to shoot him.'

I stopped eating. 'He told you that?'

'When we were in the kitchen. He told me he didn't trust you.'

'Was this before or after you offered him your millions?'

'Persuading him wasn't hard. He already knew.'

'He didn't know. He was just eager to get ahead,' I said, returning to the soup. After a time, I stopped, realizing she was staring at me. 'What?'

'How do you live like this? I mean, this is what you do? Donny tells you to kill someone, and you go out and take another person's life?'

I stopped eating. 'It's what I do. What I did. I did it for Queen and country and didn't much believe in that. This is not so different.'

She snorted derisively. 'You might tell yourself that, but you know it's not true.'

'Isn't it? I spent years fighting wars that made no sense. Liberating places that barely have roads and hospitals. Blowing countries back into the stone age. For what? A lie about stopping terror, about weapons of mass destruction? I didn't know what I was fighting for. I know that actions have consequences and that the ones who make the decisions are never the ones who pay.'

Karima listened. She thought about that. I'm not sure she was convinced, but somehow I needed to get it out.

'He saved my life, didn't he? The boy?' she said.

'How do you work that out?'

'If he hadn't shot you, you would have killed me. That hole you dug was meant for me.'

Maybe I had misjudged the kid. Maybe underneath all that swagger there was a ticking brain after all.

'He said something to you?'

'He said that he knew why you had brought him along. They told him you were going to train him, but he didn't believe that. He knew you were going to try and kill him.'

'He couldn't have. I didn't even know, not until the end.'

'He knew.'

I looked at her. 'The story you told the kid, about the money?'

She shrugged. 'It was just a story.'

Just a story, yet it cost him his life. That wasn't entirely true, but up until the moment when the kid shot me I was still undecided about what to do. I couldn't believe Donny would order a hit on his own nephew. To the Apostolis brothers, family was everything, and I still wasn't sure I believed Donny's story about Zef and the Ziyades. There were too many loose threads.

I wasn't expecting to be in this position. Working with someone like Donny you get used to the unexpected. But we'd built up trust over the years. Or at least, I had thought so. Truth be told, someone like Donny could turn on you in a flash. I'd seen it happen.

Life has a habit of crashing through the walls we build around ourselves to keep us safe, to keep all the others out. Everything we thought we had is suddenly gone. It's a reminder that we come into this life with nothing, and the only thing we can be absolutely sure of is that we go out the same way.

Karima leaned over to lift the tray away from my lap. I could smell her skin, and a mixture of soap and some kind of perfume. Strange and unfamiliar, but not unpleasant. She stepped back to survey me again, then spun on her heels and headed for the door.

'Wait,' I said.

She stopped and turned to look at me. I pulled myself to my feet and stood for a moment, swaying. I felt as if I just might throw up the soup I had eaten. Either that or collapse in a heap. I took a couple of deep breaths to clear my head. Once I was standing, it felt better.

'This is a bad idea,' said Karima.

'It'll be fine.'

'How long do we have?' she asked, breaking into my thoughts.

'Less than we think.' I shifted forward again. Balancing the tray on one arm she steadied me with the other hand. I tried to smile. It didn't feel too bad. I stood there for a moment catching my breath.

'OK. It feels better.'

Karima took her hand away and I sank back slowly to the bed.

'Cressida says you'll improve more quickly if you rest.'

'If I stay here they'll kill me. Maybe that's what you want?'

She ignored the question and offered one of her own. 'Do you at least have a plan?'

'Right now the only plan is to keep moving. There are only two rules. The first is, run as fast as you can, and the second is, never run in a straight line.'

She didn't look completely convinced, but she didn't object either.

EIGHT

The street was cold and painted with a slick layer of damp that made me shiver. Karima fetched the Jaguar from around the corner. Doctor Mallory stood in the doorway and watched us go. I saw her silhouetted against the light and wished I had managed to persuade her to leave.

'Just remember, you haven't seen either of us.'

'Don't worry, I'll be fine.'

Something told me she was going to need all the luck in the world to fool Shelby and Ramzan when they turned up. They were good at what they did, and could tell when someone was lying. It was instinctive with them. They just knew. Still, there was nothing more I could do to persuade Mallory, so I thanked her again for taking care of me. She said nothing in response. I understood that.

The Jaguar slid up and Karima hopped out to open the door for me. I managed to get into the passenger seat without too much difficulty. Karima got back in behind the wheel and we rolled down the hill away from the house. I noticed her glancing up at the rear-view mirror.

'She'll be fine,' I said.

'Are you sure?'

'She's cool, calm and collected. So long as she stays that way when they turn up she won't have any worries.'

'I'd like to believe you. If anything happens to her, I couldn't live with myself.'

'I know these people, she'll convince them.' Karima looked sideways at me. 'She'll run rings around them,' I added.

'I hope so,' said Karima.

The evening traffic was light and we drove slowly through the town.

'Which way are we headed?' she asked.

'We need to get rid of this car.' I liked the Jaguar, but even with new plates it stood out a mile. 'I know someone nearby. Follow the signs to Doncaster.'

It took us a little over half an hour to get there. The car wash was dark, but I knew where to find Gazi. A short drive away was an old working men's club that had been overtaken by new arrivals from Eastern Europe. The chipped brick building was run down. A hand-painted sign on the wall warned patrons that the television options available were limited: *No BT or Sky – too expansive.*

'You'd better wait here,' I said, when we came to a halt outside the club.

'What is this place?' She leaned over the wheel to get a better look.

'It's England.'

Inside, the tables and chairs had the same look of abandonment, as though everyone had moved out years ago and nobody had bothered to lock the doors. A cloud of smoke hung over the pool table at the far end where a group of men stood in the white glow of the neon strip lighting. Other than that, the place was almost empty. On the wall behind the bar hung a large red flag with a black, double-headed eagle.

'Gazi?' I said to the man behind the counter. He looked me up and down and then nodded to his right. I found who I was looking for sitting in an alcove just off the main area. A group of men were playing cards. Scattered between the playing cards, poker chips and tin ashtrays were bottles of beer and vodka. It looked as though they had been there for hours if not days.

'Hey stranger!' Gazi greeted me with a broad smile. The others looked wary. Gazi pushed back his chair and clapped me on the shoulder as he led me through to the main room. He waved to the bartender who handed him a bottle of Stolichnaya and two glasses in return. 'I wasn't expecting you,' he said, pouring for both of us.

'I wasn't planning on visiting. It was a spur of the moment thing.'

Gazi was a shrewd, intelligent man who had once been an officer in the Sigurimi – the Albanian security forces. He was one of the tens of thousands who had been laid off when the Eastern Bloc had collapsed back in the nineties. A tall, stooping man, the bristles on his shaven head were turning grey. He'd made a life for himself in this country, treading the thin line between running a legitimate business and the unavoidable deals you had to make to try and stay afloat. I'd used him a number of times. We'd both benefitted. I'd paid him well and he'd always been straight with me. Now he looked me over and saw the way I was moving, holding my hand to my side.

'You been in the wars, Brodie?'

'Not enough to make a fuss over.'

'Suit yourself.' Gazi dipped his head and raised his glass. 'How can I help?'

'I have a car I need to trade in.'

He refilled our glasses. I'm not sure I should have been drinking on the medication I was taking, but I wasn't going to get away with it otherwise.

'It's hot?'

'Only with me in it.'

Gazi considered. He looked at the knock-off Rolex on his wrist. 'It's late. I take it this can't wait until tomorrow?' He saw the answer written on my face and drained his glass. 'OK, let's go.'

I wasn't as quick out of the chair as him. He looked me over.

'Sure you want to do this now?'

'Nothing a little rest can't heal.'

'If you need doctor . . .'

'It's fine. Let's just do this.'

'Have you been drinking?' Karima asked when I got back into the car.

'Just a taste, for appearance sakes.'

'You're on antibiotics, remember?'

'I'll be fine.'

We followed behind Gazi back across town to a high-sided wooden fence. The lettering had faded but you could just make out the words: Hot Wheels Used Cars. Gazi had taken over the place when the original owner went down for armed robbery.

'Where do you know him from?' Karima asked as we waited for Gazi to open up the gates.

'He's a reliable fixer. Whatever you need he can get it for a good price.'

I became aware that she was staring at me.

'You don't approve.'

'It's not that,' she said.

'Let me ask you something. How did you wind up working for someone like Donny?'

'Like everything, it was just an opportunity that came along.'

That didn't tell me a lot, but Gazi was waving us in. We rolled forward through the gate onto the used car site, parked the Jaguar and got out. The air was rich with the smell of damp earth, engine oil and rust. In the sodium glow the cars were lined up in rows that stretched off towards the perimeter fence.

'What are you looking for?' Gazi asked as he gave the Jaguar a once over. It didn't take him long. He knew quality when he saw it. A little old, but still in good nick.

'Something reliable, and inconspicuous.' Gazi frowned. 'Ordinary,' I added for clarity.

We wandered around. I could feel the strain, but was relieved to find that walking wasn't all that difficult, although maybe that was the vodka. As we came back around after looking at about half a dozen cars I began to feel it.

'You all right?' Gazi asked. I heard the urgency in his voice and followed the line of his gaze down to my shirt front where there was now a dark stain.

Karima stepped forward and tugged my jacket closed. 'Maybe you should go back and sit in the car. I can do this.'

I was about to protest, but I could see that she was right. It made no sense for me to overdo things. I needed to focus on getting my strength back.

I waited in the car. It took them another twenty minutes, which surprised me. Either Gazi was putting on his best salesman pitch or Karima was having trouble making up her mind. Or maybe that was just how long it took and I was impatient. Either way, I closed my eyes for a moment. When I opened them I saw a grey Ford Mondeo.

'Really? Are you serious?' I asked when I joined them.

'It is ordinary as white bread,' Gazi shrugged. 'Ten years old. No worries. Automatic transmission.'

I took a walk around it. Anonymous. There were loads of them on the roads. You could barely distinguish them from half a dozen similar-shaped models. I nodded at Karima.

'Nice choice.'

'Thank you,' she said, with a mock curtsey.

I drew Gazi round the back of the Jaguar and opened the boot. Bending over was difficult. 'Do me a favour and grab that bag,' I said, nodding at the canvas holdall. This was my life raft. It contained everything I might need in an emergency – weapons, fake passports, driving licences and other documents, along with bundles of cash in a variety of currencies. Gazi hauled it out and, shutting the boot, placed it on top. I reached inside and pulled out a stack of notes. Gazi pulled a face.

'It's not worth that much, especially with what you're trading in.'

I held out the money. 'This isn't for the car. Someone will be round asking questions. The bonus is to make sure you give them the right answers.'

Gazi rubbed his nose with a grubby hand. I knew what he was thinking. He was trying to weigh up the money against the trouble it could bring. It was a dilemma, but not one that was going to tax his intelligence. You had to throw a lot at Gazi to stop him taking your money.

'They'll be running around all my old contacts. You tell them you haven't seen me and that's the end of it. They have no way of disproving it.'

'Sure,' he said, still not completely convinced. 'Just for the record, how much trouble are you in?'

'It's bad. More than that you don't need to know.'

'We've known each other for a while, right?' He took the money. 'It's not a problem.'

'How about the people who work for you?'

'They're good. They won't go against me.'

'I'll take your word for it.' I tapped the Jaguar. 'How soon can you get rid of it?'

'We'll get it loaded on to a ferry tomorrow.'

'Where to?'

'Riga, Gdansk, whatever.' Gazi grinned. 'They all love these old cars. Bit of English style!'

NINE

Karima took the wheel and we sped smoothly along empty roads. The Mondeo wasn't nearly as comfortable as the Jaguar; it seemed to creak and strain with every move. In time we would forget all that. On the plus side it went a lot further on a gallon of petrol. When we reached the motorway we came to a halt and Karima asked which way. We'd just driven east from Sheffield. If they traced us here they would have to work out which route we took.

'Hundred and eighty degrees,' I said. 'Let's head west.'

'Where are we going?'

'Right now we just need to put some distance between us and this place. We need to find somewhere to sleep. I need to rest properly.'

'Isn't that risky?'

'It's all risky, but if I don't heal properly I'll be easy prey.'

In the glow of light from outside I saw her smile. 'What's so funny?'

'Nothing, just that you talk as if this was some kind of game, a hunt or something.'

'That's exactly what it is.'

We drove for an hour and found a roadside motel. An ugly, low brick building with a brightly lit logo that looked like a five-year-old's version of happy. The interior was cold and impersonal to match and the woman behind the desk looked as though she hadn't had a decent night's sleep in weeks. I signed in under the name Thomas Edison and paid in cash for two single rooms. The woman barely glanced at the form. She didn't care about the details. Nobody did. The only thing she cared about was getting back to whatever sleeping arrangements of her own she had behind the door over her left shoulder marked Personnel Only. After she buzzed us through the interior door she disappeared. We walked down the carpeted hallway in silence to our rooms, which were next door to each other at the end of the corridor.

'Are you sure you'll be able to manage alone?' Karima asked. I thought I detected a note of sarcasm in her voice, but chose to ignore it.

'I'll be fine.' As I was about to turn away, I stopped. 'It's not that I don't trust you,' I said, 'but I'll sleep better if I have the car keys.'

She looked at me for a moment and then dropped the keys into my hand and turned away without another word.

Inside the room, I realized that perhaps I should have put a check on my pride. Getting undressed was not easy. I was still trying to get my jacket off when there was a knock at the door. I got up and went to open it.

'Sorry,' Karima began. 'I was being mean. Let me help you. I should change your dressings.'

I said nothing but allowed her to help remove my jacket and shirt. I lay down on the bed as she worked. The dressing had leaked, although when Karima removed the gauze it didn't look too bad. She cleaned the wound with disinfectant and taped a fresh dressing into place over it.

'You'll make a fine nurse someday,' I said, trying to inject a little levity into an awkward situation.

'Don't get the wrong idea,' she said, straightening up. 'The moment we don't need each other, I'll be gone.'

I believed her. I'd never been in a situation where I was reliant on another person. I didn't like being dependent. In addition, Karima had made it clear that she was here because she had no choice. She viewed me as an abhorrent human being and it was hard to argue against that.

I lay in the dark thinking about that long after Karima had gone back to her own room. I'd never really considered what I did as good or bad. I was a hired killer. A button man. Everything had led me to this point, as if the course of my life had been preordained in some way. I saw a natural progression from the scrapes I'd got into as a kid, to joining the army, where they turned my aggression into a set of skills. They gave me a purpose. I swore an oath of allegiance that made me duty bound to defend the realm against all enemies. I must have believed that for a time. I know I did. But later on it became diluted, watered down, distorted. You are changed by the things you see and do, so that one day the person who swore that oath seems like another person entirely.

When I came home I discovered that I was more of an embarrassment than I was a hero. I had no other skills. Soldiering was what I did. Without it I was nothing. So I went back, signed up for another tour, and another after that, and when that was no longer an option I looked further afield. But nobody was fighting for a flag any more, or an ideal. Killing had been privatized. It was about how much money you could make.

Iraq and Afghanistan had cured me of any notion that something good would come of all that death and mayhem. War is about survival and who wants it the most. It's also about luck. That's what you worked at, day in and day out, cutting percentages, making sure the odds were stacked in your favour, and even then that's not enough. At the end of the day it's your reflexes that get you through, your animal instincts, nothing more. Whether you call it Allah, or freedom, democracy or a way of life, it's about making it through the day in one piece. This is what I had learned, but for the first time in a long time I was wondering if that was all there was to life.

TEN

We got on the road early the next morning, walking out of reception with nothing more than a backward wave. The day was clear and cold and Karima took the wheel. I was still not ready to try driving. I had slept well, despite everything, and felt stronger today. Sleeping had been a good idea.

'We can stop for coffee later, if you don't mind.'

'I'm fine,' she said. 'I can wait.'

Which marked the end of that conversation. I eased the seat back into a reclining position to take the pressure off my wound. I wasn't a fan of these executive cars. Too generic. No character. But that was exactly what we needed right now. I leaned back and tried to close my eyes. I was glad she was driving as I welcomed the chance to think. We had to come up with a plan.

Instead, I found myself discreetly studying Karima's face in the light that reflected up from the slick road. She was still something of a mystery to me. What did I know about her? Not much was the simple answer. In some ways, you want to know as little as possible about a mark. It felt strange to think that if everything had gone according to plan I would have taken her life a few days ago. Right now I would be back in London taking a couple of days off, picking up my bonus for a job well done. And yet here she was, having saved my skin and now driving me away from danger. I knew nothing about her past. Who she was, where she had come from.

Most of all, I had no idea why Donny wanted her dead.

That had always been the way of things. As far back as I could remember people had sent me out to do their dirty work. It's what I did. I didn't ask questions. I didn't wonder why or question their judgement or motives. I just did as I was told. Now all that had changed.

It was as if my world had been flipped upside down. The train had gone off the rails. I wasn't sure what was happening. I didn't know who to trust. The person I had been sent to kill was now helping me, and the one person I thought I could trust was hunting me down. That much I could assume to be true.

The only place I really felt safe right now was here, on the open road. No destination in mind. Just keep moving. It was all I could count on with any certainty. The oldest rule in the book: a moving target is harder to hit.

The thing about plans is the simpler they are the more chance you have of pulling them off. And that was the problem right there. Donny's plan beat anything we had hands down. It was the simplest plan in the world: track us down and kill us. It doesn't get much simpler than that. You didn't need the services of a professional bookmaker to figure out that we didn't stand much of a chance. One wounded soldier and a civilian. We were as good as dead. But that's the thing about survival. No matter how rough the odds, you still want to believe there is some way out. Right now my body was doing its best to recover under circumstances that were far from ideal. I'd been shot before and I knew what to expect. I was going to recover, but it was going to take time.

For the most part we drove in silence. I was glad Karima wasn't the chatty kind. She kept her mouth shut and she drove well. Normally, I don't like being in a car when I'm not behind the wheel. It's a matter of trust. I didn't know much about her, but she was steady and calm, kept her eyes on the road, aware of everything around her. The more I saw of Karima Coogan, the more questions I had.

'We should eat something,' I said, as a sign floated by us announcing a service station.

'I'm not hungry.'

'We need to eat anyway. You need to eat. You're doing all the driving and there's more to come. You should have a break.'

I expected her to protest, but she didn't, she just swung the wheel and took us smoothly off the motorway and up the ramp. Once we had come to a halt in the car park she seemed to relax, as if actually relieved to be able to stop. She handed me the keys without being asked and got out to stretch. I followed suit, climbing out more gingerly and giving the stretching a miss. I held the keys up and looked at her over the top of the car.

'I don't have to worry about you running away, or trying anything, do I?'

Karima rested her hands on the roof. 'It's all about trust, right? I want out of this as much as you do. More, even. Right now, though, I don't think I have a choice.'

The restaurant was all decked out in a colour scheme that might be more suited to a kindergarten. Red counters, yellow and green tables, and a chirpy animal mascot to greet customers at the entrance, as if we were visiting an amusement park. The menu boards were vertical light boxes. All of it was somehow designed to lull you into a sense of ease. Underneath the props, however, it was the same old story. Chips and fried eggs sat congealing under hot lamps. The air was thick with the smell of frying and burnt toast. I was reminded of the stop Zef and I had made on the way up. That seemed like a million years ago now. In the bathroom there was piped muzak as I checked my dressings and replaced the gauze pad that I had been wearing overnight. A skinny teenager wearing a polyester uniform and a paper hat came in as I was clearing up. His eyes darted to the bloody dressing on the counter and he backed out of the room quickly.

Karima was sitting in the window drinking coffee and eating a croissant when I came out. She nodded at the place opposite her.

'I guessed you were the full English type.'

'You make it sound like an insult.'

'Not exactly. I'm just not that into bacon and eggs.'

'Ah, a vegetarian.'

'It's a choice, not a crime,' she said, sipping her coffee.

I surveyed my overladen plate. I wasn't actually all that hungry, and the sight of the food was frankly making me feel nauseous. Still, I needed to keep my strength up and had no idea when we might have a chance to eat again. I chewed on a rubbery piece of bacon for a time.

'The thing about trust is that it works both ways.'

'I'm listening,' I said.

'I mean, how do I know that as soon as you're on your feet you won't just carry out your orders and get rid of me?'

'You don't,' I said. I sawed through a fried egg. 'But I don't just get rid of people on some kind of a whim.'

'I'm a witness. I saw you shoot the boy.'

'That was self-defence. He was trying to kill me, remember?' I looked her in the eye. 'Acting on your recommendation.'

Karima set down her coffee mug. 'Maybe what I'm trying to say is that we have to learn to trust each other.'

'Fair enough.' I set the car keys on the table. She put them in the pocket of her jacket.

'More coffee?'

She took our mugs back to the counter to get refills. When she came back she had more questions.

'Tell me how you got into this business?'

'Do you really want to know?'

'I wouldn't be asking if I didn't.'

'I came home from the war and couldn't settle down. It turned out there wasn't much I was really qualified to do, so I went back to doing what I did best.'

'Killing people.'

'In most cases it doesn't come to that. But to have any leverage people have to be convinced that I am prepared to do so.'

'I can believe that,' she said. 'So what's the plan? I mean, we can't just keep driving in circles.'

'I agree. Sooner or later they'll catch up with us.' I pushed my plate aside. I'd eaten less than half of it. 'We need to know why. I mean, why did Donny decide to take you out?'

'I told you, I have no idea.'

'It must have something to do with the work you did for him.'

'Sure, but I left him nearly two years ago. Nothing was wrong then. So why now?'

The sugary beans were still making me feel nauseous. I took a sip of coffee. 'Can we go back to the beginning?'

'The beginning?'

'I'm trying to work out the sequence here.'

'OK, what do you want to know?'

'Let's try to establish a timeline. When did you start working for Donny?'

'About seven years ago.'

'And how did that come about?'

'A friend of mine. Actually, not a friend, a guy I used to know years ago. I ran into him by accident.'

'By accident?'

Karima shrugged her shoulders. 'I was getting off a bus in the Strand. He was just standing there.'

'Coincidence?'

'I don't know. Later, I did wonder. I mean, he could have

known I took that bus every morning, but why would he do that?'

'Why does anybody do anything? Who was this guy? How did he know you?'

'Matt?' Karima pushed a hand through her hair. 'We had a thing at uni.'

'OK, so he was after you, and he got you.' I glanced over my shoulder at the room behind me. I wanted to know where the kid with the acne was and what he was doing. People were easily spooked by things nowadays. He might have panicked at the sight of bloodstained dressings and talked to a manager, who in turn had decided it was in everyone's interests to call the police.

'And then what happened?'

'We met up for a drink, talked about old times.' Karima drew patterns on the table with the tip of her index finger, her mind going back, searching for details. 'There wasn't much to say. Actually, by the time of our second or third meeting I had already decided that it was going to be the last. Sometimes there's a reason you never really stay friends, but then you meet up again and think maybe there's something I missed.'

'So that was the end of it.'

'It would have been, but then he started talking about this friend of his, who was looking for someone like me. It was good money, so I thought I'd take a look.'

'And Matt?'

'He drifted out of the picture. Turned out he owed money to Donny. He'd lost a lot at one of his poker games.'

'Right.' It sounded plausible. Maybe he had just caught sight of her one day. London was a big place, but stand in the centre for long enough and there was a chance. A slim one, but still a chance.

'So you went to work for Donny?'

'In the beginning I was just in an office in Fulham.'

'Above an estate agent's?'

'You know it?' For a second Karima looked surprised, as if she had forgotten who she was talking to. 'You've been there.'

'A few times. There was a storeroom at the back that we used sometimes.'

'Used for what?' She lifted a hand. 'It's OK, I don't want to know.'

'What kind of work did you do?'

'Well, at first it was simple, just dealing with accounts. Donny had a lot of properties, all over that part of London. He was renting out shops and flats, office space. You name it.'

'It's his area. Donny has always had a high opinion of the property market. He thinks that's the way to respectability.'

'Tell me about it. As time went by I started to gain his trust. Donny liked me. He tried it on a few times, but when that didn't work he took me seriously. There was a lot of turnover. People came and went. One day they just weren't there and someone would tell you that you were taking over their job.' She laughed.

I watched her. It's funny the way a person's face can be transformed by a simple gesture. Karima seemed like a different person, as if a mask had been lifted. Most of the time she was chewing her lip, frowning, looking worried. 'It was crazy.'

'But you did well there,' I said.

'Somehow. It wasn't like working for an ordinary company. There was nothing ordinary about Donny. It was all so unpredictable.'

'So, where are we now?'

'Well, a lot happened just in that first year. I found myself suddenly in charge of everything. I didn't really mind. The money kept getting better. The way I saw it, the more important I became to them the better it was for me.'

'Can we get to the specifics? I mean, basically you were his accountant.'

'One of many. He had an army of them, in other offices, all dealing with different parts of the business.'

'What was your part?'

Karima sat back with a sigh. She looked out of the window for a time. 'I was basically hiding his money. I would funnel it through various accounts, banks, both in this country and abroad.'

'It didn't bother you, the fact that it was illegal?'

'That's just the thing – everything was above board. OK,

where some of the money came from was unclear. But that's the same in any business. They always have dodgy accounts that are hard to trace. But the Inland Revenue don't have time to chase all of those up.'

'So, it's OK because everyone else is at it?'

'Look.' Karima leaned forward to rest her elbows on the table. 'When you've seen tax-dodging prime ministers who make no apologies for their actions, it's hard to tell where right ends and wrong starts.'

'Fair point,' I conceded.

'After that anybody else would be a fool not to put their money into offshore tax havens.'

'So that's what you were doing?'

'We dealt with a lot of things. Donny was keen to increase his investment in property. The money was flowing in and out of the country. I helped him to set a lot of that up.'

'Do you think that's what he's worried about?'

'Part of my job was to make it look legitimate, so yes, that could be what he's worried about.'

'But enough to want you dead?'

She stared at me. 'You'd have to ask him.'

'Have you ever been contacted by the Ziyade family?'

'Why do you ask?' Karima frowned.

'It's a simple question.'

'The answer is no. Where is this coming from?'

'Something Donny mentioned.'

'He thinks I would sell him out? Is that it?'

'I don't know.'

I didn't know if I believed her. I didn't know who to believe. Donny's paranoia was legendary, but it could still get you killed. I sat back. The chair I was sitting in was uncomfortable. I had one eye on the car park, watching the vehicles as they came and went for anything out of the ordinary. I looked back towards the counter.

'We should get moving,' I said, tapping my watch.

'I was going to have another coffee.'

'Not a good idea to stay in one place for too long. People notice you.'

Karima followed my line of sight and saw what I was

looking at: the teenager in the uniform talking to an older, plumper man who could have been a manager.

'Maybe you're right,' she said. 'We should make a move.'

ELEVEN

While she drove, I lay in the back watching the rain stream down the windows. It felt good to be moving. After a time I must have fallen asleep. I dreamed I could hear the sea. The gentle soothing sound of waves rising and falling. I thought I was dreaming, but when I opened my eyes, there it was. Grey water stretching off into the distance. It looked like we'd come to the end of the earth. To the place where there was nowhere left to go.

I sat up slowly, feeling the stiffness in my body. The driver's seat was empty. I pushed open the door, only to have it wrenched from my hand as the wind nearly blew it off its hinges. I managed to get myself up into a standing position and leaned on the top of the car. I looked both ways, up and down. A long stretch of empty sand. Not a soul in sight. I was about to give up when I caught a glimpse of something. Karima was sitting far off, close to the water's edge where you could hardly make her out against the grey motion of the water. A tiny, rolled-up speck on the horizon. Sea spray blew around her, enveloping her in a cloud of windblown water.

I shut the car door and started off. It was hard-going although the sand was hard and flat, beaten down by tides and rain, which made it a little easier. It still felt like running a marathon, but I made it. I was surprised by how out of breath I was. Karima looked round to watch as I approached.

'You should sit down before you fall down.'

'I would, only I'm not sure I'd be able to get up again,' I said as I lowered myself gingerly to the sand.

'What a pair!' She laughed, reaching into the pocket of her raincoat for a cigarette. I shook my head at the offer.

'I didn't know you smoked.'

'I've been trying to quit,' she said, lighting up. 'Not the right moment.'

'You might be right about that. I gave up years ago.'

'I find the sea calming,' she said, holding her hair out of her eyes as she turned to look at me. 'Do you ever just relax?'

I lay back, propped up on my elbows. 'This is as good as it gets, I'm afraid.'

'So, it's work for you? Nothing else?' She stared out to sea as she smoked. 'I was like that once. Dedicated. No time for anything else – or anyone.'

'Dedicated to what?'

'Does it matter?' She reconsidered the question. 'History. I was good at remembering dates.'

'So how did you wind up an accountant?'

'I told you, I dropped out.'

'What happened to the dedication?'

'Other things got in the way.'

'You mean, life?'

'Isn't that always the case?' Her laugh was quick and shrill. 'I got into some trouble. Moved abroad, settled down. For a time I had another life. It didn't last.'

'What kind of trouble?'

She seemed to consider whether or not to answer the question before speaking. 'Sometimes when you're running away from something you settle for the first thing that comes along. You convince yourself that it's where you're meant to be, and for a time that works. Then, one day you realize you were wrong.'

I wasn't entirely sure I knew what she was talking about, but I didn't want to crowd her.

'So you leave again.'

She tipped her head to one side. 'Something like that.'

For a while there was only the sound of the sea, grazing back and forth against the shore. Gulls tumbled over one another above us, tangled in a dogfight none of us would ever understand.

'Did you never ask why Donny wanted me dead? Before you knew me, I mean.'

'Sometimes it's better not to know.'

'You don't want to get involved.'

'It's easier that way.' I shrugged. 'Where is this coming from?'

'I'm just curious to know what makes someone like you tick.'

It wasn't an accusation. My answers seemed to leave her resigned, disappointed even. For some reason that felt painful. I wished I had better answers for her, but the plain fact of the matter was that I didn't. I never asked.

'We're all just pawns, I suppose,' she said finally. 'Waiting to be told what to do.'

'Perhaps, but in this case the king is worried about at least one of the pawns. He knows you have something on him. It would help if we knew what that was.'

'You really think that will help us?'

'I don't know, to be honest,' I confessed. 'But at least it's a start.'

We had to turn the tables, take back the initiative. If Karima had some information that was valuable, even dangerous to Donny, then we needed to know what it was. And if she didn't, then the answer lay elsewhere. For as long as we didn't know, we were at a disadvantage. Finding out offered the only chance of us getting out of this predicament alive.

After a while we walked back to the car and drove up off the beach where we found a small café. It was right on the seafront, one of those old whitewashed structures with rounded windows got up to look like portholes. We sat and watched the whitecaps chasing one another across the water. I stared at the sea for a long time before I realized I didn't even know what part of it I was looking at.

'Where are we, anyway?'

'Ainsdale. I used to come here as a child with my father,' Karima explained. 'There were just the two of us then. My mother had left. I think he was always trying to find things for us to do together. He bought this big kite somewhere. One of those old-fashioned ones made of wood. You don't see them anymore.'

Growing up in nearby Liverpool, she went on, this desolate beach had been a kind of escape, a refuge from the sadness of the house where she and her father had lived alone.

'He was originally German. His parents had come over here after the war in the 1950s. They changed their name. Cullmann became Coogan.'

'And your mother?'

'Her family were East African Asians who came over here from Uganda.'

There was more to Karima Coogan than I understood, but I was beginning to get a better picture of her.

The woman running the café was a plump, cheerful figure in her sixties.

'You look like you're ready for lunch.' She smiled as she took our orders. Bacon sandwich for me and vegetarian wrap for Karima. 'Best time of the day.' She seemed to assume we were here on a romantic weekend away. 'Enjoy!' she smiled as she went away. The tea was good and strong. I stirred sugar into the mug.

'Any fresh thoughts on why Donny might have thought you were about to turn against him?'

Karima looked away from me. 'It just doesn't make any sense. I've always been loyal. I've done what he asked me, quickly, discreetly. Nothing more. I hardly ever saw the man.'

'And you never had any contact with the Ziyade family?'

Karima shook her head. 'We've already been over this.'

I sipped my tea and set down the mug.

'And you weren't cooperating with a police investigation?'

'No.'

'Now's the time to tell me, Karima. This nearly got you killed. You can't hold anything back. Our survival depends on it.'

'How much?' she asked, lifting her head.

'Sorry?'

'How much was he going to pay you to kill me?'

'What difference does it make?'

'I'm curious. I'd like to know how much I'm worth.'

'I'm on a retainer,' I said finally. 'I do what he tells me.'

'Really?' Karima folded her arms. 'So killing me was just an everyday, run-of-the-mill job?'

I didn't know what I could say. 'It's the world we live in. If he hadn't sent me it would have been someone else.'

'Well, that must be a comfort to you,' she said, turning away.

'Look,' I said. 'Let's try and deal with the situation we're in. How much Donny was paying me is hardly important right now.'

'You mean that the value of my life is not important to you.' She swivelled her head to lock eyes with me.

'We have to focus on what we have to do now,' I floundered, looking for the right words. 'You must have been a threat to him in some way.'

'I told you,' Karima was adamant. 'I wasn't cooperating with anyone.'

'Is there any reason Donny might think otherwise?'

Karima shrugged. 'Maybe somebody was whispering lies in his ear.'

That was certainly a possibility. Donny's Achilles' heel was that he thought he was smarter than everyone around him. He was vain, and that combination meant that he was easily misguided. He listened to people he liked, dropped the ones he didn't. Flatter him and you had his ear. Try to correct him and you were asking for trouble. Altogether it added up to a bad strategy all round. On top of that he was short-tempered and had a tendency to go off half-cocked. He would always act now and think about the consequences later. Nothing he hated more than disloyalty. If he got it into his head that someone was moving against him he wouldn't hesitate to strike first.

'Didn't you miss it?' I asked as the woman brought us two more mugs of tea.

'Miss what?' she asked.

'The life. I mean, you went from the glamour and bright lights of London to a secluded cottage in the middle of nowhere.'

'I like nowhere, and besides, by the end I'd had enough of the night life, the clubs and high living. Too many drugs. Too many broken souls. There's a lot to be said for the quiet life.'

'Really? Like what?'

'The simple things. Peace and quiet. I do a lot of reading.'

'History?'

A simple nod. 'How we got here. Everyone assumes nothing of any great importance happened before we came along.'

'We like to think we are the most important thing to have ever happened on this planet.'

'I just like to have a broader perspective.' She was twisting the mug between her hands. 'Maybe I would be better off alone,' she said finally.

'Maybe. But my feeling is that your chances would be lower. I know how they operate, and these guys don't give up.'

Together or alone, it made little difference; sooner or later they would find us. It would be unexpected. You wouldn't see a thing. It would come at a moment when you thought you were safe. Just like that. Out of the blue. It would hit you before you even knew what was happening. By the time you realized it would be too late.

'Maybe I'll stick with you until I think of something better.' She tried to smile but it only made her look weary and scared. Fear can wear you down. It's like running a marathon. You keep going until suddenly you can't.

'I'd say that's a sensible decision.'

I was glad that it was coming from her, that she didn't need persuading, that she saw the sense of it herself. She'd saved my life, after all. I was determined to keep her alive, but I couldn't force her to accept my help.

'We still need a plan,' I pointed out.

'OK,' she said. 'Where do we start?'

'I might have an idea.'

TWELVE

Ari Fenster's parents were simple folk. All their lives they'd worked in regular jobs. They didn't spend a lot. They didn't have extravagant tastes. They paid their mortgage on time. They expected their children to do the same. But Ari had other plans. He wanted the big time. Money, fame, call it what you like. If it was there for the taking, he had to have it, all of it. And he didn't care how he got it. He started out at school, where he discovered that people were basically afraid of conflict. You could get them to do what you wanted. Offer them an alternative to violence and most people would take it. He took money off the smaller kids and traded with the older ones. Cigarettes, dope, ecstasy, coke. He took no prisoners and climbed steadily through the ranks. He diversified. For a time he even traded in used household appliances, which turned out to be a good front. There was nothing he wouldn't consider. He did whatever it took. He had a couple of lucky breaks, but more importantly, he wasn't afraid to use violence.

Nowadays he ran a good portion of the drug action in the Merseyside area. He had clubs in Liverpool that were drawing in the young crowds. They came to him like a willing flock and he gave them what their ailing souls required. He had harbour masters, logistical firms and customs officers in his pocket. The port had containers coming in from all over the world, so it was the perfect spot. In recent years he'd rediscovered his heritage and he'd now made Israel his spiritual home. He had a couple of places there, a pad in Tel Aviv with a nifty beachside villa in nearby Jaffa. I knew all of this because Ari had tried to get me to come and work for him a couple of times, and because he couldn't stop talking about it. To hear him talk, he'd found the promised land.

The Gyroscope was the jewel in the crown of his little empire. A vast industrial space with non-stop music and watered down drinks doctored, or so I'd heard, with light doses of amphetamines. He had oiled strippers in glittering costumes and phantasmagorical headdresses floating over the dancefloor in cages. The music was so loud they should have sold earplugs at the bar.

Nothing was too outrageous for Ari. Not that he was a party animal himself. Nowadays he preferred the quiet life with his family. He would be home every night to tuck his children into bed, and on Friday evenings he would be back before sunset, lighting candles and reciting the Shabbat blessing. This routine regulated his daily visit to the club to check everything was running smoothly. He would always be there about an hour before the sun went down.

We waited in the car outside the rear entrance.

'Are you sure about this?' Karima asked. 'Once he sees us he'll go straight to Donny.'

'It's possible. But Ari doesn't work for Donny. He doesn't work for anyone, but particularly not Donny. That makes them rivals of a sort. It helps that they are separated by the distance between Liverpool and London. Keeps them civil.'

She didn't seem entirely convinced. 'You think that's enough?'

'I'm counting on the fact that he will see this as an opportunity.'

'An opportunity how?'

I straightened up in the seat and turned to face her. I explained about Ari trying to get me to come over to his side. 'He's always looking for an edge, something that will keep him just ahead of the competition. Me coming to him is a sign that all is not well in Donny's camp. That will interest him. He'll want to get all the angles on this thing before he decides to throw us to the wolves.'

'Equally, he could decide that handing us over to Donny will put him in good stead. He can ask Donny for a favour, for example.'

That was certainly a possibility. There were always trade-offs in this game and Ari would weigh up all the options before deciding which way to jump. I had spent too much time around men with the IQ of a brick. I had to get used to the idea that I was talking to someone whose reasoning was just as likely to hold true as mine.

'He won't,' I said. 'You have to understand how these people think.'

'Which you do.' She'd heard it all before. I decided to shut my mouth for the time being. Luckily, I saw Ari rolling up. Ever the aspiring lord of the manor, he drove a Bentley and he drove himself. We watched as he pulled into the space marked for him, getting out to remove the cones that had been left there. He got out of the car, straightened his cashmere coat and walked over to the rear door. He gave a vague wave to the security camera and was buzzed in. I gave him ten minutes to get up the stairs and settled into his office, then I opened the door. Karima made to do the same.

'Probably better if you sit this one out.'

'How so?' She was staring at me. Probably wondering if I was planning to double-cross her in some way.

'We need to keep our cards close to our chest at this stage. The less he knows about me, about us, the better.'

She thought about that for a moment. 'All right, play it your way.' She clearly wasn't happy, but she accepted it. Trust. That was what it was all about and we were still feeling our way.

'OK. So, keep an eye out. We may want to leave in a hurry.'

'I'll be here.'

Which of course was not a given. She might get cold feet and decide to just take off. Like I said, trust. Still, I didn't have much choice at this point. I got out and walked across the road and down the side street to the service entrance. I pressed the buzzer and showed my face to the camera. It would take a moment or two. Someone might recognize me, or else they would refer to Ari and he would know who I was.

It took three minutes. Then the door buzzed and I was in. The long flight of narrow stairs was a challenge, but I did my best to make it look like it wasn't. There was another camera at the top that followed my every movement. When I got there, a door to my right opened and I was ushered into the outer office where a couple of goons were lolling about comparing tattoos. They said nothing. Ari would have been following my progress from his desk. The door opened to reveal him. He was wearing a pink shirt and braces. All of it expensive stuff. He looked like a stockbroker.

'Now here's a turn up for the books. How long's it been, Brodie, a couple of years, something like that?'

'About that.'

'Come in. How's it hanging?'

'You know, good days and bad.'

'Right. I'm guessing this is not one of the good ones.'

'Meaning?'

'Meaning, you're looking the worse for wear. Been in the wars, have we?'

'Comes with the job.'

'Right, right.'

Ari sat tilted back, his hands behind his head, feet up on

the edge of the big desk. The furniture was all oversized. Made him and the room look small. A kiddie let into his daddy's office. The hair looked suspiciously thicker than I remembered it, and it had been dyed blonde. He had a bit of a tan.

'You're looking good, though,' I said, as I took a seat.

'What can I say? Life is good. Spending time outdoors. Open air, sea. Does you the world of good. Not like life down in London. Can't say that ever agreed with me.'

'Each to his own.'

'So what brings you around here?'

'I was in the neighbourhood.'

'That's a good one,' he laughed. 'Haven't lost your sense of humour, then.' He rested his hands on the arms of his chair. 'I was hoping this meant you'd reconsidered my offer.'

'I'm still considering.'

'Glad to hear it.' The feet came down and Ari swung forward to place his elbows on the desk. 'I heard you'd had a spot of bother.'

'Where would you hear something like that?'

'You know me, always keep my ear to the ground. I hear tell Donny's not a happy man.'

'Strange times.'

'That's exactly what I said to myself. These are strange times. You're a button man, Brodie. You come and go without making waves. You take care of business. In and out, no fuss, no muss.'

'Sounds like me.'

'So what's with all the histrionics, then?'

'It's complicated.'

'Right.' Ari nodded. He picked up a paperclip and twisted it open with his fingers. 'You and me go back a ways, Brodie. You've done me a few favours over the years, for which, I have to say, you were amply compensated. Am I right?'

'No complaints here.'

'Good, because I'll be honest with you, I don't like what I'm hearing. I've got some heavy-duty deals coming through and I don't want anyone to get cold feet.'

'I can't see any of this impinging on you, Ari. I came in to give you a heads up.'

'OK, and why would I need that? I mean, credit where it's due and all that but what the fuck has any of this to do with me?'

'Donny's going through some things. He's got trouble in the family.'

'I'm guessing he doesn't know you're here.'

I shook my head. 'Donny doesn't know where I am. I'd like to keep it that way.'

'So, cards on the table,' Ari said. 'What is it you want from me?'

'The thing is, Ari, I'm in a bit of a bind.'

'I can see that. What I don't get is how that is my problem.'

'I'm trying to find a way of making this beneficial to all of us.'

'No offence, Brodie, but you're a heavy. Thinking is not exactly your forte.'

'Donny's nephew. You remember him?'

'Noisy little oink? All bluff and bluster?' He reached for a rubber band and twisted it back and forth between his fingers.

'That's the one. I shot him.'

'Jesus wept!' Ari rocked back in his chair. The rubber band shot off somewhere across the room. 'You'd better be pulling my leg.'

'I had no choice. It was him or me.'

'Doesn't matter. He's family, Brodie, you know that.'

'I've been set up.'

'Fair enough, why come crying to me?'

'Donny talked about some plot involving his nephew and the Ziyades.'

'Sounds like Donny forget to take his Valium.' Ari frowned.

'That was my initial thought.'

'But now you're not sure?' Ari got to his feet and went over to a mirrored cabinet on the wall. Chintzy, like everything about him. He slid it open and pulled out a bottle of Jamesons and two glasses. He poured us both a double and handed me a glass as he went back round the desk, taking a swig as he sat down. 'The problem as I see it, is you coming to me.'

'Why is that a problem?'

'The optics of it. Donny's going to think I'm in on this

whole plot against him.' Ari studied me carefully. 'So is this what happened to you?'

'Zef nearly pulled a fast one on me.' I lifted up my shirt to show him the dressings.

'Christ!' Ari tossed down his drink and went back to pour himself another. This time he brought the bottle back with him. 'I still don't get it. Sounds like a sick fucking joke.'

'If it is, I still don't get the punchline.' I lifted my glass and then set it down again. I wasn't going to drink unless I had to.

'He's out of control.' Ari's face became more thoughtful. I could see the cogs turning. The idea that one of his rivals was losing it meant only one thing to him: opportunity. 'So, you and this nephew were sent off to do a job, right? Who was the mark?'

'An accountant. She used to work for Donny, did his books.'

'What's the angle with her? She must have been putting the squeeze on him.'

'That was my first thought too,' I said. 'She claims not.'

'I want to see her.'

'That can be arranged at some point.'

Ari sipped his drink. 'Never known you to be so coy, Brodie. Don't you trust me?'

'Right now I'm not sure who to trust.'

'Fair enough. But if she's hiding something I'd like to know,' said Ari.

'Let me think about it.'

Ari studied me for a long time. He was trying to decide whether he could trust me and what I really wanted. In Ari's world everyone had an angle.

'What made Donny think this nephew of his was in with the Ziyades?'

'He was in a hurry to get ahead. Also, he's related to them. His mother is Sal Ziyade's sister, Gina.'

'I wouldn't mess with that one.' Ari was shaking his head. 'He was in the war.'

'Sal Ziyade? Which war?'

'Which war? Don't you know anything about the world? Arabs. You know how they are.'

'Right.'

My thoughts drifted back to the image of Zef standing over me with the Uzi in his hand. I remembered the look on his face when he knew I had shot him. It was as if he had suddenly realized that his whole life as a fuck up had been leading him to this point. Everything was clear to him for that split second, and then it was over.

I knew Sal Ziyade. He'd approached me a couple of years ago, wanting to know if I was interested in coming over to him. The deal was that I would have to sell out Donny. I considered it, and in the end I turned him down. I had no guarantee that Ziyade would keep his end of the bargain and that could have left me out in the open with my pants around my ankles.

Which war? What difference does it make? To hear Sal tell it Beirut wasn't a war zone so much as a marketplace of opportunity. Goods came through from Syria, Jordan, Iraq, Turkey. And even Israel.

'I heard a rumour you did business with him in the old days,' I said.

'Now where would you hear something like that?' Ari sniffed.

'I'm the hired help. People speak freely around me.'

'I'll bet they do.' Ari was staring intently at me. 'Where are you going with all this?'

'Donny knows you two were pals. He'll be wondering if you're working with Ziyade now.'

'You're wrong. Donny doesn't want a war.' Ari reached for his glass and realized it was empty. He poured himself another shot. I was still nursing my first drink.

'The state he's in? Donny can be unpredictable at the best of times,' I went on. 'A loose cannon. He has his rational moments, but he also has another side.'

'You don't have to convince me of that.'

'If he's starting a war, Ari, everyone will get hit. He's done it before, and you know what that was like. When Goran Malevich went down a lot of people got hurt in the fallout, including yourself.'

'Things change. People come and go. It's the nature of the business.'

'Well, exactly, and Donny knows that better than most. He's been trying to go legit, investing his money in property.'

'Smart move.' Ari nodded approvingly. 'I've done the same myself.'

'Sure you have. The point is that maybe there's a way of making this work for both of us.'

'How's that then?'

'You reach out to him. Tell him you've seen me. You're worried about what you've heard. You want to know what's going on.'

'He'll think I'm trying to stitch him up.'

'He trusts you, Ari.'

'Trust is for the birds, Brodie.'

There was a knock at the door behind me and I turned to see one of Ari's men standing there. He gave the boss a curt nod and then withdrew. I was willing to bet it was a pre-arranged interruption. That didn't bother me. I had Ari's full attention now.

'I came to you for protection,' I said.

'I told you, Brodie. I don't want to get mixed up in a war.'

'If Donny has already decided to go to war with the Ziyades, then it's just a matter of which side you're on.'

Ari squinted at me. 'I'm a peaceful man. War is never good for business.'

'If this plays out it could be very lucrative for you. You've got nothing to lose. If Donny has gone off the rails, you'll be ready. You'll know when you speak to him. On the other hand, maybe all of this has a simple explanation.'

'You're taking a bit of a chance coming here. I could just sell you out.'

'That would go against your best interests.'

'Fair enough. How do I know you're not working for Ziyade?'

'Call him and ask him.'

'Funny.' He laughed. 'I always thought of you as just a muscle man who takes care of problems, and here you are making deals.'

'I've no choice. None of this makes any sense. Either Donny's got an explanation for all of this, or he's lost it.'

Ari studied me over the top of his steepled fingers. 'Where's the accountant?'

'She's safe.'

He mulled this over and came up short. 'I need to think about this. Where are you staying?'

'Doesn't work that way.' I got to my feet slowly, twisting my grimace of pain into a forced smile. 'I'll contact you. Give me a number where I can reach you.'

Ari looked up at me. 'I thought this was all about trust.'

'That's the thing about trust,' I said. 'You need to build it first. Go ask the birds.'

THIRTEEN

We drove out of Liverpool and up the coast, looking for somewhere to stay. Nothing fancy. We settled on one of those identikit models. They all look the same. Interchangeable like those building blocks kids play with. A bad dream from the future that's come back to take a bite out of the present. This one was no different. The unbeatable combo of uptempo colour scheme and cheery logo to distract your mind from the fact that it had about as much charm as a funeral home. Still, they provided anonymity. You could walk into one anywhere in the country and not be able to tell the difference.

The front doors slid open silently to admit us to a deserted front lobby. A woman appeared out of somewhere behind a vending machine. She was small and pale with lank hair that needed washing and a plastic tag that identified her as Lucy. I used one of my fake passports. Some of them work fine for this kind of thing but probably wouldn't stand the scrutiny of an airport scanner. They had two singles opposite each other and I paid in cash. I was in no doubt that Donny had access to credit card checks. I didn't know if he would be trying to trace mine, and I had a number under different names, but I didn't want to use them just yet. We took the lift to the second floor, walked down the corridor and through another fire door. As she turned to go into her room, Karima paused.

'Do you really think you can trust him?'

'Ari? This is the only way to find out.'

'Bit of a risk, though, don't you think?'

'Any move we try will be a risk, but this way there's a chance we might learn something about what's going on in Donny's mind.'

She was staring at the floor. When she lifted her face she was looking straight at me. 'Do you really think we have a chance?'

'There's always a chance. We just have to keep the odds in our favour,' I said. 'It would be helpful if we had something more. Try to think back. There has to be something that we have, that you have, that Donny wants.' As she turned to go into her room, I called after her, 'And don't make any phone calls.'

The door whispered shut behind her. I wasn't sure she'd heard me, but I had to assume she already knew better than to give us away like that.

Still, it made me wonder. So far Karima had given no indication of anyone being worried about her whereabouts. No mention of a partner or boyfriend, no children. Was it really possible there was nobody in her life? I was beginning to wonder if she was secretly in touch with her loved ones. It was strange. She was an attractive woman. Anyone would be lucky to have her, yet as far as I could tell there was no one waiting for her at home or anywhere else. Nothing too unusual about that. Not everyone felt the need to have a partner in life. I was the same, I guess. I hadn't been in a steady relationship in years. After the breakdown of my marriage that side of things never seemed to work out for me somehow.

Getting into bed was too complicated, so eventually I just shrugged off my jacket, took off my shirt and shoes and lay down on my back in my T-shirt and trousers. I sprawled across the bed and stared at the ceiling. I needed rest. I could feel that I was getting better, my wounds were healing, the sutures were beginning to knit, but I was still moving too much. Ideally, I needed a long rest with no movement. I wasn't going to get that, not yet at least.

I closed my eyes but couldn't sleep. There was something bothering me but I couldn't work out what.

The telephone on the bedside table began to buzz. I stared at it for a while and then decided there was only one way to find out who it was, so I reached for it.

'Were you asleep?' asked Karima.

'If I was, I'm not now.'

'Sorry, I just . . . I should go.'

'No, it's OK.' I sighed. 'I wasn't really sleeping. What's on your mind?'

'I don't know. I can't help wondering if we're doing the right thing. How do you know we can trust this man, Fenster?'

'I don't, not for sure. But I know the way he thinks. Ari is always looking for opportunities and he'll jump at the chance of getting some kind of edge over Donny. They're old rivals.'

'Rivals change sides sometimes to become partners. What if he decides to sell us out? I mean, what if Donny makes him a better offer?'

'I'm counting on it.'

There was a moment's silence. 'So how do you think it'll play out?'

'He'll call Donny, tell him a funny thing happened at the office today.' I shifted position to get more comfortable. 'Donny will pretend he doesn't care, then, just as a matter of interest he'll ask casually if Ari knows where we're staying.'

It was funny lying there talking. Listening to her voice in the dark had a calming effect. It felt as if there was already a level of trust between us. I wasn't sure if that was a good or a bad thing. The fact of the matter was that I still really knew nothing about her.

'As soon as he hangs up,' I went on, 'maybe even while he's talking to Ari, Donny will be passing the information to his men.'

'You know who he's going to send after us?'

'I can hazard a guess.' I heaved a sigh. I didn't like to think of myself as a target. 'My money would be on Shelby and Ramzan. They're reliable.'

'You know them?'

'A little bit, yes.'

'That doesn't bother you, I mean, knowing who is coming to kill you?'

'Not really. If things were the other way round, I would be going after one of them.'

'Don't you find that strange?' She waited, and when I said nothing, went on, 'I mean, you know each other. And you just accept that you go out to kill one another?'

'It's just what has to be done.'

'If you ask me, you live in a pretty weird universe.'

'You might be right about that.'

'So these two, Ramzan and whatever. They'll be on their way here now.'

'I would think so. As soon as they know we've been near Ari. They'll be waiting for us to go back to him.'

'So what's the point of all of this?'

'Well, first off, this is an embarrassment for Donny, having his family business out in the open. He'll try to discredit us, certainly he'll deny that he ordered a hit on his nephew, but Ari is important. He's a smaller player but he has a lot of clout in the port and Donny knows that. He needs him. So he has to treat him with respect.'

'And you think he might agree to some kind of a truce?'

'It's possible,' I said quietly. I reached over to switch on the bedside lamp. 'There are two ways this could play out. Ari could convince Donny that this needs to be handled quietly. He could act as an intermediary and we could come in and sort out whatever the problem is.'

'OK,' said Karima. 'What's the other option?'

'That Donny convinces Ari to do him a favour. Help him get us in return for something somewhere up ahead. A sweet deal, distribution of some kind as compensation for his cooperation and silence.'

'That doesn't sound so good for us.'

'It isn't. It means that they'll be waiting there for us to show.'

'And in the meantime, we are doing what?'

'Moving in another direction.'

'That's it? That's all you've got?' she asked.

'That's all there is. It might keep them tied up for a couple of days. They'll wonder why we haven't shown. I'll make another call, explain there was a delay.'

'They won't stop looking for us.'

'No, they won't.'

She went quiet. I wished I had more, but I didn't, and there seemed little point in trying to pretend that I did. Time, as I saw it, was the only way that she would learn to trust me, at least enough to tell me what was really going on. Why Donny wanted her dead. What she had on him. I didn't buy her story that she had no idea. If someone wants you dead, you can be pretty sure they have a good reason, even someone as crazy as Donny.

So long as she didn't tell me the whole story there was always the chance she might decide to set me up, or dump me somewhere along the way and make her getaway alone. If at any point she decided she was better off on her own, that I was more of a liability than a help, then she might skip out, and who could blame her? From what I had seen of her so far I was inclined to bet against that happening, but you never knew. Plan for the best, prepare for the worst. I had the car keys and the money, but there was no reason why she might not have resources of her own. Trust. For it to work it has to go both ways.

After she hung up I switched off the light and lay there in the dark. I wondered why she hadn't left me on that hillside to die. She could have turned her back and gone ahead on her own. I didn't know what the reason was. I couldn't explain it. Perhaps she wanted to know why Donny wanted her dead. Or maybe she thought she stood a better chance with me. Or maybe it was just pure human compassion. I couldn't say. I'd been over it in my head countless times. All I knew was that the simplest explanation was probably the best, even though it was the most difficult for me to accept. Maybe, at the end of the day she was just a good person.

FOURTEEN

Ari Fenster sounded happy to hear from me. I called him the next morning on a pay-as-you-go burner that I had picked up at an Argos warehouse an hour earlier. It was overcast, the sky a gunmetal blue as I stood in the drizzle and listened to his voice.

'I spoke to Donny.'

'And?'

'He tells a different story.'

'How so?'

'Well, he knows nothing about asking you to take out the kid. That's apparently all your doing. Says he loved the kid.'

'He's lying.'

'Yeah, well, I don't see how you can prove it. He agrees the kid was headstrong, but that's as far as it goes.'

'What about the kid making a deal with the Ziyades?'

'According to him, he knew nothing about that.' I could hear Ari moving around, the rustling of clothes. I thought at first he was in his office. 'Look, Brodie, I don't have to tell you, none of this is playing out in your favour.'

'I can hear that.'

'The way Donny tells it, you're a burnt out case that just went off the rails.' Ari sniffed. 'This accountant lady.'

'What about her?'

'Donny says she took some money from him. He was cagey about how much but he suggested it was a substantial amount.'

'There's no money.'

'No? Well, the way it seems to me, you're running out of options.' Ari cleared his throat. 'He's put out the word, Brodie. A reward for anyone who brings you in, dead or alive.'

'What kind of reward?'

'A generous one.'

There was a long pause.

'I put in a good word for you, Brodie, for old time's sake.'

I said nothing.

'Donny's willing to meet. He thinks this whole thing can be put aside.'

I watched Karima walking towards me in the rain. She was carrying two cups of coffee on a cardboard tray and a paper bag.

'I need to call you back,' I said.

'Where are you?' he asked. 'This is a one-time offer, Brodie. You need to take it.'

I hung up without answering.

We sat in the car and ate croissants and drank coffee.

'What do you think?' she asked.

'I think Ari's full of it.'

'I had a feeling you might say that,' she said.

I looked over at her. 'You think I lack empathy?'

'I think the level of faith you have in people is low. Generally.' She tossed her head. 'It's a vocational thing, I get that.'

'Glad to hear it,' I said.

'You're welcome. These are good.' She held up her croissant before popping the last piece into her mouth and dusting her hands off. 'So what do we do now?'

'We drive over there and take a look.'

Ari hadn't told me exactly where he was, but in the background I'd heard shouting. The kind of shouts that you might hear on a training field. I'd done work for Ari before and I'd done my research. I knew that he had a twelve-year-old daughter who was keen on football. She trained every Saturday at a club in Mossley Hill. I was willing to bet that that was where we would find him.

Traffic was light. It took us twenty minutes to get there. There was a church on the north side of the field where we parked. A short walk put us in the shelter of the trees. I had a small field telescope in my bag and through it I could see Ari Fenster. He stood apart from the other parents. He was wearing a purple tracksuit that looked out of character; an unathletic man trying to look like a champ. Like all the other middle-aged parents trying to remind their kids, and themselves, that once upon a time they too had run up and down muddy fields.

On the field in front of him two teams of girls were chasing a ball. It was a spirited match and there was a lot of shouting from the sidelines. Ari was doing his part to cheer his daughter on, cupping his hands to yell orders and waving signals that could have meant anything. Clearly, he thought he knew what he was doing. The daughter did her best to ignore him.

I ran the scope along the row of adults standing nearby. The usual collection of proud parents enthusiastically supporting their kids. Bored out of their minds, some of them were looking at their phones, others were chatting. The ball could have grown wings and they wouldn't have noticed.

I carried on, sweeping left and right. I found what I was looking for at the far left-hand side of the field.

The two men stood well back, away from the field, close to a parked car. It was a silver BMW, with the shark-like front grille.

Shelby had put on weight. I could see that even from a distance. Too much soft living and junk food. Ramzan, on the other hand, looked as lean and hard as he always had. He was wearing a snazzy beard these days, shaved to a thin line along his jaw. His hair glistened with some kind of hair gel. They were leaning on the car and watching the game.

Ari was looking around now, his attention drawn away from the match. Behind him girls yelled to one another as they pounded up and down, kicking mud. As if to confirm my suspicions, Ari glanced over towards Shelby and Ramzan and gave a kind of shrug.

'What's going on?' Karima asked. I handed her the eye glass and she peered through. 'What am I looking at?'

'Guy in the purple tracksuit is Ari Fenster. Move the lens over to the left and you'll see two men. The heavy one is Shelby. The other is Ramzan.'

She studied them for a while and then handed the scope back to me.

'Who are they?'

'They're the men Donny sent to kill us.'

Karima looked at me. 'Just like that?'

'Just like that,' I said, folding the sight back into its case. I wondered a little at Ari, allowing his family to get so close to the firing line, but then again, maybe he didn't have that much choice. It looked as though Shelby and Ramzan were calling the shots on this one.

'If there's one word that you won't find in Donny's dictionary, it's forgiveness,' I said. 'He's more of the erase and move on type.'

'So we're back to square one?'

'It looks that way.' It had been a gamble, and we had lost. 'We pick up what we've learned and move on.' I turned and started heading for the car. Karima followed a few paces behind.

'I'm sorry, I don't understand. What does that mean exactly?'

'It means Donny's not interested in reconciliation. So we have to change strategy.'

Karima leaned on the top of the car. 'How do we do that?'

'We have to go on the offensive.'

She took the wheel and we circled around, away from the playing field, making sure to keep the trees between us and them. When we reached the motorway we took the southbound carriageway. At the first service station we passed I told Karima to pull in. I got out of the car and strolled around the parking area until I found a suitable opportunity. I taped the phone I'd used to call Ari to the underside of an articulated lorry. At the next exit we turned around and went in the opposite direction. We drove for about ten minutes before Karima swerved suddenly to take an off ramp. She swung through the roundabout at the top and pulled to a bumpy halt on a muddy patch of ground at the side of the road and turned to me.

'How long is this game going to go on?'

'Time is on our side,' I said. 'The longer this takes, the stronger I get.'

She laughed. 'Are you seriously thinking of taking them all on?'

'I'm thinking about surviving, that's all I'm concerned about. If we came up against those two right now we wouldn't stand a chance.'

'This is some kind of macho bullshit. We can't fight them. Even if you were a hundred percent. And if we did, Donny would just send more. Are you going to fight them all?'

'Then what do you suggest?'

'I don't know.' Karima flipped the sun visor down for no

reason that I could see other than it was there in front of her. 'Those two guys back there,' she said. 'They're good at what they do, right?'

'They're the best.'

'So, sooner or later they're going to find us.' She thumped the steering wheel. 'It's all hopeless. We'll never outrun them.'

She was hyperventilating, her chest heaving as she tried to get air into her lungs.

'Try to take deep breaths,' I said. 'It will pass.'

'Fuck you!' she yelled. Then she kicked open the door and got out. I watched her pace away from the car. A farmer driving by in a van slowed to see what was going on. I didn't think there was much I could do to reassure her. There really wasn't anything I could say that hadn't been said before, but I knew I had to try. I opened the door and eased myself out. She was still pacing up and down along the muddy grass verge.

In the end I didn't have to say anything. She saw me standing there, leaning on the top of the car and she carried on pacing, but already she was becoming self-conscious. She stopped and came back to the car, starting the engine without another word.

We drove on in silence. The road was dry ahead of us. The sun was breaking through the clouds now. It was going to be a nice day.

'Maybe it's not about me,' she said, turning to look over at me. 'I mean, isn't that possible? Couldn't it be something to do with you, something you're not even aware of?'

It seemed like an absurd idea. Here she was, an accountant who had spent years working on the inside of the organization. I was just a heavy. I did what I was told. Go here, go there. Lean on him, take them out. That was all there was to it.

'I'm nobody,' I said. 'I'm just a hired hand.'

'Nobody is just anything,' she replied. Her hands moved on the wheel. 'Tell me about how you met. How did you get involved with Donny in the first place?'

I stared at her for a time. It didn't make any sense, but I still needed her help and I knew that if I wanted to keep her on my side I had to give her something. I sat back in the seat and let the air out of my lungs slowly. I looked straight ahead through the windscreen and thought back to how it all began.

FIFTEEN

When I came home from the war, I found myself lost. I wasn't the only one. It was tough trying to fit back into civilian life. Combat changes you and, aside from that, in the service your every need is taken care of. You're there to do a job and there is a whole network to get you to where you need to be. There are people to organize your transport, your lodging, every aspect of your life, even your food. You don't have to think about any of that. It's all covered. All you have to do is train for the specific task you are expected to perform. And I was good at what I did. I was quick to learn and I was dedicated. The army was my life. I'd signed up when I was still at school, joined the territorials for weekends away, and first chance I had I went for the paras. That was hard but back then I wanted that red beret more than anything in the world. I was nineteen when I went through basic training, learning to jump, to navigate, to shoot. I loved all of it. The long hikes with a thirty-five-pound pack plus rifle. The night jumps into the sea when you had to hit your harness release just before you hit the water or you would drown tangled in your chute. Hit it too soon and you'd break your neck. I loved every part of the training and I watched the others around me and knew they wouldn't stick the course. I watched them drop out one by one. It was a matter of when not if. Not for me.

For the next ten years I travelled. I started out being stationed in Colchester, then Germany, then Gibraltar. I didn't mind. I'd never felt particularly rooted. I liked the routine, never getting too cosy in any one place. Make your camp, break it up and move on. It's a cliché, but the army is your home, your family. And it was a fairly cushy life, being paid to do what you loved. We were the best, and there was pride in that. People talk about the Navy SEALs, but we were up there with them. We made less of a fuss about it, and we didn't go whining for air support the first sign things were turning against us.

Then 9/11 happened and suddenly it was all real. We were at war. Everything we had been training for had a purpose. I remember walking out of a transporter plane in Iraq and thinking that it couldn't have been more alien if it had been a distant planet. But alien was now our new reality. We had to understand how it worked, how people thought, how they reacted, and fast. The enemy were not fellow recruits on a training exercise. They weren't shooting paintballs. We were in their country and they hated us. They weren't playing games; they were trying to kill us.

Surviving those first few months was like learning a new language. You had to forget everything you thought you knew, because now it no longer counted. Everything meant something else. A lot of men couldn't cope with that, being out of their element. Enlisted men or officers, it made no difference. The problem was the same: they couldn't let go of who they were. They carried it around with them like a ball and chain. Then there were the others, the ones like me, who thrived. We shrugged off the baggage and became what we had to be to survive. This was our reality and nothing else mattered.

In war every man is different. It doesn't matter who you think you are or where you come from. Once people start lobbing mortar shells at you, everything changes. You had to embrace that, let yourself go, and become someone else. The simple fact of the matter was that the world had changed. We were engaged in something that we did not fully understand. Every corner we turned took us away from what we knew. The complexities of the conflict were beyond most of us. You can't think about the big picture. Take that line and you'll more likely than not become roadkill. The devil is in the detail. It's the small things that make all the difference. You don't have to understand why the Shia hate the Sunni, you just have to accept it as fact. Being a member of the Baath party didn't mean you were a supporter of Saddam, but it meant that you had gone from being in the gravy to being on the menu. You want to move in their territory, you have to understand how they think.

It wasn't all that complicated. You could be unlucky – an IED can come for anyone, anytime. You take precautions, learn to spot the tell-tale signs – bits of junk, wire, newly dug earth along the side of the road. If you want to spend your time sitting there chatting to your mates then you've got no excuses. You have to be alert 24/7. Never let your guard down.

I got through it. I got my three stripes. I came out of it a changed man. Being in a war twists your whole sense of reality. It doesn't take place in some faraway galaxy. They have roads and streets and buildings and cars over there just like we do. There are women and children walking along. There are men driving vans, selling bread and sugar cane, kids hawking cigarettes, gum and telephone cards. War means that at any moment this reality can be ripped asunder. Cars explode, kids are blown apart by a stray bullet. A mate who was talking to you one minute is transformed into a mess of blood and guts lying in the dust the next.

All of that becomes a part of you. The difficulty is leaving it behind when you come home. I saw the steadiest of men and women crumple into rags, unable to function. It happened to me. I turned into a zombie. I couldn't sleep or eat. I couldn't function. The drinking felt natural. I couldn't deal with normality without it. I could drink all day and it just about kept me afloat. I lost everything I had. My life fell apart, not that there was that much of it to lose. I had no wife and kids, and maybe that was a blessing, but I lost any sense of purpose. In time, I began to see that the only cure for war was to go back to it. So I did.

For the next three years I was a contractor. I worked with a number of outfits. They sent me to Kabul, back to Baghdad, and then further afield, running security details for visiting officials in Libya and Mali. The difference wasn't just the paycheck, it was the fact that we had none of that bullshit about our mission. We weren't there to bring democracy, or to safeguard the civilized world from savagery, or any other line of crap they had been selling us. We were there to do a job: protect some official moving around the country and get them out in one piece. We did our work and we got paid. Nothing else was of concern. It was clean and for the most part it was a lot easier. We were on the move. I liked that. Never stopping. Never on patrol. The people I was working with were a mixed bag. There were Navy SEALs and Marines

along with Dominicans who'd signed up to get their Green
Card; members of the Special Operations Police in Brazil who
were used to fighting gangs in the favelas; the French Foreign
Legion. Every stripe of elite soldier you could imagine. The
private sector was just that. There were Russians, Ukrainians,
Poles. You name it, we had them.

I thought going back into the danger zone would cure me,
but it didn't. It just gave me more of a taste of the habit I
should have been trying to kick. Earning ridiculous sums of
money was added to the danger and the power that comes
from carrying a high-powered automatic weapon in your hands.
By the time I came home for good I knew I would never really
kick it. What I needed was a way of channelling that life into
this one. And that's where Donny came in.

SIXTEEN

I felt as though I had been talking for hours. My jaw hurt
and the stream of images that had come running through
my head had brought with them a mixture of feelings that
I couldn't even begin to describe.

'I don't usually talk this much,' I said quietly.

'No need to apologize,' said Karima, taking her eyes from
the road. 'Really. You don't have to tell me everything if you
don't want to.'

And that was the strange thing. Now that I had started I
felt that I wanted her to know everything. I couldn't explain
that. It went beyond the urge to convince her to trust me.

'I haven't even got to the bit about Donny yet.'

'That's OK,' she said. 'It can wait until you're ready.'

She was right. I could feel that I was done with talking for
a while, and so for a long time we drove on in silence. I fell
asleep. When I woke up it was to the sound of her singing.

'*Before they come to get me, I'll be gone. Somewhere . . .
they can't find me.* Sorry,' she said, realizing she had woken
me. 'You were sound asleep.'

'Simon and Garfunkel? I'd never have guessed.'

She reached over to flick the radio off. 'My music teacher at school was a fan of harmonies.'

'What instrument did you play?'

The look she gave me suggested this was asking for too much information. She was uncomfortable with talking about herself. Understandable really, under the circumstances.

'Don't worry about it,' I yawned. 'Where are we?'

She told me. 'I'm still not sure where we're headed,' she said.

I thought I had told her, but realized now that I hadn't. I also wasn't sure how much I wanted to tell her.

It was raining again, heavily. Through the swish of the wipers I could make out a road sign up ahead that read: A6 Kendal.

'Marko Peric,' I said.

'Sorry?'

I shifted in my seat. I was trying to work out the odds, or if anyone would remember him. Marcus had been living in Grozny during the Chechen war back in the 1990s. On the list of terrible things to see, Marcus had ticked off most of them. I directed Karima as we came off the main road and drove slowly through the grey limestone walls of Kendal. The pavements were slick with rain. Ramblers wandered along in bright cagoules with heavy boots and rucksacks looking unhappy.

'The Kendal Bowmen,' Karima murmured.

It was my turn to say sorry.

'They were decisive in winning the battle of Agincourt,' she explained. 'Tell me about this Marko.'

'We worked together in Africa a couple of times.'

'He's a mercenary?'

I winced. 'We don't really use that term.'

'Oh, right, excuse me. So, what do you call yourselves – soldiers of fortune?'

'Too romantic. Contractors.'

'Right.' She nodded. 'Well, that sounds neutral enough, could be builders or plumbers.' She was silent for a moment. 'Won't Donny remember you two worked together?'

'I've been thinking about that. It was a long time ago,' I reasoned, more to myself than to her. 'Marko got out of the game early. I'm not sure how many of the new people would remember him.'

'How about those two back in Liverpool?'

'Shelby and Ramzan? Marko was before their time.'

Karima seemed satisfied with that. 'And you trust him?'

'As much as I trust anyone.'

Marko Peric was in the Russian army when he was taken hostage by Chechen warlords. The things I had heard from him were horrific. We would sit out there under the stars in the desert and he would tell his stories of people being held for ransom. They had fingers amputated, teeth knocked out, one man was sawn in half while still alive. In another case they decapitated one man and then kicked his head around like a football afterwards. Marko was lucky; as an officer he was valuable because he would fetch a good ransom. Eventually he managed to escape. He killed three of his captors and then spent months travelling through the mountains to make his way home.

'Quite a story.'

'He's quite a guy.'

I had only been up here once before, but finding the place proved less difficult than I had anticipated. I had a clear memory of the road we had taken going out of town and after a couple of wrong turns, I managed to find it again. We left Kendal and headed north-west along a narrow road with trees and hedgerows on both sides.

'Crook?' Karima read the sign announcing the name of the next village.

'No idea,' I confessed. 'I'm guessing he picked it at random off a map.'

'So not some kind of cryptic message?'

'Marko's not the literary type.'

We drove on. The village wasn't much more than a bend in the road. We slowed as I searched for the next link in the chain. Finally I spotted what I had been looking for. A post box in a stone wall, almost hidden beneath an overgrown hornbeam hedgerow. We cut down the narrow lane, the wheels bouncing through potholes and coarse branches scraping against the sides of the car.

'You're sure about this?' Karima asked.

'As sure as I am about anything,' I replied.

We finally emerged from what felt almost like a tunnel through the mud and undergrowth to find ourselves on the shoulder of a hillside. To our left the landscape opened up and we paused for a moment to admire the view of patterned fields and woodlands stretching into the distance. To our right the track traversed along the hill leading to a small cottage. Next to it was a roughly assembled barn made of breezeblocks. A lick of green paint covered one corner, adding a touch of colour and a sense of hopelessness, of things left unfinished. The cottage itself looked in need of attention. One window was covered by a piece of plywood and the roof had been patched up with blue tarpaulin held down with bricks and string. The Land Rover poking around the side also looked as though it had seen better days.

We parked the Mondeo and got out. The rain had lifted and the sound of birds chirping filled the air. It was peaceful and the view of rolling green hills brought a sense of calm. Karima walked away from me and I let her go, sensing that she needed space. Up until a few days ago she had had a life in a tranquil place much like this. Now she was on the run with a man she barely knew and there wasn't much chance of her going back to her old life anytime soon.

I walked around the side of the house to find an old wooden barn. I could hear the sound of chickens coming from within. The big doors stood wide open and I walked through them into the gloom. There were bales of straw on one side and a green tractor with flat tyres on the other. The voice came from behind me.

'Stand perfectly still.'

I didn't need to be told twice. I froze and lifted my hands slowly.

'Hello, Marko.'

I took my time turning around. I was still healing and I certainly didn't need any more holes in me.

'Brodie?' The shotgun was cradled in the crook of his left arm. For most people that would reduce your chances of accuracy, but not with Marko. He'd lost his left hand to a machete in a place called Tessalit on the Mali-Algerian border. I'd come off a little better than him on that occasion. I had a scar just in front of my right ear. The blade had missed my jugular vein by inches. It had been a bad time, but we'd come through. He lowered the rifle.

'You ought to know better than to sneak up on a man like that.'

'Sure. Next time I'll arrange an appointment with your secretary.'

'Right.' He nodded. 'Good to see you.'

'You too.'

We moved to stand in the doorway where he lit a cigarette. The rain was starting up again. The drops trickled through the leaves in the trees behind us.

'Peaceful here,' I said.

'It has its moments.' Marko nodded at Karima. 'You're not alone.'

'Well, that's the thing.'

He looked me over. 'You're in some kind of trouble?'

'You could say that.'

Karima stood watching from a distance. She seemed in no hurry to join us. Maybe she was waiting to see if Marko was going to use the shotgun on me. Smart move.

'We'd better go inside,' said Marko. 'I'll make coffee.'

'Sounds good,' I said, waving for Karima to join us.

You can learn a lot about a man when you see their living space. In Marko's case, the first thing you realized was that he lived a solitary life. The inside of the cottage looked like a survivalist's hideout. Everything was cut back to a bare minimum. The second thing was the sense of order. Everything was in its place. The bare shelves, the single pot on the stove. Not a crumb in sight, and no dishes piled up in the sink. Not the kind of person to just let things lie where they had dropped.

The interior was dark. Light came through low windows. The kitchen ran along one side. It was basic but functional. There was a window above the sink that looked out over the valley behind the house. The cupboards and furnishings looked like they had been installed maybe thirty years ago, but every-thing worked. I recalled that Marko used to have a wife, but

I saw no sign of a woman's presence. When he opened the
pantry door to reveal neatly stacked shelves of tins and packages, I saw a couple of rabbits hanging.

I sat down at the kitchen table and waited while Marko
went about the business of making coffee. Karima disappeared
in search of a bathroom. I studied the photographs on the wall.
They were what you might expect, pictures of places he'd
been, taped in place. I guessed he could clear out of here in
under fifteen minutes flat, leaving no trace. I stood and stared
at the dusty landscapes. I recognized a few familiar faces.

'My hall of fame,' said Marko from across the room without
turning.

'Funny how you forget people.'

'A lot of them are gone now.'

'It feels like a lifetime ago.'

Marko shrugged. 'Time moves on. People move on.'

I knew what he meant. You can be out there fighting a war
one minute, and the next moment ten years have gone by and
nobody can remember what it was even about, let alone who
died in it.

'Like they say, yesterday's soldiers are today's forgotten
heroes.'

'Yeah,' I murmured, wondering whether he had heard that
somewhere or made it up. I was thinking there was a reason
I never went to the trouble of keeping pictures, let alone
hanging them on the wall. I didn't want my life to be defined
by a bunch of dead men – the ones I had known, or the ones
I'd put in the ground. I didn't need snapshots taped to my wall
for that.

Karima joined us. She'd cleaned up and tied her hair back.
She looked good. We sat around the table and drank coffee.
Marko set a bottle of Scotch on the table.

'If you want to take the edge off.'

'Don't mind if I do,' I said, pouring a shot into my mug. I
made to hand him the bottle, but he shook his head.

'I haven't had a drink since Marsha died.'

'I'm sorry to hear that, man.'

He gave a shrug, as if to say what can you do. Now I
remembered hearing about his wife dying, somewhere in

passing. The mention of it underlined the fact that we'd always been colleagues and never really close friends. I recalled that Marsha was the reason he was living in this country.

'So, what's this all about?' Marko asked.

'We're in a bit of a jam.'

'That much I could have worked out for myself.'

I sipped my whisky, ignoring Karima's look of disapproval. 'I'm not sure it makes sense for you to know too much.'

'Right.' Marko glanced at Karima and then back to me. 'You know you don't have to explain anything to me.'

'I appreciate that. It'll only be a couple of nights. Then we'll move on.'

Marko lifted his good hand and let it drop. 'Stay as long as you like. Whoever it is, I'm not afraid of them.'

He showed us where we could sleep and we brought our bags in from the car. The house was a simple old structure. It was made up of two parts. A door led from the kitchen through to another large room. Here, the furniture was even more spartan. A fireplace that looked as though it was well used and swept clean; a stack of chopped wood and a crate of newspaper was beside it. In one corner by the window stood a battered armchair next to a wooden chest. Alongside this was a flat sofa bed covered with a check blanket. There was another, almost identical, on the opposite side of the room.

'I hope you don't mind sharing. It's the best I can do,' Marko said as he went over to kneel by the fire and started piling logs in it.

'It'll be fine,' said Karima, without looking in my direction.

Marko glanced back at me and I nodded my agreement.

'I'll get a piece of lamb out of the freezer for supper,' he said. He lit the fire and got to his feet. Having only one hand hardly seemed to slow him down. Once he was satisfied with the fire he turned and disappeared out of the house without another word. Karima and I stood there for a moment.

'How well do you know him?' she asked.

'I don't know. Over the years . . .'

'You trust him?'

'With my life.'

She stared at me for a long time but said nothing. After we had finished settling in, I decided I would lie down for a bit and have a rest. I must have been tired because I instantly fell asleep. When I opened my eyes again the window was dark. I could hear voices from the next room. I got up and realized that I was getting better. My wounds were finally knitting together. I went through to find them in the kitchen, Karima chopping and slicing vegetables, a glass of wine at her elbow. Marko was stirring the fire, putting an extra log on. The room was cosy and warm.

'Something smells good,' I said as I came in.

'How are you feeling?' Karima asked, sliding vegetables into the pot.

'Better,' I smiled. 'I feel better.'

'I hear you've been in the wars,' said Marko. 'Want me to take a look?'

'Can't hurt,' I said. Marko had trained as a medical orderly early in his military career. I'd seen him administering first aid in the field. I lay down on the couch and he fetched a medical kit and pulled a pair of gloves on before undoing my shirt and examining the dressings.

'You're coming along, but I can see you've ripped a couple of stitches. They'll take longer to heal. And we have to watch out for infection. You still need to rest.'

'There hasn't been a lot of time for rest,' I said, glancing over at Karima. She looked more relaxed than I had seen her. I wondered how much she had told Marko while I was sleeping. He seemed to sense my question.

'Whatever you guys are mixed up in, you need to grab yourselves a time out.'

As I sat up to rearrange my clothes, I caught Karima watching me out of the corner of her eye. She turned away and went back to her cooking.

The leg of lamb came from a neighbour who reared his own sheep. The vegetables were from a woman down the road.

'We live well up here.' Marko smiled. 'Simple. Off the land.'

Karima was hitting the wine pretty hard, I noticed. We finished one bottle and Marko went to fetch another.

'How much did you tell him?'

'Only the basics.' Karima's eyes sparked with anger. 'What's the matter? I thought you trusted him with your life?'

I heard the doubt in her voice, but there wasn't time to answer. The rest of the evening was spent chatting about other things. The climate, what was happening in the world, and of course the past. Our past. Marko had a huge stock of stories about our escapades. Maybe it was seeing me again that brought them back, but he was in full flow. We had seen a fair bit of action together, one way or another, not all of it deadly serious.

'You should have seen the look on his face,' Marko was chuckling. 'He'd gone behind a shed to take a piss and right at that moment the ambassador decides he wants to leave. So everyone scrambles and we take off, forgetting all about Brodie here.'

'It's true. Not my finest hour.'

Marko was in stitches. 'It took him four hours to catch up with us, in a taxi with all his gear on. He only just made it. We were about to take off.'

When I turned in, Karima was off on the other side of the room, hidden in the shadows. I had stayed talking to Marko while she prepared for bed. I thought she would be asleep when I finally came in and eased myself down on to the sofa on the opposite side of the room. I listened to the sounds of the house settling down. Marko was pottering about in the kitchen tidying up the last few things before there came the creak of the stairs as he went up to his room. Then her voice came out of the darkness.

'He seems to like you,' she said.

'When you go through that much together you build up a certain trust. Your lives are literally in each other's hands.'

'And you think that explains it?'

It was a question I realized I had been avoiding ever since we arrived. I had always liked Marko. I trusted him. When you've been through combat together a bond forms, but we were never buddies and Marko's warmth had been unexpected, slightly over the mark. Once I'd turned that corner I realized there were other, small things, that had been bothering me. The fact that Marko hadn't seemed all that surprised to see me, or by Karima being there with me. Marko had always known me to be alone.

'We should try to get some sleep,' I said finally.

She didn't answer. I lay there until I heard the sound of her breathing become steady. I couldn't sleep. I heard every tiny creak, the trees outside bending in the wind, the little sounds a house makes as the temperature drops overnight. I dropped off only fitfully. At some point I woke up and remembered listening to Karima and sensing that she too was not sleeping easily.

SEVENTEEN

In the early hours I got up and dressed silently. I slipped out of the room and then out of the house. The air was cold and the grass damp against my boots as I crossed towards the barn where I had first seen Marko the day before. The valley below the house was bathed in a blue glow. Here and there the odd winking lights broke through the mist, marking out houses and clusters of streets. A car's twin beams drifted in and out of sight across the landscape.

Inside the barn I stopped for a moment to look around me. I wasn't sure what I was looking for. Something that would tell me Marko was all right, or the opposite. I didn't know what that might be, but I knew I'd recognize it when I saw it.

Ten minutes later I found what I was looking for. It turned out to be something as simple as an old flip-top phone, tucked in behind the doorframe. Maybe there was a practical explanation for Marko keeping it out there. On the other hand, maybe there wasn't. I flipped up the lid. It was charged and unprotected by a pin code. I scrolled down through recent calls. There was an incoming call at three p.m. the previous afternoon, which would have been just before we arrived. Another call to the same mobile number some three hours later. That would have been around the time he went out to fetch the lamb from the drop freezer. There were no more calls registered after that.

I stared at the phone in my hand. It might not have been definitive evidence, but it was enough. I could have called the number back and found out it was a local vet or a supplier. But if it wasn't then I would be giving myself away. I replaced the phone where I had found it. I didn't like the idea that Marko had sold us out, but I could understand where it came from. We were comrades in arms. Old-style warriors whose time was up. He was living up on this hillside by himself, dealing with the death of his wife. That would bring with it a level of despair I couldn't imagine. At the end of the day we're all alone. We construct our own version of history. Marko had his memories and his photographs. He told his stories the way he wanted to hear them. In some ways, I was no more alive to him than those dead men on his walls.

I crept back into the house. Nothing was moving. In the room next door Karima was still sleeping. I placed a hand over her mouth and she came awake in an instant, kicking and spluttering, her eyes wide. I motioned for her to remain quiet.

'Get dressed. We have to leave,' I whispered.

Karima's eyes narrowed, but she said nothing. She nodded and I took away my hand. I turned my back and threw my stuff into my bag. It couldn't have taken more than a couple of minutes to get ourselves ready. All the while I listened for any signs of life from upstairs. The sun was a pale glow on the horizon, but I suspected that Marko was an early riser. Outside, in the grey light we climbed into the car, closing the doors softly. It was time for me to drive. I put the key in the ignition and turned it to release the steering lock and switch the electrical system on. I put the automatic gear into neutral and let off the handbrake. We began to coast silently down the track.

The sky ahead of us was ruffled with ominous cloud. A heavy downpour was coming. Already the silver sheen of rain could be glimpsed falling across the hills on the other side of the valley.

'Look out!'

I heard Karima's shout in the same instant as I saw him.

Marko was standing right in the middle of the track. The shotgun was resting in the crook of his arm, just as it had the previous day. I turned the key and the starter spun ineffectively. I listened to the whine, turned the key back off and then tried again. This time it came to life. I put it into drive. The car didn't like that, but the engine engaged. When Marko saw that we had no intention of stopping, he didn't step out of the way. Instead, he swivelled the barrel of the shotgun towards us. We were on an incline and he was too far away to be accurate. He fired anyway. I felt rather than saw the side mirror on my right explode. Shotgun pellets slammed into the windscreen, splintering the glass. It could have been meant as a warning shot, or else his aim was off. I put my foot down and felt the impact as we hit him. The car reached the bottom of the track where it met the lane. We were going too fast to make the turn. I swung the wheel into it and then the other way as I slammed my foot on the brake. I felt a stab of pain in my abdomen from the effort. The car skidded sideways, slamming into the fence. The engine stalled.

I looked in the rear-view mirror. Marko was lying on the ground. He wasn't moving.

'Where are you going?' Karima asked as I opened the door.

'Stay here.'

I walked up the track, gun in hand. There was no longer any doubt that Marko had intended to sell us out. Still, I was curious. As I approached, I saw him come to life. He must have been momentarily stunned by the impact. He rolled over on to his belly and began to crawl away. I could see what he was aiming for, the shotgun that lay in the mud. There was something wrong with him. His legs didn't seem to be working.

I overtook him and placed a boot on his shoulder. He stopped crawling and lay there face down for a moment. I flipped him over and squatted beside him. There was blood on his face. He looked past me, up at the sky.

'Why?' I asked.

'You know me, Brodie. It's nothing personal.'

'We're buddies, Marko. We look after each other.'

That produced a heavy sigh. 'Maybe, a long time ago, but in the end, you know, we all have to make peace with our actions.'

'What did they promise you? Money?'

'I don't care about money.' He coughed for a moment before he caught his breath. 'I just wanted it to end. I can't do this anymore.'

'Look at us,' I said. 'When did we stop having each other's backs?'

'It's the way of things.' Marko sighed. 'Time stands still for nobody.'

'True.' I nodded. 'How long have we got?'

'Not long. You should go.'

I straightened up and looked back down the track. Karima was standing by the car.

'Brodie?'

'What is it?'

Marko looked me in the eye and said, 'Do an old pal a favour, will you? Finish it.'

I looked at him, then I looked back at Karima.

'I can't do that,' I said. I nodded at the shotgun. 'Is that thing still loaded?'

He nodded.

'Then you have your answer. So long, Marko.'

'So long, Brodie.'

'Are you just going to leave him there?' Karima asked as I walked by her.

'It's what he wants,' I said. I stopped to look at her. 'We can't wait around. They'll be here soon.'

She considered that for a moment, looked back at Marko where he lay, then she came around the car. 'At least let me drive now,' she said.

EIGHTEEN

We drove in silence for an hour or so. I was lost in thought. When Karima finally spoke I knew what was coming.

'It was wrong to leave him there like that.'

'I know,' I said. I stared out of the side window at the trees and undergrowth. Everything was coated in a layer of grey. 'It's what he wanted.'

'Do you really believe that, or is that what you'd like to think?'

I dragged my eyes round to study the side of her face.

'It doesn't matter what I think.'

She was angry. I remembered the previous night when we had sat with Marko, drinking his wine and eating his food. It had been a nice evening. I could see that he had taken to Karima and she to him.

'He had nothing left to live for.'

'Maybe that's just a convenient way for you to think about this.'

'Maybe.' I could still recall the look in his eyes when he asked me to finish him off. That would stay with me for the rest of my days. 'We'd talked about it often enough.'

'About death?'

'In our line of work it's always there, a real possibility. We had talked about the idea of being so badly wounded you can't ever go back to doing what you loved.'

'What is that, some kind of old-fashioned macho crap? Bushido, something like that?'

'I don't know what you'd call it. I suppose it was just about being prepared for the worst.'

I wasn't sure I had managed to convince her, but I felt I had to say it anyway, to get it out there for Marko's sake, or for mine, I'm not sure. 'Either way, we agreed that if it ever came down to it, we would be ready to do that for each other.'

'Very noble.'

'It's what it is.' I shrugged.

That brought a snort of laughter from her. 'You make it sound as if you didn't have a choice.'

'You don't believe me?'

She looked at me levelly. 'I believe that we all have a choice. If you make killing people your profession, that's your business. There are other things in this world.'

I stared out through the windscreen. 'Violence came to me early. I learned not only that I could defend myself, but that

I was good at it.' I paused before adding, 'I never hurt someone just for the hell of it.'

'Whatever. You can make out you've some kind of samurai code or something, if you like, but don't expect me to swallow it. Somebody pays you to go out and take people's lives. You hurt people for a living.'

There was no arguing with that, so I didn't try.

After a long time, Karima said, 'What do we do now?'

It was the obvious question. We'd been running the whole morning. Ultimately, playing a defensive line was simply a means of putting off the inevitable.

'Have you considered that maybe the best thing we can do is go to the police?'

'I don't really think that's an option.'

'It could be,' she argued. 'I mean, if you were willing to become a witness, to tell them all about Donny's operation.'

'It doesn't work like that.'

'Why not?' she laughed. 'Is that some other kind of bullshit code?'

I could see a lay-by coming up. I pointed ahead. 'Pull in there,' I said.

The look on her face told me she was wondering what I had decided. Maybe I'd had enough of defending myself. Maybe I'd come to the conclusion that there was an easy way to end this partnership.

'Much as I would like to bring this happy journey to an end, I don't think that's the solution,' I reassured her.

Karima pulled off the road and drew the car to a halt. It was a narrow space. A row of hazel trees on one side were like thin staves thrusting from the ground, grey with exhaustion. The slipstream from the heavy lorries going by made the car shudder and shake. She switched off the engine and sat back in her seat.

'I can see that there would be certain drawbacks to turning yourself in,' she said.

'For both of us. Donny has plenty of informants inside the police and I've seen them screw up before. Witness protection is a nice idea, but you need competent people to run it.'

'So what's next?'

'I think we can assume they are not right on our tail. They'll throw the net wide, but we need to keep changing the game.'

'Maybe we need to forget about your contacts. How about that for an idea?'

She wasn't far wrong on that one. We could no longer afford to rely on them. Now we had to assume they might be one step ahead of us. I nodded my agreement.

'We need a strategy, a way of turning the tables.'

'How do you think we can manage that?'

'We need to go back to understanding why Donny wanted you dead. Still wants you dead, I should say. The sooner we figure that out, the sooner we can plan our moves.'

'I've told you, I have no idea why.'

'Now's the time to come clean, Karima.' I turned sideways and leaned against the door to face her. 'The only two things that matter to Donny are his family and money. As far as I know you haven't threatened his family in any way, right?'

'Not at all. I mean, I wouldn't know how.'

'OK, that's what I would have thought. So that leaves the obvious. You were his accountant. You know where the pot of gold is hidden.'

'We've been over this.' Karima pulled a face. 'I just did as I was told.'

'Sorry,' I said. 'But that's not going to cut it any longer.'

'What do you mean?'

'I mean, you've been holding out on me since the beginning. You promised Zef money. I'm willing to bet you know where some of Donny's hard-earned cash is stashed.'

Karima looked at me for a moment, then stared straight ahead out of the windscreen.

'You have to trust me,' I said. 'Otherwise we're not getting out of this.'

She thought about that for a long while, her forefinger tapping on the steering wheel. Finally, she began to speak.

'Donny was concerned about cleaning up his profile.'

'Meaning what exactly?'

'Meaning that he felt it was only a matter of time before he was taken down, either by a rival or by the law.' Karima shrugged. 'His general paranoia.'

'Which has come true finally in his troubles with the Ziyades.'

'It would seem so, yes.'

'Let's stretch our legs,' I said, cracking open the door. There was one of those mobile trailers parked in the middle of the lay-by. We walked over. They had fairground lights running around the sides and an old album of hits by Dean Martin was playing somewhere within. No doubt the crooner of choice as far as the truckers and long-haul drivers who stopped here were concerned. We ordered coffee and stood off to one side, blowing steam off Styrofoam cups.

'So, what was Donny's plan back then?'

'He wanted to steer money away from the dodgier parts of his operation by shifting it to more legal investments, mainly in property.'

'He talked about that. How exactly did it work?'

'It's quite simple really. There are plenty of ways of moving cash abroad and bringing it back in to the UK through a foreign investor.'

'So the property would be owned by someone entirely different?'

'Well, sure, on paper it would belong to a consortium of some kind, but in effect you would remain the sole partner.'

'And this is your area of expertise?'

'More or less, yes. You buy a business and the bank arranges a bridging loan and the money comes in from various foreign banks, typically in the Gulf or the Far East, Singapore, the Cayman Islands. Once the basic infrastructure is set up you can keep moving funds from one place to another as you wish.'

'So, what are we talking about, how much? Millions?'

'Altogether? If you put the investments together, it would be hundreds of millions.'

I let out a low whistle. 'And you were keeping tabs on all of this?'

Karima looked down into her coffee. 'I wasn't the only one.' She tossed her hair back. 'Donny has trust issues. He likes to keep things compartmentalized. Nobody has the full picture.'

'Except himself.'

She hesitated, as if trying to decide just how far to bring me in.

'Donny is pretty smart in his own way, but these financial transactions are complicated, if you get my meaning.'

'So you're saying that there were areas of Donny's investments that he actually couldn't really understand.'

Karima nodded. 'He couldn't be bothered with all that stuff. He just wanted to hear that it was there.'

I thought about that for a time. From inside the trailer came the sound of 'You're Nobody Til Somebody Loves You'. Donny was always afraid of making too much of his wealth, didn't like flashing it around. So he kept on driving around in the same old car, year after year, trying not to draw attention to himself. He liked comfort as much as the next man, but he took his time about it, kept his head down. Unlike his nephew, Zephyr, who loved nothing more than living it up at the clubs, driving a Maserati. He spent money on clothes, girls, expensive champagne. Living the life. Or he used to. I couldn't help feeling a moment of regret. We all make mistakes. However misguided he was, the kid had deserved a chance to learn from his.

'So you never had any contact with these other accountants?'

'No, like I said, Donny liked to keep things separate. We weren't supposed to even know of the existence of the others.'

'But you did.'

'It was obvious. I mean, to anyone with an ounce of intelligence.' She poured the remains of her coffee on to the ground and tossed the cup into the bin next to the trailer.

'Obvious, how?'

'I noticed little anomalies, transactions where money has gone in and out of somewhere and you know it was nothing to do with you.' She saw the look on my face. 'There is always some overlap. There has to be. The accountants and lawyers running the legit stuff have to be above board, but it's impossible to keep all of his businesses and investments completely watertight.'

'So there was some kind of a back door between one side of the business and the other?'

'Yeah, that's one way of putting it.' Karima reconsidered her answer. 'I was in on it in the early days when the system was being set up.'

'Before everything was separated.'

'Exactly. There was a lawyer called Nathanson. He was fired from a big company for something or other. He was a key player in the beginning.'

'Maybe we should talk to him.'

'He's dead. He was killed during a break-in at his flat in London.'

I remembered that. 'That wasn't so long ago. Did you know him?'

'I'd heard of him, but never met him,' said Karima. 'Much later I read about his death in the paper.' She was looking straight ahead so that I could only see the side of her face. It wasn't easy to read.

'OK, what is it you're not telling me?'

There was a long pause. I could hear the wind in the high trees and the swish of cars along the wet road. The high-pitched whine of a motorcycle went screaming by, disappearing into the distance.

'I need to know, Karima. I can't protect us if I'm in the dark.'

She reached into the pocket of her jacket for a cigarette. I waited while she lit it, blowing smoke into the damp air.

'This is a while back. I was getting nervous. There had been some bad business and Donny was in trouble. This would have been around the time Nathanson was fired from Clayton Navarro. I wasn't sure how serious it was, but I was sure the police were going to come down hard on all of us. I wanted an insurance policy, in case I was caught.' She chewed on a thumbnail. 'One day I downloaded everything I could. Codes, account numbers, names, dates.'

'You made a copy of his files?' I couldn't believe I was only just hearing about this. In a way, I understood it. I couldn't exactly blame her for not trusting me.

'Where is it? At your house?'

'That would be too risky. I was careful. Up until the time you showed up I thought nobody knew I had this material.'

'Let's assume that's not the case.'

'Donny didn't mention anything about it?'

'No. This is the first I've heard.'

'Well, I couldn't risk keeping anything like that at home. They knew where I lived. They had people who could break in and search, professionals.'

I knew that. Donny had a stable of experts who could get in and out of a place without leaving so much as a cat's whisker folded the wrong way.

'Then where?'

She was studying the tip of her cigarette. Finally she looked up. 'Amsterdam,' she said.

'Amsterdam?'

'I used to live there. It's stored on a hard disk drive. I left it with someone. He was part of my history, before I even met Donny. There was nothing to connect us. It seemed like the safest option, away from me, out of the country.'

'Who is this guy? I mean, are you still in touch? Is he still there?'

'Rinke?' Karima blew out her cheeks. 'He's not going anywhere.'

'What if he decides to do something with the disk for himself?'

'He doesn't even know it's there.'

'Are you sure? He might have found it.'

'Rinke's not capable of that. Believe me.'

'So you think it's still there?'

'I'm sure it's there,' she said. 'Unless he's managed to burn the boat down.'

'It's on a boat?' I was incredulous. The more I heard about this the less I liked it.

'A houseboat.'

'Great.' I sipped my coffee and decided I'd had enough. It was bitter. I'd tasted worse, but not often. I tossed my cup into the bin alongside Karima's. The man inside the trailer looked up from the magazine he was reading. He didn't seem to take it personally.

As we walked back to the car I thought about the idea. Taking a trip across the Channel to Amsterdam might help to throw our friends off the scent.

'How long is it since you and Rinke split up?'

'Oh, nearly ten years now. A long time before I started working for Donny.'

'So, there's a chance they wouldn't know about Rinke or his houseboat?'

Karima lifted her shoulders. 'I don't see how they would.'

Which was not the same as saying they didn't know anything about it, but it was better than nothing. When we got back to the car I went round to the boot to fetch the holdall. It was the first time Karima had seen my collection of documents. She watched me filing through them.

'Isn't that the sort of thing world-class spies have?'

'They come in useful at times.' When I straightened up we found ourselves face to face. 'Do you have your passport with you?'

'It's in my bag.'

I knew there was a possibility Donny had contacts inside the UK Border Force who would be keeping an eye out for us. Nowadays everything passed through a centralized electronic system. All you needed was someone somewhere in the chain with access. Any movement into or out of the country could be flagged. If they were looking for us trying to leave they would spot us the moment we crossed the border. That was a chance we were going to have to take. I would have preferred to get a false passport made up for Karima, but that would take time and involve reaching out to my contacts. I didn't want to break the surface unless I had to. For now it was better for us to stay low and keep moving.

'You really think it's worth going over there?' she asked. We were back in the car. I was thinking about the name on the passport I had in my hand. Andrew Manuel. A schoolteacher of mine when I was around nine. He'd seen potential in me and once tried to protect me from my father when he turned up drunk one afternoon to collect me.

It took us a few minutes to find out there was a ferry service still running from Newcastle to Amsterdam. We could get ourselves on to the four o'clock departure if we got a move on.

'What if it's not there?' Karima asked as we started up and crunched over the gravel towards the road.

I looked over at her. 'I thought you said you were sure it would be?'

'I did. I just. Well, I don't really know.'

'It's a place to start,' I said. 'And right now that's the best thing we've got going for us.'

NINETEEN

On the ferry we split up for a time. I felt less concerned about letting Karima out of my sight now. I told myself that it was good for me to get used to the idea of trusting her. After all, so far she'd done nothing to indicate she was planning to try and get away from me, or turn me in. She seemed to have concluded that until things were straightened out with Donny it made more sense for us to stick together. I could live with that. I was still surprised that she had held out for so long and wondered how much more she hadn't told me. I also knew that the only way I would find out was to get her to trust me more, so letting her walk around away from me served its own purpose.

I was relieved that we had managed to slip aboard the ferry with only the most perfunctory of checks when we'd arrived at the terminus in North Shields. I was counting on the Dutch being even more relaxed at the other end. The last thing anyone expects is illegals moving from Britain to the Continent. It's usually the other way around.

Every once in a while I got up from the Pullman chair and did a circuit of the lounge area. I was looking for anything out of the ordinary, but also any familiar faces. I tried to commit to memory as many details as I could about our fellow passengers. If anyone here showed up later I wanted to know about it. It was an old habit. Stay aware of your surroundings. People, vehicles, repeating patterns, coincidences. All of these were warning signs that you needed to be conscious of.

Mostly it was what you would expect. With the autumn holidays coming up there were families travelling by car to spend their holidays in some dreary seaside hotel. They looked reassuringly dull, living the kind of lives that I wouldn't have exchanged with them for all the tea in China, despite my current predicament. Something about the ordinary life has always repelled me. Not that I looked down on them or anything. Everyone has to find their own way in life, I suppose. I just knew it wasn't for me.

My eyes lingered for a while on a couple dressed in bike leathers, before deciding they were not a threat. Next to them another couple was travelling with two small children. They had one of those ergonomic pushchairs that looked like they were designed with a robot in mind. The woman was wiping something off her dress that looked like baby food. The table in front of them was littered with fluffy toys and Tupperware containers. Having children along was a pretty smart move. It certainly would deflect attention. In the end I found myself dismissing them as a threat and instead thinking about my own life. Somehow the idea of having children had never appealed to me. I understood that it often happened simply by accident. There wasn't much you could do about it, and I supposed most people went along and accepted the facts. To me, choosing to bring children into this world seemed like an act of the most unadulterated selfishness.

I found Karima on the upper deck, leaning against the railings with her sunglasses on, face upturned to receive the maximum rays. I didn't recognize her at first and stared for some time before realizing it was her. Most of the time she carried herself in such an unassuming way you could be forgiven for not noticing she was there. She was good at blending in, observing the world around her. It added to the sense that there was more to her than met the eye. I found myself wondering again what it was that I wasn't seeing.

'Enjoying the fresh air?'

She laughed. A carefree, happy sound. 'It's great. Reminds me of all those childhood holidays.' She swivelled away from me to look at the sea. 'My father and I used to travel a lot. I think he was restless after my mother died. With him there was always a new adventure to be had.'

'Sounds like you were very close.'

'I suppose we were. Sometimes we only value things after we've lost them.' She glanced round at me. 'Don't you find that?'

'I don't think about it so much.' I shrugged. Then I thought I should try a little harder. 'I think we sometimes tell ourselves things because we like the sound of them.'

She laughed again and turned back to the sea. 'Not the most romantic view I've ever heard.'

Romantic wasn't a quality I'd ever associated with myself, but the observation intrigued me.

'I'm curious,' I said.

'About what?'

'This life of yours across the sea.'

'Oh, that.' She flicked her lighter, holding it inside her jacket to light a cigarette. 'Are you going to grill me about my past now?'

'How long is it since you've seen him?'

Karima blew smoke into the air. 'I haven't been back for nearly four years.'

'So you and this guy, you're still friends?'

'In a way,' she said. It sounded like a concession, like something she hadn't really thought about. 'We've stayed in touch.'

I didn't know exactly what that meant. I wondered if she was trying to tell me that they still had some kind of a relationship. I sensed she was still being economical with the truth. I'd learned enough about her to know that pressing her on the subject wasn't the way to go, however. We stood side by side and leaned on the railings, watching the gulls flutter around our wake.

The rest of the voyage passed without incident. We rolled down the ramp on to the quay and found our way through the maze of lorries and container parks to arrive at a motorway, then followed a ring road that took us into the heart of the city. The traffic was slowed to a crawl by the number of HGVs and a lengthy stretch of roadworks. Eventually we arrived at a quiet area of canals and narrow streets. We drove under a railway bridge and turned again. Ahead of us was a traditional

lifting bridge over a small, quiet canal. Two high arches were
linked by a truss structure. We came to a halt before it and
Karima turned to roll slowly along between a row of houses
and the canal, which widened into a secluded enclosed area
of water. There were houseboats moored all the way round at
uneven intervals.

The one we came to a halt beside was an old iron hulk that
sat low in the water. The wheelhouse was on the left-hand
side. The wood panelling looked worn and in need of attention. The nameplate on the stern read *Jannetje*. A low, roofed
passage extended some twenty metres forward from this,
almost the full length of the vessel.

We parked the car and got out. A tall, stooping man leaned
out of the wheelhouse. He looked like a mythical creature, a
giant with wispy brown hair threaded with grey that hung to
his shoulders. His face was a puffy mess, striated by burst
capillaries and punctuated by a large red nose. If you were
looking for a poster boy for recovering addiction problems,
he would be it. Over the top of the car Karima read my gaze.

'Go gentle on him, will you? We need him on our side.'

I had no objection. The truth was I was trying to reconcile
what little I knew of her with this man I was looking at. Maybe
I was too quick to judge, but it was like trying to match up
two sides of a picture that Picasso had painted in his sleep.

Rinke was surprised to see us but didn't seem too worried
about it. It didn't look like there were a lot of things Rinke
worried about. We stepped aboard and went through the
wheelhouse and down a set of steps that gave on to a long
living area.

'I wasn't expecting visitors,' he said with a loud sniff, as
if to explain the mess.

'We should have called ahead,' I said, although I had the
feeling it wouldn't have made all that much difference. Karima
slipped off her jacket as she looked around and rolled up her
sleeves to go straight to work, hauling dishes out of the sink
to make enough space to fill the coffee pot. Rinke seemed to
know from experience that it was best to stand back and let
her do it. He went around the kitchen to find tobacco and
papers and proceeded to roll himself a smoke, leaning against

the wall behind him with the ease of a man who had had plenty of practice.

'So, are you on holiday?' he asked, glancing up at me. The two men were having a conversation while the only woman among us took care of domestic matters.

'I have some old business contacts here I'd like to look up,' I said.

'What kind of business?'

'Maritime insurance.' I had no idea what that was and had yet to meet anyone who did.

Rinke's hair bobbed on his shoulders. He nodded as if it didn't make any difference to him either way. He licked his cigarette paper and rubbed his stubbly chin at the same time. Karima was silent throughout all of this. She said nothing as she went through the kitchen cupboards until she found the coffee. She filled the percolator, switched it on and then folded her arms and leaned against the counter.

'So, how are things with you, Rinke?'

'Oh, you know, the same as usual.' He shrugged, studying the floor for a moment. 'I'm clean now. Three months.'

'That's good.'

It was more than good, and from the deflated look on his face he had been hoping for some encouragement. I assumed that Karima's reserved response was connected to their history. Maybe she'd been through all of this before. I was still having trouble seeing them as a couple.

We drank coffee sitting around the long wooden table in the middle of the room. Despite the mess, there was something quite homely and peaceful about the place. The windows offered a view across the canal. Houseboats of various shapes and sizes sat along the waterside with rows of high buildings behind them that would once have been warehouses. A quiet, residential area. The one we were on looked like a real vessel that might once have worked the canals, carrying goods through the country. Other houseboats were more modern structures, clearly designed as a living space. Nothing much was moving out there, save for the occasional cyclist going by. That suited me fine. Less movement, more chance of spotting anything out of place.

'How long are you staying?' Rinke asked.

'Just a couple of days,' I said, taking up the story. 'I have some business contacts to see.'

'Where are you staying?'

'We haven't decided that yet,' I said, looking over at Karima who was staring out of the window as if she wasn't paying attention, maybe running back over the episode of her life that she had passed here. No matter how distant, there was a connection to Karima here and I didn't want to risk it by staying too long. We needed to locate the disk and be on our way.

Rinke slapped a hand to his forehead. 'I just remembered. You can stay here.' He saw the look on Karima's face and quickly added, 'Not here, of course. Next door. Harry and Hella are in Portugal. You know, they bought a house down there. I'm looking after their place.'

'That's OK,' Karima said. 'We'll find a hotel.'

But Rinke was adamant. 'No, really. I'm sure they'd love it if you stayed there. They often ask after you.' His English was good, if a little rough around the edges, and I was getting used to his accent.

'Maybe we should take a look,' I said softly. I wasn't sure how far Donny's reach could stretch, but I knew he had connections in Amsterdam. A lot of drugs floated in and out of this country, and drugs were part of Donny's enterprise. As far as I was concerned, the smaller our footprint the better. 'It can't hurt.'

Karima was clearly not happy with the idea. You didn't have to be a mind-reader to see what was written on her face. This was too much like going back to her past, and clearly that thought didn't fill her with joy. Still, she was smart enough to see the sense of it too. So, when we'd finished our coffee, we all trooped round. Unlike Rinke's houseboat, the one next door was built to spec. A low, simple rectangular wooden box set on a pontoon. The wooden sides were painted a blue-grey colour. The deck that ran along the front was dotted with large plant pots.

'I promised to water them too,' Rinke explained as he fumbled with the keys.

'Looks like you've been neglecting your duty,' said Karima, crumbling dried leaves from a rose bush.

The glass doors slid aside to reveal an interior that was musty and smelt of cat. Three steps took you down to the main living area which was spacious and simple. A corridor to the left led to what must have been sleeping quarters, while to the right we moved past a small kitchenette to a living area with low sofas and a coffee table. The owners were clearly more concerned about tidiness than Rinke. I guessed they were also older. A record player and a stack of faded vinyl LP covers testified to a taste in Creedence Clearwater Revival and Janis Joplin. It was pleasant enough. The windows came down level with the water. A couple of ducks floated by.

'It looks great,' I said, just to say something. 'Are you sure they won't mind?' I noticed the expression of horror on Rinke's face and looked down at my shirt and the growing stain.

'You're bleeding.'

'A hernia operation.' I smiled weakly. 'Impatient to be over it, I suppose.'

'I should change your dressings,' said Karima. She took me by the hand and, picking up her bag along the way, led me towards the rear where there was a bathroom.

She helped me off with my shirt and removed the gauze pad carefully. The wound wasn't doing badly. It was only bleeding slightly on one side.

'You're trying to do too much,' she said, as she cleaned the wound and applied a new dressing. She had everything she needed in the bag. Dressings and disinfectant. I watched her as she worked.

'Tell me about him, about you.'

'Why are you interested?' She didn't look up.

'He doesn't seem your type.'

'My type?' She dropped a ball of cotton wool into the sink and reached for another. 'What would you know about my type?'

'Sorry,' I said. 'It's none of my business. I'm just curious about this whole thing. Settling in this city. What was it about Amsterdam?'

'I don't know how to explain it,' she began. 'Maybe it was

just being away from England, being in a strange place. Everything seemed different. I felt free. All the old problems I'd had were wiped out. I was beginning again. Does that make sense?'

'I think so.'

She paused and took a moment, soaking the ball of cotton wool with disinfectant.

'As for Rinke, well, what can I say?' She went back to work on me. 'When you're young you don't think so much about consequences, you just carry on.'

'You had a habit?'

'For a time.' She looked up to meet my gaze. 'It wasn't all roses. I wound up here with an abusive boyfriend who kicked me out. I had no money and nowhere to go. Rinke helped me.' She finished what she was doing and straightened up. 'He's a kind person.'

'I understand,' I said. 'Thanks.'

'You're welcome.'

I watched her tidying up as I buttoned my shirt. 'So how long were you together?'

She turned to fix me with a look, the kind that said it was really none of my business. 'Where's all this coming from?'

It was my turn to shrug. I really didn't know how to explain it. 'Natural curiosity, I suppose. You seem like an odd couple.'

Her hands were clenched around the medical kit. 'Have you never made a decision and then spent the rest of your life trying to work out what the hell you were thinking? Or maybe your life has just been one perfect step after another. Somehow, I doubt it.'

'Karima,' I began. I put out a hand to touch her shoulder but she shook me off. We stood like that for a moment, close together in that narrow space, neither of us speaking, nor making a move.

'It happened,' she said finally, staring at the floor. 'I needed somewhere safe, with someone I could trust. Rinke was there for me.'

'You don't have to explain,' I said quietly. I made to move past her towards the door. She rested a hand on my chest and looked into my eyes. I'm not sure what she was looking for, or whether she found it. Neither of us spoke. Finally, she took her hand away and stepped aside.

'The hard disk should be in the utility room on the *Jannetje*. I just need to find the right moment to go down there and get it. Rinke doesn't know it's there and I'd rather keep it that way. He might be angry to think that I had hidden something on his boat without telling him.'

'So staying here makes sense.'

'I suppose so.' Karima gave a sigh of defeat. 'It'll only be a day or so.'

'Twenty-four hours. No more. You have a history here, remember, which means someone might hear about you being back. It's not safe.'

'Everything all right?' Rinke called.

Karima stuck her head out into the corridor. 'We'll be right out.'

'Better be,' he called. 'Or I might start to get jealous.'

I raised my eyebrows quizzically but Karima just shook her head.

'It's his way of being funny.'

When we got out Rinke looked me over. 'You could use a new shirt.'

'I've got one with me. I'll change when we get the bags from the car.'

'I'd better take care of that,' he said, holding his hand out for the key. I gave it to him. We needed to establish trust. And besides, even if he went through the bags he wouldn't find anything. I had hidden all the weapons underneath the spare wheel in case we ran into a nosey customs officer on the way over. I doubted Rinke would go to the trouble of opening that up.

I stood on the deck and watched a jackdaw sitting on the railing. It seemed to be asking me what I was doing here, so far away from home. I wondered that myself.

TWENTY

That evening Karima made supper for all of us. She disappeared on her own and returned more than an hour later laden down with shopping bags. Rinke grinned as he surveyed them.

'You remembered all the old places.'

'Some of them have gone,' she said. 'Everywhere changes, I suppose.'

'Yeah, tell me about it.'

There was no alcohol, out of consideration for our host, I assumed. Instead, we drank sparkling water and ginger ale. Karima had bought fish and sautéed vegetables to go with it. She'd even found an apple tart and cream for dessert.

The conversation circled around how we had met and what had brought us to Amsterdam. Rinke was curious and Karima and I had taken a moment to knock together the makings of a story about meeting in London while she was working there. Rinke didn't seem to know she no longer lived there and was happy to accept it.

At one point Karima disappeared to go to the toilet and I stepped up the conversation to keep Rinke occupied. I asked him about how long he'd lived on the boat. He took that as a reason to talk about Karima and the old days. I hadn't intended to pry, but I was happy to let him talk.

'She was really young when we met. I mean, she was still a kid, maybe seventeen, a little lost. I was older. I took care of her.'

'This would have been twenty years ago?'

'Yeah, something like that.' He frowned, trying to be accurate. 'A little more.'

Despite his wayward, distracted appearance, his memory was clearly still sharp.

'We were together for nearly five years. I think, actually, we were good for each other.' He sounded contemplative, rather than bitter or annoyed. 'Taking care of her somehow made me more aware of myself, of how I was behaving.'

'Why did you split?'

Rinke gave a philosophical shrug, staring down at his hands. 'I guess I was still too much thinking about myself, you know?'

'So you took care of her until you couldn't.'

'Something like that. I was unreliable.'

'You had your own problems.'

'You could say that, yeah. Old habits die hard. They come back with a vengeance.'

'Still, it doesn't sound like it was a bad time for either of you.'

'Oh, no. It was good. I mean, I messed up. I like to think we were all happy.' The corners of the big eyes crinkled as he smiled. 'It's like that song. You don't know what you've got till it's gone.'

I didn't know what song he had in mind. I wanted to ask him what he meant by 'all', but our conversation was disrupted by Karima. She said she was feeling tired from the journey and really needed to sleep. Rinke told her to go. He would finish clearing up. I found it hard to imagine, but to his credit that's exactly what he started to do. Maybe Karima was a good influence on him.

On the way back next door, I took a slight detour, first to the car, where I retrieved the Browning from the wheel hub and tucked it into the back of my belt. Then I went back along the quay, across the little bridge. I walked a long circuit and saw nothing out of place. There was hardly anyone about. A couple on bicycles talking loudly as they made their way home. Other than that, everyone seemed to have settled down for the night. It was so quiet I could hear a cat mewing on the far end of the canal.

When I got back, Karima was waiting for me. She was stretched out on one of the sofas facing the water. On the coffee table next to her was a bottle of whisky that she must have found somewhere. She raised the tumbler in her hand.

'I needed a drink after that.'

'I understand. All of this must be tough on you.'

'The fact is,' she said, staring out the window, 'I thought

I'd put all of this behind me, but the memories come back anyway.'

'They have a habit of doing that.' I found a glass on the kitchen counter and came over to join her.

'Did you find it?' I asked as I sat down on the opposite sofa. I poured myself a long shot of Scotch. I saw her shake her head.

'It wasn't there.'

Surprised, I set the bottle down. 'Could Rinke have found it?'

'I doubt it. I mean, I don't see how. I was careful, all right. It was well hidden.'

'I believe you.' I sipped the whisky which was mellow and expensive. This houseboat sitting wasn't all bad. 'But just to be clear, how well hidden was it?'

'Why is it that whenever you ask a question you sound like you're talking to an idiot?'

'Unintentional, I assure you. I just need to know. Where was it?'

She considered for a moment before relenting. 'It was taped inside an old air vent. Something that's never used.'

'You can just open it up?'

'You need a screwdriver. There's a toolbox down there.'

I nodded. It sounded solid enough.

'It couldn't have fallen further inside?'

She was shaking her head as I spoke. 'If it's gone, it's because someone took it.'

'OK, let's assume that's the case. Who?'

Karima gave a loud sniff but said nothing. I had another question building up, just morbid curiosity, but I had to ask it anyway.

'I'm curious. You and this guy split up years ago. How is it that you're still in touch?'

'I don't know.' She gave a light shrug. 'Maybe we were always better suited to staying friends than, you know, being in a relationship.'

'I still don't see it. I mean, the two of you seem so different.'

She was frowning at me over her drink as I went on.

'You're smart, attractive . . . alert. He's, well, none of those things.'

'Sometimes it's nothing to do with that, it's just, you know, things you went through together.'

I wasn't entirely convinced, but short of holding her feet to the fire I couldn't see a way of getting her to tell me more.

We finished our drinks and while she prepared for bed I went outside and paced around again to make sure that nothing was out of place. Nothing was moving.

'Don't you ever relax?' Karima asked as I came back in.

'It's just habit, I suppose.'

'Some habits are worth shaking,' she said as she went by. I found myself smiling at that long after I had tucked myself in on the sofa. I had always been that way, overly cautious, observant, watching everyone and everything around me. It wasn't a habit so much as an obsession.

Karima had the bedroom and for a time I listened to her moving around before she settled down and went to sleep. For a long time I lay there on the sofa listening in the dark to all the unfamiliar sounds. Cars in the distance. A high-pitched motorcycle. A police siren. The sounds came and went, leaving only the gentle lapping of the water against the hull next to me. Eventually I gave in and allowed myself to fall asleep. I must have been tired because I slept soundly. When I woke up the sunlight was streaming in through the windows and Karima was behind the kitchen counter making coffee.

'Sleep well?' she asked. She was wearing a long, loose shirt, which I assumed she had slept in. Her legs were bare and her hair was down, pulled round to hang over her right shoulder.

'I did actually, surprisingly.' I sat up and pulled my trousers on. Such routine manoeuvres were getting easier, which was a good sign. I was glad to note that no blood had leaked through the dressings overnight. I went back up to the entrance to look around. The jackdaw was back, perched on the railing. It all felt remarkably peaceful and domesticated. That generally made me nervous.

After coffee, I waited while Karima showered and dressed. Together we walked over to Rinke's boat next door where a surprise awaited us.

The wheelhouse door was open.

'What the hell?' Karima said as we stepped inside.

The whole of the interior had been turned over. If I thought the place had needed tidying up the day before, now there could be no doubt. Tables and chairs were overturned; the kitchen cupboards had been emptied, their contents strewn all over the floor.

'Jesus!' muttered Karima. Then called, 'Rinke!'

He was in the back, tied to a chair, his hands bound together with wire that had cut deep enough into his wrists to draw blood. At first sight, I thought he might be dead. His face was covered in blood. But there was a pulse. I found a pair of pliers in a toolbox in the wheelhouse and cut him free, then we helped him up. I cleared a space for him on the couch under the window in the living room. Karima knelt beside him with a cloth and a bowl of warm water. His eyes were swollen and he looked like he'd lost a couple of teeth. Somebody had given him a good going over.

'What happened?' I asked.

Rinke tried to speak. His jaw moved but he seemed to have trouble getting his tongue to work. I wondered just how hard they had hit him.

'Water,' said Karima. 'He needs water.'

I fetched some and she took the glass and held it to his lips. It helped. While Karima tended to his wounds, he began to talk.

'I don't know where they came from. I was asleep. Suddenly, they had me.'

'They?' I asked. 'Can you describe them? How many were there?'

'A man and a woman. I'd never seen them before.'

'Why did they do this?' Karima asked, looking at me.

'We have to assume they followed us.'

Rinke was having trouble getting his mouth to work. He was in shock. Karima used a cloth to clean away some of the blood from around his mouth and chin. It flowed back out as soon as she took her hand away.

'I need a drink,' he moaned. 'A real drink.'

'That's probably not a good idea,' I said.

'I don't care,' Rinke whined, pointing a trembling finger. 'Under the sink.'

I looked at Karima. She shrugged. 'Get him something to drink.'

There was a bottle of vodka gathering dust behind a bucket of cleaning products. I fished it out and found a glass. Rinke gulped down a shot and held out a shaking hand for more. After his third he cocked his good eye at me.

'This story about being over here for business is bullshit, right?'

I glanced at Karima before nodding.

'So why are you here?'

'It's complicated, Rinke,' Karima said.

'Sure, everything is too complicated for old Rinke to understand.' He grabbed the bottle from me and poured himself another glass, full to the rim.

'Maybe you want to go a little easy on that,' I said. 'You took quite a blow to the head.'

'Yeah, and now you're a doctor, I suppose.'

'I know something about getting hit in the head.'

Rinke just glared at me with his good eye before reaching for the glass.

'OK, this is not getting us anywhere,' Karima said. I had to agree with her.

I went back up to the wheelhouse and scanned the area around us, three hundred and sixty degrees. The canal, the houseboats and quays across the water. I didn't see anything. I knew that every minute we stayed here increased the chances of Donny's men catching up with us, but this attack didn't seem to match their style. Nevertheless, I needed to know who the attackers were and what they had been after. I tried to work out how they would have found us. Coincidence, or resourcefulness? Could one of Donny's contacts have spotted us in Newcastle? It was possible. A security camera might have picked us up in the port or coming aboard the ferry. Karima had used her own passport which might have sent up a red flag somewhere. My first instinct was to run, but that was tempered by a need to know. I don't like surprises and I was pretty sure we had been careful, calculated the risks properly. I went back below to find Rinke had passed out on the sofa. Shock and a good measure of vodka will do that. Karima waved me over to the kitchen area.

'He went out like a light,' she whispered.

'Did he say anything?'

'We need to give him time.'

'We don't have time.' I paused. 'There's something here that doesn't quite add up.'

'How do you mean?'

'I mean, how did they find us? We were careful. We avoided airports. They would have to be tracking us, but that doesn't make sense either.'

'Why not?'

'Because if they were tracking us in some way, it would have made more sense to get to us at Marko's place. There's something else.' I turned to look out the window as a gull swept by low and twisted round in the air. 'Why pick on Rinke? Why turn the place over?'

'They were looking for something?'

'How big is this disk?'

Karima held up her left hand. 'About the size of my palm.'

'OK.' I nodded in the direction of the couch. 'We need to talk to him.'

'He's not in a fit state. He should really go to hospital. I think he's had a concussion.'

I shook my head. 'Not an option, not yet at least.'

It was clear that Karima was unhappy with this, but she could see that we didn't have all that much choice. There was a groan from the sofa as Rinke struggled to sit up. I bent over him.

'Listen, Rinke, I'm sorry about all of this. It's possible the people who did this came here looking for us.'

He was mumbling something and shaking his head.

I turned to Karima. 'Can you try?'

She crouched down in front of him and started talking. Rinke began to speak, only this time it wasn't English.

'What is he saying?'

Rinke was still mumbling. Karima held his head up to let him drink. Water this time. He was in a bad way and I suspected he wasn't going to be much help. He was getting quite worked up about something. I looked at Karima for clarity. She set the glass down on the table.

'Ziggy,' she said. 'They were asking for Ziggy.'
'Who's Ziggy?'
She looked up at me. 'He's my son.'

TWENTY-ONE

We left Rinke on the sofa and went back up to the aft deck. The sun was out and I scanned the road alongside us though I assumed that our assailants would not come back in broad daylight. Our situation had changed. I was no longer as worried as I had been. This was not about us, or rather, not in a way that involved Donny. That left a number of gaps that needed plugging, starting with Ziggy. Now I understood what Rinke had meant by them having 'all' been happy.

'So you were quite the little family here.'

'I'm sorry,' Karima said. 'I didn't think it was relevant.'

'It's quite a big detail to leave out, don't you think?'

'I don't mean it like that. I just . . .'

Karima sank down on to a rough wooden bench that rested up against the bulkhead. Someone had nailed a couple of wooden pallets together and painted them fire engine red. Rinke's handiwork, I guessed. The wind ruffled her hair and she raised a hand to shield her eyes from the sun as she looked up at me.

'It was a long time ago. I was a mess.' She hesitated again, trying to find the words. 'I was too wrapped up in my own problems to be any kind of mother.'

'How old is he now?'

'He was eighteen in January.'

She lowered her face and looked down at her hands.

'I get the feeling you haven't had much contact with him?'

Karima gave a quick shake of the head. 'I was just a kid myself.'

'So Rinke looked after him?'

'For a time, but he had his own ups and downs. In the end

Rinke's mother, Esther, came to the rescue. When I decided to leave, I left him with her.'

'Sounds like a lot to ask.'

Her eyes flared and her face glowed as if she had been slapped. She took a moment before going on.

'It was a difficult decision, but the way I saw it, I was the problem. They were better off without me.' She looked at me. 'And I knew that if I was to have any chance of surviving I had to get away from here, from the whole toxic environment I was in.'

I sat back and stared up at the sky. Clouds were scurrying by over the rooftops. When the sun was hidden the wind turned chilly.

'I'm assuming Rinke is the father.'

She hung her head. 'Actually, that was part of the problem.'

'This is the story that just keeps on giving. Who is the father?'

'He's just a guy, someone I met. We had a brief thing.' Karima swore under her breath and pushed a hand through her hair.

'Does he know? That he's the father, I mean.'

'No, of course not.' She looked at me. 'Rinke was the only father Ziggy knew growing up, but eventually that wasn't enough.'

'You told him.'

'He asked me.' She leaned forward, resting her elbows on her knees. 'Ziggy went through a difficult time. The usual soul-searching, I suppose. I was doing all right by then. I was clean. I had a steady job.'

'Doing Donny's accounting.'

'Eventually. It took a while and I couldn't really pick and choose. I took whatever came my way.' She picked at the seam of her jeans with a fingernail. 'I think Ziggy's in some kind of trouble. We have to find him.'

'That's not why we came here.'

She looked up at me. 'He's the only person who might have found the hard disk.'

I nodded. 'Then maybe that's a good reason to find him. Any idea where he might be?'

'No, but Rinke might. I don't think he's still staying with his mother.'

It was a plan, but as it turned out, not one with legs on it. Rinke was, as I feared, next to useless. He had recovered somewhat, but claimed he'd had no real contact with the boy for ages.

'Every now and then he turns up without a word.' He shrugged, pointing across the living area at the sofa. 'I just wake up and find him there. He stays for a day or so, takes a shower, eats. I try to feed him.' He was shaking his head. 'I've never really had much of a relationship with him. I mean, I think he likes me, but he's in his own world.'

There was something resigned about Rinke, as though he'd given up trying to understand how he had come to be in this position.

'How about money?' I asked.

Rinke looked at me. 'How do you mean?'

'I mean, does he have a job?'

'No, not as far as I know. He's always short. He asked for money, but, you know . . .' He looked around him as though the answer was obvious.

'So he asked for money and you told him you didn't have any to give him?'

'Yeah,' Rinke nodded, as though this was a fair assessment of his position.

'OK. Do you have any way of reaching him?'

'I have a number. Not sure if it still works.' By now Rinke was beginning to look agitated. 'You want me to call him?'

'No, not call. I want you to send him a message. Tell him you've found some money and he can have it.'

Rinke frowned. 'He's not going to believe that.'

'Tell him his mother sent some money for him. Will he believe that?'

'I don't know,' he said slowly.

'If he needs money bad enough,' I said, 'he'll believe it, right?'

'Maybe.' Rinke's eyes darted back and forth between us. 'What is this all about anyway?'

I looked at Karima, who was standing with her arms wrapped

around her. She'd been silent for a long time. I turned back to Rinke.

'He has something that we need. A computer disk.'

'A what?' Rinke's eyes were dull with incomprehension. 'I don't . . .'

'You need to send him a message,' Karima said quietly.

Rinke blinked dully around him. 'I have to find my phone first. I haven't seen it since last night.'

As he set about looking, I led Karima to one side.

'You need to tread carefully,' I said. 'If Ziggy has the hard disk, we need to get it back.'

'I don't like it,' Karima said quietly. 'I don't understand. Why would he take it?'

'We can ask him when we find him, but that disk is our only chance of finding out why Donny wants you dead. We need to get it back.'

'I'm not sure coming here was such a good idea.' Karima was biting her nails. It felt like I was watching her unravel. 'This is not easy for me. The whole thing with Ziggy . . . I'm not sure . . .'

'Look,' I said, putting a hand on her shoulder. 'It's not that difficult. If he's in some kind of trouble we can help him, lend him some money, or whatever he needs.'

Karima shrugged herself free. 'I'm not sure I'm ready.'

'It doesn't have to be bad,' I said. I could see she was suffering and there wasn't much I could do to reassure her. This was about her relationship with her son. I was in no doubt that all of this was bringing back memories of that time and why she had walked out on him.

Down below, Rinke had managed to locate his telephone. He waved it with a big smile.

'Don't call,' I said. 'Text him.'

'OK.' He shrugged. I watched him picking out the letters with his thumbs. It made no sense to him, but phone calls could be monitored quite easily. Text messages couldn't. While he was doing this Karima disappeared up on deck again with Rinke's tobacco and cigarette papers.

We waited ten minutes for a reply. Ziggy was keen. Rinke read out the message.

'He says he'll come over right away.'

'No,' I said. 'Tell him it's better to meet somewhere. Tell him a place that he knows. Somewhere he's been with you.'

Rinke considered the idea before nodding. 'The playground in Westerpark. We used to go there with my mother. It's close by.'

'Perfect.'

Twenty minutes later found us in the park. The sky had grown dark as heavy clouds swarmed overhead, threatening a downpour.

I held back with Karima under the trees while Rinke stood out in the open, in the middle of the playground. We waited another twenty minutes. I began to wonder if Ziggy had changed his mind or decided he didn't like the idea. Maybe he was just being cautious. Then I caught sight of him. A skinny figure in dark clothes, black jeans and a hoodie. His clothes were worn. He seemed to be hesitating. I put out a hand to stop Karima from moving forward. She was trembling.

'Wait for him,' I whispered. 'He's scared.'

Rinke was smoking a cigarette and kicking the ground with his shoe, his thoughts who knows where. Either way, he hadn't noticed Ziggy, which was perhaps a good thing.

When he was satisfied that the coast was clear, Ziggy stepped forward. He moved quickly, with his head down, staying close to the shadows. He approached Rinke from behind, startling him as he appeared seemingly out of nowhere. You could see Rinke was spooked and Ziggy knew it. He stood at a distance, looking over his shoulder in the direction Rinke was sending nervous glances, towards us.

'Now,' I said, nudging Karima forward.

When he saw us stepping out from the trees, Ziggy stared at us for a moment, frowning, as if unsure what he was seeing. Then he began to back away. I could see Rinke say something to him and the young man stopped. He looked at us again and seemed to recognize Karima. He waited, twitching, hands thrust deep into his pockets. He was still looking around him, making sure his line of escape was clear, but now you could see he was compelled to stay. He was curious. As we drew closer, I could see that curious was the wrong word.

'Hello, Ziggy,' Karima said. The boy spat something that I took to be a curse.

'Why are you here?' he asked in English.

'I wanted to see you.'

It was a nice try, but clearly he wasn't buying it. He shook his head at Rinke and said something I couldn't understand.

'It's not his fault, Ziggy,' I said. He looked me up and down and decided he didn't like what he saw.

'Who are you?'

'I'm a friend. I'm trying to help your mother.'

'My mother?' Ziggy's laugh was tinged with bitterness. 'She ran out on me when I was a baby. She's not my mother.'

'I knew this was a bad idea,' Karima said.

'You see, even she knows it makes no sense.' Ziggy was shaking his head as he laughed. 'I don't need you; I don't need any of you.' He turned to walk away.

'Wait,' I said. 'If you won't talk to her, at least listen to what I have to say.'

'Why should I do that?'

'Because you're in trouble and maybe we can help you.'

'Help me? Why would you do that? I don't even know you.'

'I told you, I'm a friend of your mother's.' I glanced at Karima to see if she would object. She was silent.

'That doesn't mean anything to me. *She* doesn't mean anything to me.'

'Ziggy, they came to the house,' Rinke said quietly. 'They were looking for you.'

'That's my problem,' Ziggy snapped. 'I can take care of it.'

'Really?' I asked. 'How are you going to take care of it?'

'I don't know,' he shrugged. 'I'll think of something.'

'Yeah?' I asked. 'Because it didn't look like these people have a lot of patience. The next time they come back it might not work out so well for Rinke. Did you think about that?'

From the look on his face, Ziggy hadn't thought about it, or anything else really. He was young and he wouldn't believe he couldn't handle the situation until it was too late. I was reminded for a second of Zef, but that was long ago, or it felt that way, and Ziggy was smarter than Zef. You only had to look at him to know that.

'What do they want from you?' I asked.

'Tell him,' Karima urged.

Ziggy's response was predictable. 'Why should I do anything you tell me?' he scowled.

'Because whatever I've done, however you feel about me, I'm still your mother and nothing is ever going to change that.'

It was a nice try, although I didn't think her words would have much impact on him. To my surprise Ziggy actually seemed to reconsider his position.

'Money,' he said, staring grimly at the ground. 'I owe them money.'

'How much?' I asked.

'Not that much.' He shrugged and tried to wave the question aside. 'I'll pay them. They just, you know, these guys, they like to play tough.'

'How much?' I repeated.

Ziggy gave a deep sigh. 'Ten grand.'

'Ten thousand euros?' Rinke was incredulous.

'Oh my God!' muttered Karima.

Ziggy wasn't swayed by this response. 'It's not that much. I mean, I would have made three times that if things had worked out.'

'So what is this all about?' I asked. 'You owe them for something you were going to sell?'

'Sure. Pills. You know, speed, ecstasy . . .' Ziggy's voice tailed off.

'So what happened? Why didn't you sell them?'

'Someone took them off me.'

This whole business was getting more convoluted by the minute. I gestured to Karima and led her aside.

'This is getting too complicated. We don't have time to get involved.'

She stared at me, as if she couldn't believe what she was hearing. 'You were the one who wanted to help him, remember? We're here now. We can't just walk away.' She was looking at me as if I had lost my mind.

'Whatever he's into, whoever he owes money to, he'll have to straighten it out himself.'

'You want to just ditch him? Leave him to these animals? Who knows what they might do.'

'Our business is more pressing. We're here to find out why Donny wants you dead. We need to get hold of the hard disk. The rest is a distraction.'

'A distraction?' she echoed. 'My God! How did you get like this?'

'Like what?' I couldn't see why she was so shocked. 'I mean, it's not as if you've been the perfect mother to him all these years.'

'That's unfair!' she hissed. I realized I had crossed a line.

'I'm sorry. You're right, that was unfair.'

Karima didn't say anything and for a time we just stood there.

'No wonder that poor kid was scared of you,' she murmured eventually.

I wasn't expecting that. 'You're talking about Zef? He was scared of me?'

'Terrified.' Her eyes searched mine. 'Why do you think it was so easy to turn him against you?'

'You told him you were going to give him a share of the money you took from Donny. And besides, he had a thing for you.' Zef had a thing for any woman his eyes fell on, but I wasn't going to mention that.

'He didn't want money, or me.' Karima shook her head. 'It wasn't like that. He was desperate for respect, any kind of respect.' Her voice fell. 'We were both desperate for a way out.'

It tallied with what little I had known of Zephyr. He was young, cocky, too sure of himself. A part of me regretted having to kill him. Another part of me knew I had had no choice.

'I didn't have to talk him into killing you, he came up with that all by himself.'

I nodded. I understood. 'I was asked to show him the ropes. He saw me as a rival. It was bound to end badly.'

'You should listen to yourself some time. When did you lose all faith in humanity?'

It wasn't a question I had any kind of answer to, but even if I had, Karima wasn't interested in hearing it. She turned and walked back over to Ziggy.

'If we can get you the money, will that straighten things
out?'

'You can do that?' Ziggy looked from her to me and back
again. 'You can get ten grand just like that?'

I stepped in. 'If you pay these guys off, is that the end of
it, or will they still want more?'

'They just want their money.'

I wasn't sure I believed him, but I couldn't really argue.
'There's one condition,' I said. 'We need the hard disk back.'

'The what?' He frowned, feigning ignorance. Whatever
Ziggy was, he wasn't a good liar.

'The hard disk you found on the boat. It belongs to your
mother.'

'It's important, Ziggy,' Karima said.

'And there was me thinking you missed me.' He had a
tight-lipped grimace on his face.

'This doesn't have to be complicated,' I said. 'Get us the
disk and you get the money.'

Ziggy sniffed and rubbed the back of his hand across his
nose. He was feigning uninterest, but you could see he was
hooked.

'You really have that kind of money, in cash?'

'Yes, but we have to do this the right way. Where's the hard
disk?'

'What if I don't have it?'

'We don't have time for games, Ziggy,' I said.

'OK, but how do I know you'll give me the money?' He
had a silly grin on his face, like he didn't believe he had much
leverage.

'The way I see it, you don't have much choice.'

'Maybe.' He shrugged.

'There's no maybe about it,' I said. 'You want these people
off your back, don't you?'

'Please, Ziggy,' Karima said. It seemed to work. Her being
nice to him was wearing down his resistance. His expression
changed.

'Where is it?' I asked.

He pushed his hands into the pockets of his jeans. 'It's at
my place.'

'You need to take us there, now.'

Ziggy thought about that for a time and finally nodded. We made our way back to the car and he directed us. Karima took the wheel and we drove along the side of a canal headed out of town. It was pretty. There were ducks in the water and grey herons standing like sentries here and there along the banks. They were scruffy things, but they had something regal and dignified about them, as if they were removed from everything around them. I watched one spread its wings and take off, flapping away in great beating arcs as it vanished into the quickening dusk.

TWENTY-TWO

We followed Ziggy's directions to a tree-lined street where Karima parked the Mondeo. I had been keeping an eye out all the way, checking the side mirrors to be sure we weren't being tailed. When I stepped out of the car I discovered that we were standing in front of a long grey building with wide, high windows. It looked like a school of some kind and that's exactly what it turned out to be.

Ziggy entered a code into a digital pad beside a metal door which he then pulled open. It gave on to a corridor that led through the building. We came out on the other side in a square courtyard with trees and flowerbeds in the middle. The building walled the four sides of the open area with the same concrete structures. These all looked as though they might once have housed classrooms or training facilities of some kind. Ziggy led us round to a glass-fronted door in the far corner. There was trouble waiting for us on the other side.

The room we entered was about twelve metres long and around the same in width. The walls were high with long, narrow windows at the top to let in the light. The windows were covered in black drapes that had been hung haphazardly. The single space was broken up by a number of tables that had been pushed together in the middle of the floor. Around the side were mattresses on which sleeping bags, duvets and other assorted bedclothes were scattered. There were also sports holdalls, rucksacks, shoes, plastic bin liners and heaps of clothes. Out of one of these emerged a young woman. She was clearly frantic.

Like Ziggy she was in her late teens. Like him she wore torn jeans and a sweatshirt. Her hair was braided into long, thick ropey dreads that hung down past her narrow shoulder blades. They were dyed blue and purple, with a touch of blonde creeping through here and there. She was in tears. Sobbing hysterically, she ran to Ziggy and threw her arms around him. He seemed embarrassed by this display of emotion. I couldn't understand what she was saying but she clearly wanted to know where he had been. After a moment she looked around in bewilderment, as if she had suddenly noticed that he was not alone.

'Rinke?'

'Hello, Fleur.' He beamed.

Her big shining eyes turned to take in the rest of us.

'My mother,' Ziggy explained. 'And her friend.'

Fleur's gaze rested on me only for a moment before moving on.

'What happened here?' I asked. She looked at me, still trying to work out who I was.

'I was asleep when they came. I don't know how they got in, but suddenly they were turning everything over. I mean, look at it.' She began to cry again as she looked about her. 'It was horrible!'

'What did they want?'

'I don't know!' She sobbed. 'They were looking for you.' She looked at Ziggy, who said nothing.

'They didn't hurt you?' I asked her.

She bit her lip and shook her head. 'Next time.' Her voice dropped to a whisper. 'They said that if they had to come back they would do terrible things to me. Then they laughed.'

'Who?' I asked Ziggy, who was staring at the floor like a condemned man. 'Who are they?'

'Momo Khelifa,' said Ziggy softly.

'How do we find him?'

He looked at me as if I was mad. 'You don't find him. He finds you.'

'Then you need to call him and tell him you're ready to talk. But first,' I said, 'we talked about that hard disk, remember?'

'It's gone.'

Again, we all turned to Fleur.

'Gone how?' I asked.

'They took all the stuff they could.' She shrugged. 'Laptops, screens.' She pointed at the table where a tangle of computer cables was strewn about. I hadn't really paid it much attention, but I could see it now: the overturned chairs, the cables, the electric power lines that snaked around the floor. Not bohemian carelessness, but the outcome of a ransacking.

I turned back to Ziggy. 'What exactly have you been up to here?'

'We're the Global Avengers,' Fleur said, as if this was self-explanatory. I looked to Karima for an explanation and got a blank shake of the head in return.

'The Global . . .?'

Fleur glanced over at Ziggy who was trying desperately to light a cigarette with a lighter that was out of gas. He clicked it over and over until Rinke stepped in to help him. Fleur carried on talking.

'We're eco-warriors, changing the world from inside the Web.'

'Does this have anything to do with this Momo character?' I wondered.

'No, that was just a way of making some cash,' Ziggy said, trying to explain. 'To finance our operation.'

'Wait a second,' said Karima. 'What exactly were you doing?'

Ziggy noticed the change in her voice and became evasive once more. Less reticent than him, Fleur was only too happy to explain. Underneath the nervous flow you could sense that she was proud of what they were doing. Ziggy didn't look too happy, but Fleur went on anyway.

'The whole point is to break into the banking system. Hit them where it hurts.'

They were switching in and out of English, which meant I was having trouble following it all, but Karima seemed to understand.

'You were breaking in, you mean, hacking into the banks? To do what?'

Ziggy had shut down, puffing hard on a cigarette. When Fleur started to speak again, he snapped at her. She was annoyed about that. You didn't have to understand the words to recognize the tension between them. She clasped her hands together and looked away.

Karima pressed Ziggy. 'What were you trying to do?'

'He wasn't trying,' Fleur couldn't help piping up, despite the glare Ziggy shot her. 'He's very good. They're all good.'

'All?' I asked, gesturing at the table. 'You mean, there's a group of you doing this?'

'You need to be a group to break in,' she explained, as if talking to an idiot. 'You have to attack several points at once.'

'I don't get this,' I confessed, turning to Ziggy. 'If you were breaking into banking systems, why waste your time with pills?'

'Because this isn't about making money.' Ziggy sounded indignant, as if insulted by the mere idea of stealing for himself.

'So what is it about?'

Fleur answered. 'It's to bring down the system. The whole system? World collapse? Anarchy? The end of capitalism?'

'Right.' I nodded. 'Great. I get that. Then what?'

'Then we start again, redistribute the wealth.'

I nodded at our surroundings. 'And you were going to do all of that from here?'

'It was Ziggy's idea. He had found a way in.'

Karima swore quietly. 'You used my hard disk.' She stepped forward to confront him. Ziggy avoided her gaze. 'That's what you did, right?' She glanced over at me, keeping her eyes on her son. 'That drive contains banking information from all over the world. Transfer codes, account numbers, telephones, emails.' She threw her hands up and stepped away. 'How could you?'

'I just found it. I didn't know it was yours.'

'Whose did you think it was?'

'I don't know. It was hidden behind a ventilation panel. It could have been anyone's.'

'What were you looking in there for anyway?' Karima asked.

'I was looking for somewhere to stash some of my merchandise.'

'You never asked me about it,' said Rinke.

'I know. I'm sorry. I just didn't think it could belong to you.'

'It was on my boat.'

Ziggy shrugged as though that piece of information was neither here nor there. We were going round in circles. I turned to Fleur for more information.

'These people who were here. What exactly did they say when they took this stuff?'

'They said it was . . .' She fished around for the word. 'Compensation. We would get it back when we returned their pills to them.'

'I still don't get why you needed to sell the pills. Surely that confuses everything? You were breaking into banks. Why did you need money?'

Ziggy was silent.

'Tell them the truth,' Fleur urged him.

'That sounds like a good idea.' I turned back to Ziggy. 'Why don't you tell us everything?'

Ziggy was frowning fiercely at the floor.

With a sigh of resignation, Fleur explained. 'The pills were for Rasha.'

'Who's Rasha?' Karima asked, echoing the question in my head.

Ziggy found his voice again. 'She's just this girl I met.'

'He's in love with her.' Fleur pulled a face, clearly unhappy.

'I'm not,' insisted Ziggy.

'Yes, you are. You might as well admit it.'

'Met where?' I asked, breaking in on what might have been an endless discussion. 'How?'

Ziggy shrugged. Again, it was up to Fleur to fill in the blanks.

'She's from Syria. She escaped. We met her in a coffee shop.'
'She's a refugee,' I said.
Fleur nodded.
'So the money is for her? Why?'
Now it was Fleur's turn to shrug. All eyes turned to Ziggy.
'She has nothing. She works in a window.'
I'd seen enough of the red-light district to know what he was talking about. It was one of the city's most notorious features. Women sat behind glass windows waiting for customers. When someone came along who was interested, they let them in and drew the red curtains.

This was not a good development. Those windows were valuable pieces of real estate and the people who ran them made a lot of money. Behind the bright lights and scantily clad girls there were some pretty dark characters. The girls were brought in from all over the place. Often they had no choice. The liberal myth that these women were exercising their free right to sell themselves, that they were in control of their bodies and earnings, that they had free healthcare and all the rest of it, was exactly that, a myth.

'So, let me get this straight. You wanted to sell the pills to make enough money to buy this girl's freedom?'
'Rasha, yes.' Ziggy nodded with something that finally resembled conviction.
'Well, that's very noble of you,' I said. 'The man who owns her, is that the same one you got the pills off?'
Ziggy hesitated and then gave a furtive nod. 'If I could just have sold them I would have had more than enough,' he protested.
'You've ruined everything!' Fleur cried. 'Why is she so important to you?'
Ziggy was silent.
'My son, the idealist,' murmured Karima. I couldn't be sure but I thought I detected a note of pride in there somewhere.
'The best laid plans and all that,' I said to Ziggy. Now that I understood what he had been trying to do, I had to admit I felt some sympathy for him. He was making our lives a lot more complicated than I had bargained for, but what the hell.

'You have to call them,' I said to him. 'Tell them you have the money.'

He looked at me strangely. 'I can't. They won't believe me.'

'You have to make them believe.'

'You have the money?' He still didn't look convinced.

'I just want this business wrapped up. It's a distraction.'

Ziggy looked to Karima for confirmation and she nodded. While Ziggy found his phone and stepped away to make the call, she took me aside.

'This is bad,' she said, keeping her voice low. 'If they have used those codes, then they could be exposing all kinds of things.'

'Could that have prompted someone in Donny's firm to get suspicious?'

'Definitely.' She nodded.

Ziggy finished his call and sidled back over. 'No dice. He says he wants another ten grand interest.'

'What?' Fleur erupted into tears. 'We're never going to get out of this. They're going to rape me and then kill us both. Not that you care.'

'Don't be silly.' Ziggy sounded as though he was trying to make amends.

'Calm down,' I said. 'Everyone calm down.' I tried to get Ziggy to focus. 'Did you speak to the man in charge?'

'What? Momo? No way, he doesn't talk to people like me, but he was there. I could hear him in the background. He was yelling.'

'What did he say?' Karima asked.

'It was in Arabic. I couldn't understand.'

'But he said another ten thousand in interest, you're sure of that?' I asked. Ziggy nodded. 'OK, then we need another plan. We need leverage on this guy.'

'Leverage?' Karima echoed.

'What do we know about this Momo?'

'He's Moroccan,' said Ziggy. 'He runs everything.'

'Not everything.'

We all turned towards Rinke who was standing in the corner, leaning against an old filing cabinet that had been dragged in from the street by the look of it. He was rolling himself a cigarette.

'I used to know some of these guys,' he continued, before licking his cigarette paper. 'In the old days. One guy in particular. He handed the business over to the Moroccans.'

'Who are you talking about?' I asked.

'Kenny Broek. Old school.'

'Is he around, can we talk to him?'

'Sure, he's always around.' Rinke shrugged. 'I can call him.'

TWENTY-THREE

R inke made the call and Kenny Broek agreed to meet. We all got into the Mondeo and drove for an hour. This was turning into a side-track of epic proportions. On the way we dropped Fleur off at her parents' place in the suburbs. A nondescript house in a row of identical houses. The kind of place you dreamed of getting out of and never coming back. By the look on their faces as they opened the front door, they were surprised to see her. There was a chance Momo would find out where she lived, but all in all it was the safest thing to do, keeping her out of harm's way until this was sorted out. After that we got back on the highway and drove south, before turning on to a small, deserted street on the beachfront.

The rain was lashing across the top of a low dyke that separated the road from the actual beach. Facing the dyke was a row of buildings, apartments for retired people, restaurants and shops that were either shuttered or closed.

'Are you sure this is the right place?' Karima asked, voicing my thoughts exactly.

Rinke craned his neck left and right. 'This is what he said. There should be a sushi place somewhere along here.'

It was on the corner. Yumio Sushi. Sounded as authentic as hell. A red and black façade with an interior that looked deserted.

'The place is empty,' I said.

'He'll be here,' nodded Rinke. I wondered why he was so

sure. Right now I didn't trust anyone. We parked the car and went inside. There was nobody around, not even behind the counter.

I indicated a table by the window. Nobody seemed to object, so we sat down there. I looked at my watch. It was ten minutes past the hour. We were later than we had agreed, but still, I expected him to be here.

'We'll give him fifteen minutes,' I said to Rinke. 'No more. Tell me again how you know this guy.'

'I knew him back in the old days. He was one of the few dealers you could actually talk to. The rest were just brutes. Kenny always treated people well. He had style.'

'So how long is it since you've seen him?'

'A while.'

A waitress appeared. A small woman wearing a set of black pyjamas with red piping. Her features looked Chinese and I was willing to bet she didn't speak more than a couple of words of Japanese, but I let it go. Karima asked for green tea and I nodded. It was as good as anything else at this point.

Where we were sitting offered us a view of the street and parking area. I had my back to the wall, so I was the first to notice the silver Audi as it rolled up. It was new, a couple of years old at the most. I watched it pull in to the kerb and come to a halt. For a long time there was no movement. The driver was taking his time. As far as I could see he wasn't doing anything. He was just sitting, watching. A few minutes later he climbed out.

Kenny Broek was a large man, in his early sixties, tall and bulky, wearing a baggy grey tracksuit. What was left of his hair was white and receding. He didn't much care about his appearance. I watched as he stood there for a long time, looking up and down the street before finally crossing over and entering the restaurant. He stood in the doorway, tossing the keys in his hands. We were the only people in there. Even the waitress had vanished. Finally he came over. Rinke got to his feet and they shook hands and exchanged greetings. Then he introduced us. Finally, Broek sat down. He insisted on facing the door, so Rinke changed places.

The waitress reappeared and smiled at Broek. She clearly

knew him and knew what he wanted to eat. Ziggy was studying
the menu like it was a rocket manual. Broek ordered for
everyone.

'It's my favourite place. I come here all the time,' he said,
his eyes roving around, sizing us up. 'Of course they're not
really Japanese. How would they end up here at the ends of
the earth?' He chuckled at his own humour. 'But they do know
how to make sushi.'

I wondered at the wisdom of what we were doing. I had
no idea who this man was or what he was capable of. All I
knew was that right now we needed his help, and he knew
the same thing, which put us at a disadvantage. With a nod
to me, Rinke started to fill him in. Kenny's face was expressionless as he listened. He looked Karima over, then me, and
finally his eyes came to rest on Ziggy.

'So this is all your doing?'

He was speaking English for our benefit. Ziggy managed
to give a small nod.

'You're messing with some serious people,' said Broek. He
looked up as the waitress brought him a can of Coke and a
glass without being asked.

'You know this man, Momo Khelifa?' I asked finally.

'I've dealt with him.' Broek paused to study me as he took
a sip of his drink. 'So tell me where you come in?'

'You're the odd man out here,' he summarized when I had
finished. 'What's your interest in this?'

'I'm just trying to help.' Kenny Broek looked as though he
wasn't sure he believed this. I put that to one side and went
on. 'My feeling is that reasoning with this guy is not going
to be easy, which is why we thought you might be able to
help.'

'That would be my feeling too,' Broek agreed. 'Look, I
only agreed to meet because Rinke and I go back to the old
days when we were all young and good looking, and poor.'

That amused Rinke. The more I watched him, the more I
saw how he admired Broek. I tried to imagine Broek in the
old days, when he didn't look like a scruffy retiree. I was
beginning to see that his appearance was anything but casual.
The unkempt hair, the baggy sweatsuit. He didn't look rich

and he didn't look like a threat. Kenny Broek was a lot smarter than you might assume.

'Correct me if I'm wrong, but you look as if you have some experience of this kind of thing.'

'Like I said, I'm just trying to help a friend.'

'You don't look like the philanthropic type, but let's drop it. Momo is a difficult character. He has a temper and can behave in a rash way. You have to be careful how you deal with him.'

'What would you suggest?' I asked.

'Look, I'm out of the game, as you know, and I'd like to keep it that way. But with this guy you can't show any weakness. That only encourages him.' Broek glanced around our group. 'You can't go up against him. You need to take him by surprise, keep him off balance.'

'I just want to end this as quietly as possible,' I said.

'Of course. You want to get the boy out of trouble.'

'I'm not a boy,' Ziggy objected.

Broek ignored that. The food began to arrive and he inspected each lacquered tray carefully as it was set down. The waitress stepped back and waited for his approval before moving on. Broek unwrapped his chopsticks and helped himself, popping a piece of salmon into his mouth and chewing contentedly.

'I don't care where they come from, this is the best.'

'Salmon is unsustainable,' said Ziggy. 'That's why they carry so many parasites.'

'What are you talking about?' Broek lowered his chopsticks slowly. 'Parasites?'

'I'm just telling you the facts.' Ziggy was unrepentant.

'He's joking,' Rinke said hastily. 'That's all. It's just his way of being funny.' He glared at Ziggy. We all did. The kid was about to derail the only chance we had of solving this problem.

'Who talks about parasites when you're eating?' Broek's disgust was plain. The discussion continued as they switched into Dutch. I waited for them to finish. By then nobody was eating. We all just stared at the food on the table. Broek threw down his napkin and pushed back his chair. 'Well, I'm sorry, but I'm not wasting any more time on this.'

As he headed for the door, I went after him. Behind me I could hear Ziggy protesting his innocence as Karima and Rinke turned on him.

Outside, I found Broek standing on the pavement. He hadn't been in such a hurry as it had appeared. In fact, it seemed to me that he was actually waiting there.

'He didn't mean it,' I began. 'He's just a kid. He wants to change the world.'

'Then he'd better start learning how to live in it.' Kenny Broek looked me over. 'I've been in this game long enough to recognize a soldier when I see one. You're connected, over there in England?'

'I know people,' I conceded.

'So you've had dealings with characters like Momo before?'

'Some.'

'OK, well, that's a good thing. What I said in there still counts. You can't expect Momo to play nice. You have to hit him, that's the only thing he respects.'

'What do you suggest?'

I listened while he told me. When he had finished and I had all the details straight, I asked him why he was helping us.

'When I decided to retire, my associates and I had to pick a successor, someone to take over the business. The decision went in favour of Momo, but I didn't like him and he knew it, so he screwed me over on a couple of deals.'

'I don't want to get caught up in a turf war.'

'You won't. Nobody wants that, least of all me.' Kenny Broek nodded at the Audi. 'Believe me, I have more than enough. I don't need anything. No, this is just a way of getting back at him. It won't do too much damage, but it will hit him. One thing.' He held up a finger. 'Whatever happens, I need your word that this doesn't come back on me.'

'You have it. That's not a problem.'

'Maybe for you, but that kid's got a mouth on him.'

'I'll talk to him. He's scared. He knows this is his only chance.'

'Well, for your sakes, I hope you're right.' He looked up and down the street which was deserted. In the distance a small red car started up and drove towards us. Broek waited where he was, watching the car approach. The only occupant was the driver, an elderly woman wearing a scarf. We waited in silence until it had vanished round the corner. Kenny Broek was a cautious man.

TWENTY-FOUR

We drove back to Amsterdam and Ziggy's studio in the converted school. The whole building appeared to be occupied by artists and oddballs of one sort or another. A group of young men preparing a meal on a portable hotplate on the floor of one of the other rooms waved and shouted greetings as we passed them.

'Who are all these people?' Karima asked.

'Some of them are artists, musicians, theatre groups. That whole section is refugees. They have nowhere else to go.'

It sounded like a description of chaos, but it was also a reminder that this was Ziggy's world. The boundaries were fluid. People came and went. It was the perfect setting for a bunch of young people to plan their takedown of the financial system. Everyone was still hungry after the sushi debacle so Karima and I walked out to fetch pizzas from a nearby place. It gave us a chance to talk in private.

'What do you make of this guy, Broek?' Karima asked.

'I'm not sure. He could be setting us up, but I have a feeling he's being straight with us. He genuinely has a grievance with this Momo. This is a way of getting back at him without being drawn into it.'

'Sounds pretty sick to me.'

'You've been around enough of these types to know how they think.'

'So, you think we should go along with him?'

'I don't think we have much choice. This is the only way of putting pressure on Momo. We want him to lay off Ziggy and we want that hard disk.'

Karima nodded. She could see it made sense. That didn't

mean she had to like it. We were sitting at a small table waiting for our order. Behind the counter three Moroccan kids in their twenties were chatting to one another in a mixture of Arabic and Dutch as they worked. The rest of the place was empty.

'What is it that's bothering you?' I asked.

'I don't know.' Karima rested her hands on the table, locking her fingers together. 'I just feel we are getting further and further away from what we came here for.'

'If it's any consolation, I feel the same.'

'I mean, what are we actually doing? How did we get so deep into this?'

'Look,' I said. 'We came here for that disk. We had no way of knowing that Ziggy and his friends had been using the information on it in their bid to save the planet. Maybe that's why Donny decided to take you out.'

Her eyes lifted from the table to look at me. 'You think that they might have set something off with their hacking?'

'Is that possible?'

She thought about it for a moment. 'If they were digging into people's accounts and using them to launch some kind of attack, they might have triggered an alarm.'

'In which case, the banks might have warned their clients. And that could have led to you.'

Karima nodded. 'Only a limited number of people have access to certain information. It would have been a process of elimination.'

It made sense. Ziggy and his friends had set something off that had somehow got back to Donny.

'Maybe we don't need the hard disk,' she said. 'I mean, we know what happened. Can't we leave it at that?'

'That's information out there with your name on it,' I told her. 'We need to get it back.'

Karima could see the sense of it. She just didn't like it.

'I can't put him through this.' Her head dropped and she stared at the table. 'You don't understand the guilt I've felt all these years for having left him. I was never a good mother. I've told you that already.' She looked up. 'But I never stopped feeling guilt about leaving him behind.'

'You're trying to help him now. He knows that.'

'I did something terrible and the thing is, I can never make it right.'

'You didn't have to do it this way. You didn't have to come here.'

'He knows I'm basically only here to help myself.' She seemed to be unravelling again. I put out a hand to take hers. 'I didn't expect this reaction, these feelings. But the truth is I care. I don't want him to hate me anymore. I don't know how to explain this.'

'You don't need to explain.'

'Meneer!' One of the kids behind the counter was waving me over. Karima pulled her hand free.

We walked back in silence. It felt strange, as though my soul was in turmoil. I realized I was beginning to care about this woman who, only a few days earlier, I had been planning to kill.

'So, Ziggy, take me through it. What exactly were you guys doing?' I asked, when we had all settled down to eat. Ziggy lifted his face from his pizza and looked around him. The black drapes, the anarchist symbols spray-painted on the walls. He didn't seem unhappy with what he saw.

'We broke into banks. Not just here, all over the world. Nowadays, the fat cats move their money. Dubai, the Cayman Islands, the Bahamas, the Baltic states. Capital is fluid, as is corruption. National boundaries are a joke, or rather . . .' He held up a finger for a moment as he wiped his mouth with a paper napkin. 'It's all part of the plan. Politics, borders, it's all there just to keep us occupied, right? Too busy fighting each other to see what they are up to. Right?'

'If you say so.' I wasn't going to argue with the guy. He seemed to have it all figured out for himself. Underneath that anarchic exterior there was a little Napoleon proud of his conquests.

'Politicians keep talking about protecting the country, taking us back to some lost age when we lived in perfect isolation. That's all bullshit. It's a story they are selling us. The money flows round and round making them richer and us poorer.'

'So you hacked into the accounts of people you knew, companies, firms?'

Ziggy grew edgy. He avoided looking at Karima.

'We used the information I found.'

'That was my property,' Karima said angrily. 'The details on that hard disk are private.'

'Then why did you have it?' He didn't seem too bothered about the accusation. 'And why hide it on Rinke's boat?'

'I needed somewhere safe, somewhere nobody would think to look.'

Ziggy shrugged. 'Well, too bad. If it was so valuable to you, you shouldn't have left it so far away. Anyway, it's too late now.'

I tried to bring him back on course. 'How far did you get with your plans?'

'We were doing fine until all this crap came along. Now we'll have to start again.'

'That's not going to happen,' I said.

He didn't like that. He balled up his napkin and threw it down. 'What the fuck has this got to do with you anyway?'

'I'm here to get that hard disk back and I'm not leaving till I have it.'

'Fuck you!'

Ziggy stalked away and threw himself down on a mattress on the far side of the room.

Karima fixed me with one of her looks.

'What?'

'I'm guessing that parenting skills aren't your forte,' she said, getting up.

I looked at Rinke, who shrugged and turned away. After that we all withdrew to our own corners of the old classroom. It would have been more comfortable to find a hotel but this felt safer. I didn't want to risk surfacing. Hotels ask for passports and I had to assume Momo had contacts. Until this whole deal was over and done with, I preferred to stay out of sight as much as possible. There was always the chance that Momo's men would come back. They had taken the computer equipment and I was guessing now they would give us a day to see whether we turned up with the money.

Across the gloom of the big schoolroom I could see the glow of a screen and went over to where Ziggy was lying down.

'Listen, I don't have to tell you that you should probably stay offline. We don't want to announce where we are.'

He finally consented to remove the headphones and look up at me, slowly setting the phone down before sitting up.

'So what exactly is your deal?' he said.

'My deal?'

'You and my mom.'

'There is no deal. I'm just helping her.'

'But you're banging her, right?'

I took a slow breath. 'Why do you assume that?'

'Because, what I don't get, right, is how you're mixed up in all this. Why do you give a fuck? Also, I think you're a dangerous person.'

'What makes you think that?'

'I saw you and that guy, Kenny. Looked like the two of you had a lot to talk about.'

'Listen, Ziggy, you need to stop thinking of me as your enemy. Right now, we both want the same thing. Try to get some sleep. You need to be on your toes tomorrow.' I started to walk away and then turned back to him. 'And you should cut your mother some slack. She may have made mistakes in the past, but she wouldn't be here if she didn't care about you.'

'Care about me?' His voice dripped with scorn. 'Oh, I get it, you haven't banged her yet, but you're still hopeful.' He set his headphones back in place as he turned on his side. 'Fuck you!'

I returned to my side of the room and lay down on the mattress without getting undressed. I slipped the Browning underneath the pillow. I didn't know what might come for us in the night but I wanted to be ready. To my right I could hear Karima's even breathing. I wondered how much she had heard of Ziggy's words.

It was still dark when I woke early the next morning. I felt strong, my wounds finally knitting together. I pulled on my boots and went round waking everyone up. Karima was already awake and dressed. Rinke said he was tired and would prefer to stay behind, which was fine by me.

'We'll get coffee on the road,' I said to Ziggy before he started complaining.

Our destination was Tilburg, a small town in the south of the country. The motorways were crowded and fast-moving and the drive took a little over an hour. On the way I outlined the plan I had worked out the night before. Everyone seemed happy to leave the decisions up to me, all except Ziggy who was in the seat behind me mumbling to himself as I spoke. I chose to ignore him. I was pretty sure that once things got underway he would buckle down, and if he didn't, well, we would have to deal with that as things unfolded.

The directions Kenny Broek had given me brought us to a small yard at the end of a quiet street. Beyond were flat green fields. An idyllic, rural setting for an illegal drugs plant. The factory itself was discreetly located inside an old farm warehouse. The brick building stood on the far side of a small compound surrounded by high walls. The front gate stood open. There was an abandoned air about the whole place. A thresher machine was rusting off to one side. To all intents and purposes it looked like the kind of place a farmer might use to store equipment out of season.

I got out of the car and went round to the back. I opened the boot, lifted up the spare wheel and picked out a small automatic. I emptied the magazine and handed it to Ziggy. I had the Browning tucked into the back of my waistband. I took another gun from the bag. A .357 Magnum revolver. Large and impressive. I didn't want trouble with these guys. I wanted them to back off and comply.

'Why are you giving me an empty gun?' Ziggy asked.

I looked at him. 'You ever used one of these before?'

He stared down at it and shrugged. 'How difficult can it be?'

'Exactly my point,' I said, shutting the boot. 'Nothing more dangerous than someone with a loaded weapon who doesn't know how to use it. There's a lot of chemicals in there. One stray bullet and the whole place could go up.'

Ziggy weighed the gun in his hand. He raised it and sighted

along the barrel. I pushed his arm down slowly and looked around us. The street was deserted but I didn't want to risk being seen by a nosy neighbour.

'Keep it down. No theatrics. Forget what you've seen in the movies. Try to be discreet. People who know how to use guns don't make a big show of it.'

He gave no indication that he was listening to what I was saying.

'Are you hearing any of this?'

'Sure,' he mumbled. 'So what's the plan?'

'It's real simple. You follow my lead. You do exactly what I say. You don't question my orders.' He looked sceptical. 'If you don't think you can do that, then you should stay here. I don't want any trouble in there. I can take care of this by myself.'

'No,' he said. 'I'm OK.'

'Good.' I turned to Karima. 'Stay behind the wheel with the engine running. We might have to leave in a hurry.'

There was a nagging thought at the back of my mind as I said this. There was still a chance, slim, but still there, that she might decide to take off and leave us both behind. But Ziggy was her son, so I was hoping that would have some influence. I pushed the idea firmly out of my mind. Her hair blew across her face and I had to stop myself reaching out to tuck it aside. I stepped closer to her.

'Are you OK?'

'I don't like it. I don't like any of this.' She indicated the gun I was holding.

'It's the only way.' I rested a hand on her shoulder. 'It'll be fine. I promise.'

'I'm not dealing with all this very well, am I?'

'You're doing fine,' I said.

She hung her head. 'I just want this over with.'

'It will be,' I said. 'Very soon.'

The car was parked just out of sight, up against the wall. I motioned for Ziggy to move and together we walked in through the open gates.

TWENTY-FIVE

As we came into the yard, I signalled for Ziggy to circle left while I followed along the wall to the right. I wanted this to go as smoothly as possible and that meant we needed the element of surprise on our side.

The big set of double doors on the front was closed with a latch and a heavy padlock. Rudimentary, but giving the impression that there was nothing of great value within. The locked doors implied that nobody was home but when I reached the corner of the building I glimpsed the front end of a van sticking out from around the back. I motioned for Ziggy to carry on circling the main building and meet me on the other side. That meant he would be out of my sight for a few minutes, but I would have to take the chance he could manage that without getting into trouble.

I peered around the corner. The grey Volkswagen van was parked parallel to the building, alongside a large rear doorway that had been slid open. The van's side and rear doors also stood open. They appeared to be about to start loading something into the vehicle. I could hear music playing somewhere inside. Looking across the rear of the building I saw Ziggy appear through a clump of weeds and wild shrubbery on the far side. He was holding the gun and creeping along sideways as if auditioning for a role in a cop show. I signalled for him to stay put, but either he didn't care or he was pretending he didn't understand. He carried on moving towards the entrance to the building. I couldn't do anything to stop him. He stepped round into the open doorway, presenting himself as a perfect target. I hoped for Karima's sake that he didn't get himself shot. There was a long moment when nothing could be heard but the music. Some kind of hippy dippy pop hit from the eighties. I was about to step forward and pull the kid out of the way when someone else did it for me.

The guy was big, with the kind of shoulders and biceps that told you he had spent some serious time doing steroids and weight training. The tattooed arms and pumped-up pecs were now accompanied by a swelling belly which indicated that he had let himself slide. Too much fast food had turned some of that muscle to fat. How much was hard to say at this stage. He was holding a baseball bat. Where he'd come from I couldn't say. He struck Ziggy on the back of the neck and the kid went down like an ox in a slaughterhouse. Then the muscle man zipped up his pants, explaining where he'd been. I stepped in behind him and pressed the barrel of the Magnum into the back of his neck.

'Drop the bat and get on the ground, now.'

He took it well. I half expected him to start swinging. But he must have felt the size of the gun barrel and realized this wasn't the wisest way to go. Instead he let the bat drop to the floor and got down on his knees in a slow, lumbering way.

'Face down, arms behind your back.'

He did as he was told. I took a zip tie from my jacket pocket and locked his hands together. Ziggy was groaning so I decided I didn't have to bother checking on him. Instead, I stepped inside and took a look around the interior.

One wall was taken up by stacks of large blue plastic drums with chemical stickers on the sides. I stepped closer to read them, but I already knew what they contained. Acetone. Methanol. Methyl ketone. All the ingredients for making amphetamines, methamphetamines and MDMA.

On top of muscle man's head was a ventilation mask, rubber with serious-looking filters on it. The fumes from these chemicals could kill you, or fry what was left of your brain.

The cooking area was to the left, separated from the main storage space by a rough plywood wall. The inside was lined with heavy PVC plastic sheeting – walls, ceiling, even the floor. I could see a production line of weighing machines, mixers, cookers, extractors, all ranged around the wall in some kind of order that culminated in an area where transparent bags filled with coloured pills were stacked in transparent plastic boxes.

There was a movement behind me. I turned to see Ziggy climbing to his feet. He sagged against the doorframe, one hand to his head.

'You don't look too good,' I said.

'I think I'm going to be sick.'

'Well, go outside. You don't want to be leaving any of that here.'

Ziggy nodded at muscle man. 'Where did he come from?'

'If you'd listened to what I told you, it wouldn't have happened.' I pushed past him and went back over to the man lying on the floor. I crouched down in front of him. 'Are you the only one here?'

'Fuck you!' he swore, going into Dutch after that.

I straightened up again and placed my boot on the crook of his arm, just above the elbow, leaned my weight on it until he began squealing.

'Play nicely and this will all go away.'

'You don't know who you're messing with,' he snarled when he got his breath back.

'I know exactly who I'm messing with. In fact, I'm going to call him as soon as we're done here.' I waved Ziggy forward. 'Start loading the van.' I pointed at the stacks of transparent boxes filled with bags of pills. The man on the floor began swearing again.

'You still didn't tell me, is there anyone else here?'

'It's just me.' I leaned on his arm again until he started cursing. 'I swear! I was just doing a pick-up.'

'OK. Do you have a phone?'

'Fuck off!'

I leaned on his elbow again. 'This will go a lot smoother if you cooperate.'

He swore some more. I ran a hand over his pockets and found what I was looking for.

'What's the code?' I asked and got the same response. I placed the barrel of the gun against his leg. 'You want to walk with a limp for the rest of your life?'

He must have believed me because he gave me the code without further delay. I scrolled through the list of numbers until I found what I wanted. After that we carried on loading

the van. Ziggy carried. I couldn't lift anything, but I could
help push the trolley. It took longer than expected, but when
we had finished we had filled three-quarters of the space
with flat boxes.

Ziggy licked his lips nervously. 'How much do you reckon
this is worth?'

I would have estimated anywhere between two and five
million euros, but I didn't want to go giving him any ideas.
Ziggy's eyes were already like saucers.

'I thought you were idealists? You don't care about money,
right?'

He shrugged.

'Right,' I said. 'Well, all this goes back to Momo when
we've got what we want.'

'All of it?'

'All of it.' He looked sceptical. 'I mean it, Ziggy. If you
get in the way, I won't hesitate.'

'OK, OK. I get it. Christ!'

'Good. You're driving.'

I went back to our prisoner and bent over him again.

'When we are safely away from here I'm going to give
Momo a call and let him know you're here. Hopefully, he'll
send someone to free you.'

'You're going to regret this,' he said, twisting his head to
look up at me.

'I'm already regretting it.'

We drove out of the yard to find Karima was still there. At
least that was something. I signalled for her to follow us. As
we drove back towards the highway, I took out the phone I'd
taken back at the yard and flicked through the numbers for
Momo. He answered right away.

'You may want to reconsider your position regarding a
young acquaintance.'

'What are you talking about? Who is this? Where's Tommy?'

'Lying face down in your warehouse.'

'What the fuck do you think you're playing at?'

I ignored the question. 'You should get somebody over
there before he catches a cold. Call me back.'

I placed the phone on the dashboard. We would have to

play this carefully. Taking on Momo was like poking a rattle-snake with a stick. You couldn't be sure what he might do.

'I'm sorry about what happened,' Ziggy said. 'Back there.'

'Don't sweat it. We all make mistakes. A lot of people never get the chance to realize that, so consider yourself lucky.'

'What I said about my mother . . .'

'It's forgotten, but you really should give her another chance. This is nothing to do with me, but whatever happened back then, she did it because she was in a difficult place. You can't judge her on that, none of us can.'

He thought about that one for a time, but said nothing. We drove on in silence.

It took twenty minutes for Momo to call back, so he must have had somebody close by.

'You're making a big mistake. Nobody steals from me.'

'I'm not interested in stealing from you,' I said. 'All I want is the stuff you took from Ziggy.'

'What? That loser? Are you serious?'

'I tried to do this the simple way. I made you a reasonable offer, but that wasn't good enough for you. Now the stakes are higher. I reckon what we have is worth about five million, so it's up to you. Either you work with me or you can say goodbye to all that.'

'So what my boys took must be worth a lot to you.' I could hear that Momo was smiling. He was pleased with himself.

'Don't get ahead of yourself. It's not worth anything to you.'

'So you say.'

'Look, I've dealt with people like you before. I know how it works. You keep pushing. You ask for ten and then ten more and then another. It's never really over. I'm in a hurry. I don't have time for all that bullshit. You get your merchandise back and we get the kid's stuff. End of story.'

'How did you find my place out there?'

'You're not thinking clearly, Momo. I found it, and the point is I can find more of them. You don't want to do this with me.'

'Tough guy, huh?'

'I told you, I know people like you.'

'OK, so how do you want to play it?'

'We pick a neutral spot. We meet, exchange the goods and that's the end of it.'

'There's a parking area out by the airport. Near the Ibis Hotel.'

I had him on speaker. I looked over at Ziggy, who nodded.

'All right,' I said. 'Let's try and do this the easy way.'

'Whatever you say, you're the boss.' He clicked off the line.

'You can't trust him,' Ziggy said.

'We have no choice. This is the only way.'

'You're not going to just drive in there and hand over the drugs?'

'No, of course not. I'll take the car and if all is cool I'll let him know where the van is.'

Ziggy was shaking his head. 'You don't know this guy, man. He's evil.'

'We have to trust him, up to a point. He wants his merchandise. That's our trump card.'

The kid still didn't look convinced. He was nervous and driving too fast. The last thing we needed now was to be pulled over for speeding.

'You need to slow down,' I said, looking in the side mirror. 'We're losing Karima.'

'I'm hungry,' he said. I realized I was too. I checked my watch.

'We have time. Take the next exit and stop at the first place we see.'

As he swung on to the off ramp he was still hammering the speed, but I put this down to youthful impatience. I didn't want to ride him too hard, so I kept quiet. We reached an intersection and he cut straight through the corner and turned right without slowing down.

'You're going to draw attention to us if you keep doing that,' I said.

'It's fine. In this country there are hardly any cops anywhere now.'

I couldn't argue with that. It was true that I had seen very few patrol cars.

'You know where you're going?' I asked him.

'Yeah,' he said. 'We'll find something just up ahead.'

I looked in the side mirror but couldn't see the Mondeo. As I reached for the phone to call Karima, Ziggy swung the wheel suddenly and swerved off the road.

'Hey! Take it easy!' I yelled.

'Sorry, but I really have to piss.'

'Can't you wait?'

'I've already waited too long,' he said.

We pulled to a halt in a small area of bare trees just past an abandoned petrol station. I was worried Karima wouldn't be able to see us for the trees. She would be driving fast to catch up and there was a good chance she would go straight past. As Ziggy disappeared behind the van to take care of business, I cracked open the door and stepped outside. We were making good time and would easily be able to make the rendezvous with Momo. The phone in my pocket began to ring. It was Karima.

'Hey,' I said.

'Where are you?'

'It's OK, we had to make a pit stop. Ziggy couldn't wait. We're just . . .'

As I was talking, I was turning, looking for some way to identify where we were. I was preoccupied, concerned with reassuring Karima that everything was all right. I wasn't paying attention and that's why I never heard it coming. I didn't feel it until everything went black.

TWENTY-SIX

When I opened my eyes the world was dark. I was on the ground, face down. My body was cold. The temperature had dropped. I looked at my watch. So far as I could tell I had been out for about half an hour. I put a hand to my head. When it came away it felt sticky and damp.

The only light came from the headlights of passing cars that raced by on the highway a few metres away. I struggled to sit up. My head felt like it was split open down the middle. The Volkswagen van was nowhere to be seen. Five million was clearly too big a temptation. Ziggy had decided he was going into business for himself.

As I tried to think what my next move should be, a patch of leaves to my left lit up with a blue glow as the telephone began to ring. Ziggy had been in too much of a hurry to stop and look for it. Or maybe he didn't think he needed to worry about it. One of many mistakes.

'Karima? Listen to me, Ziggy has taken the van. You need to circle back and find me.' She immediately began asking questions. When, how, what? 'I'll explain everything when you get here. You need to drive back to where you were when we last spoke. Then you need to double back to the next exit.' I gave her a rough description of where I was. Luckily she had done the smart thing. When she lost contact she had pulled over and waited.

'I didn't know what had happened.'

'You did the right thing. Now you need to find me. He's taken the van.'

'But why?' she asked.

'I think he's planning to try and make some money for himself. We have to stop him before he gets himself into worse trouble than he already is.'

My head throbbed and I thought for a time that I was going to throw up. I walked back to the exit and waited, standing in as visible a spot as I could find. The cars rushed headlong towards me. Each set of lights seemed to hold promise, only for that promise to be swept away as they raced on by.

Finally, after what seemed like hours but couldn't have been more than fifteen minutes, I spotted a car that began to slow. The headlights drew nearer before turning off the road. It was the Mondeo. Karima jumped out and rushed over to me.

'Are you all right? What happened?'

'I'll explain as we drive,' I said.

'But your head, it's bleeding.'

'I'll be fine.'

We got back into the car and drove on with Karima still behind the wheel.

'I don't get it,' she said. 'You were trying to help him.'

'I should have seen it coming. It's not that complicated. He thinks he can solve the whole thing by himself, get enough money to start a new life for him and this Rasha.'

'The girl in the window?'

'Exactly. The kid's in love.' I winced as I shifted in my seat and felt a jagged pain cut through my ribcage.

'Are you all right?' Karima asked.

'It's fine, just a twinge.'

'You're still not healed.'

I was looking up the spot we were headed for on my phone. Momo's directions were on the other phone which was still on the dashboard in the van, but I remembered enough of his instructions.

'A parking space opposite the Ibis hotel out by the airport.'

Karima didn't need directions. As we headed towards Schiphol I described what had happened.

'But why would he do that?'

'Because he thinks he can get Momo to pay him a lot of money for the drugs in that van.'

'What about his computers?'

'Once he has his hands on five million euros he can buy as many computers as he likes.'

Karima nodded. 'But you think Momo won't let him get away with it?'

I was trying to clean up the blood on my neck and face using a paper napkin and some water, looking at the result in the vanity mirror on the sunshade in front of me. 'If Momo is as smart and as ruthless as we have heard, he'll sucker Ziggy in, and once he has his hands on the merchandise he'll kill him.'

Karima let out a small whimper and put her hand to her mouth. 'Oh my god!'

'That's why we have to find him before he tries negotiating with Momo.'

I didn't tell her that Ziggy also had a loaded revolver now, the Magnum that I had placed in the glove compartment of the van and which was still there when he took off.

We drove in silence for the next twenty minutes, speaking

only of practical matters referring to where we were going and what we were going to do when we got there.

An enormous jet airliner appeared ahead of us. There was something surreal about seeing the sheer size of it moving from left to right along a bridge over the highway. I pointed at the map on the screen of the navigation system.

'We're almost there. We need to stop for a moment. Around here.'

I spotted the illuminated hotel logo across the other side of the highway as we pulled off. We moved slowly along until I saw headlights parked off to our right and recognized the shape of the van. I indicated for Karima to stop and she pulled on to the hard shoulder. I got out and went round the back to open the boot. I pressed a hand to my shirt and felt it was wet. With everything that had happened I must have opened some of the stitches again. I needed this to go easily. I couldn't take much more wear and tear.

Inside the boot I found a shotgun under the spare wheel. The old-fashioned kind: sawn-off double barrel and butt cut down to a hand grip. Easy to find and easy to get rid of, difficult to trace. I wasn't fond of them, but they had their uses. They made a lot of noise and scared people off.

I checked the Browning was loaded; I had a spare clip in my jacket that I hoped I wasn't going to have to use. I shut the boot and went round to Karima who was pacing up and down smoking a cigarette.

'OK, here's how we're going to play it. You drop me off and keep driving. Go back out on to the ring road and drive around before heading over to the hotel. Park up there and wait in the car with the lights off until you hear from me.'

'He's my son, Brodie,' she implored. 'I can't just sit back and do nothing.'

'That's the best thing you can do for him at this point. Play it any other way and you risk getting in the way, being taken hostage, or worse.' I fell silent. 'I don't want that to happen,' I added softly.

She looked into my eyes. 'I need to know what's going on.'

'I understand. Believe me. If all goes well, we'll straighten this out and be on our way.'

'And if not?'

I looked at her. In the gloomy shadows cast by the overhead light her eyes were hidden. There was something about that mystery she carried within her that I wanted to know. There were a lot of things that I felt I needed to tell her, but for the moment I seemed to have run out of words. I snapped the boot shut.

'Let's cross that bridge when we come to it.'

I waited for her to drive on, then I stepped over the iron barrier and moved carefully across the open ground, circling around to come in from the opposite side.

There were three stationary vehicles within the area of white light marked out by the lampposts that surrounded the parking area. The van was at the centre, all its doors open, front, side and rear. The other two cars were unfamiliar to me. One was a Mercedes saloon, low and white with a black roof and expensive aluminium wheels. The man standing next to this had a muscular build and a thick beard. I guessed this was Momo. He wore a baseball cap and leather jacket, with workout pants and bright sports shoes.

The other car was smaller, a two-door BMW. Black this time, parked facing the front of the van. Both doors were open. Between car and van were three men. One was on his knees. Of the other two, one was holding what looked like an aluminium baseball bat. As I watched, he brought this down on the shoulder of the man kneeling in front of him. I hadn't spent much time studying this last figure, because I knew most of what I needed to know about him already. Ziggy collapsed from the blow, falling forward and putting out his hands to stop himself hitting the tarmac. The second man followed up by stepping in and kicking his arms out from under him. Ziggy gave another cry as his face hit the ground. The men were laughing. They let him lie there for a moment. Behind them, Momo put away his telephone as he came forward. He said something and the two men laughed again. I could see that one of them was very young, a teenager. The one holding the bat was in his twenties.

Momo walked past Ziggy, pausing only to lean down and

say something to him, before going round behind the van to look in through the open doors.

I crossed the ground between us quickly and quietly, keeping the van between me and them. He might have heard me if his telephone hadn't started to ring. He was still fishing it out of his pocket when I pressed the barrel of the shotgun to his ear.

'Let it ring,' I said.

He held his hands away from him without being asked. I nudged him and he moved. The other two looked up as we stepped out, and for a moment they seemed to be trying to work out what was happening. The young one reached under his hoodie to produce the Magnum.

'Tell him to drop it,' I said. Momo spoke and the boy, sensibly, bent down to set the gun on the ground.

'You're making a mistake,' said Momo.

'It's funny how often I hear that.'

I pushed the gun hard against his skull and he moved until we were level with Ziggy.

'Are you OK?'

He didn't respond at first. He was still bowed over. If he was unable to get up by himself we would have a problem.

'Can you stand?'

I was talking to Ziggy, but I kept my eyes on the two men. They were watching me closely, waiting for a chance to jump me. The younger one in particular. You could feel it in him. He wasn't afraid of anything, which made him dangerous.

'Tell them to be cool,' I said to Momo. He said nothing. I tapped the barrel against his head. He told them. It seemed to make little difference. The younger one was twitching, shifting his weight from one foot to the other. Slim, in skinny jeans. He would be a fast mover. In the event it was the other one who moved first, producing a Glock from behind his back. He was the older of the two, but he was still young and very scared.

'Tell him to put the gun down.'

Momo told him. The man shook his head. Momo gave a tut of annoyance.

'He's not listening.'

I could see that. It was easy enough to understand. You take some kid out with you on a routine run and nine times out of ten everything is cool. But if something goes awry you have an unknown quantity on your hands. I could see the younger one telling him to put the gun away also. He wasn't listening. He was wide eyed, shifting his grip on the gun. It was easy to let off a shot by accident, carrying on like that. The barrel of the gun was wavering, lifting and dropping like he was on the deck of a ship.

'Ask him if he's ever been shot.'

Momo half turned his head in query, but then decided to go ahead and ask anyway. The kid managed to shake his head.

'Tell him I've been shot four times.'

Again, Momo turned his head. This time he looked at me, perhaps wondering who I was.

'Tell him.'

That information didn't have much impact either. The kid was frozen. I didn't want to shoot him, but if this carried on, I wasn't going to have much choice.

'Tell him it hurts more than you think. It never goes away. If you're lucky enough to walk away from it, you'll remember that pain for the rest of your life.'

The gun barrel was beginning to sag. Either his arm was getting tired, or the message was finally getting through.

'If he wants to live to my age then he needs to learn that the trick is knowing which battles to fight and which to leave.'

Momo hesitated and then conveyed my words. The gun finally lowered. The kid bent down and placed it on the ground. Everyone took a breath. My hands were sweaty.

'Let's go, Ziggy.'

To his credit, Ziggy put some effort into it. It was a struggle but eventually he got up and stood there, swaying.

'You really think you can just walk away from this?' Momo asked.

'I'm counting on it. We brought your pills back, so now all we want is what's ours.'

Momo considered his options and decided that getting rid of us would be a blessing. He muttered something and the other two went over to the BMW and started unloading Ziggy's equipment on to the ground.

'Tell them to leave it in there,' I said. 'And to step back.' I nodded to Ziggy. 'Go and check it's all there.'

He hobbled over towards the BMW and leaned over to vomit. Most of it hit the ground, but some of it landed on the rear wheel. The two men made disgusted sounds. Finally, Ziggy made it to the back and peered into the boot. Everything with him seemed to be happening in slow motion. It took ages.

'When this is over,' I said to Momo. 'You'll leave him alone.'

'And if I don't?'

'If you don't I'll have to come back here, and neither of us wants that.'

He turned his head slightly to look back at me, but said nothing. Ziggy finally poked his head back up from behind the boot. He gave a thumbs up.

'Can you drive?' I asked him, nodding at the BMW.

'Wait a minute,' said Momo. 'The car's not part of the deal.'

'It's just a loan. You'll get it back.' I paused. 'There is one other thing. A girl.'

'What girl?' growled Momo.

'She works in one of your windows.'

'I don't own the girls, I just lease the windows out.'

'Well, one of them is going to disappear and nobody is going to try to find her.'

'You drive a hard bargain,' said Momo. 'I don't care about any girl. Just get out of my life.'

'I intend to do just that. Fetch the keys from the van,' I called to Ziggy. He did what he was told. I held out my hand. 'You have the keys to the Mercedes?'

With a heavy sigh, Momo reached into his pocket.

'Throw them out there,' I nodded in the direction of the darkness. With a heavy sigh, he did what he was told. 'When we're safe I'll call you and let you know where the car is. The keys to the van will be in it.'

It was touch and go at the end. Ziggy picked up the Glock and Magnum and tossed them into the car before getting behind the wheel. I wondered if he was fit to drive. We would find out, I guessed. Once he had got it started I ordered everyone to lie down on the ground. There was some protesting.

None of them liked to get their fancy clothes dirty, but they knew this was how it was going to play out. Then I climbed into the car and told Ziggy to step on it.

TWENTY-SEVEN

We drove round towards the main road, heading west before taking the first exit and swinging back in the opposite direction. As we drew level with the hotel I told Ziggy to turn off. Karima was sitting in the Mondeo over on one side.

'What took you so long?' She sounded frantic.

I climbed out of the car. Hurrying, I felt burning pain through my chest with every move. We had to be quick.

'Move everything over to the Mondeo,' I told Ziggy. He did as he was told, emptying the boot of the BMW. Karima went through the boxes of stuff they had taken from the schoolroom and soon found what we had come for. She held up the disk drive.

'Hold on to that,' I said. I unloaded the weapons from the Mondeo and put them into the holdall. Then I handed Ziggy a bundle of cash wrapped in rolls. 'I don't know how much that is,' I said. 'Must be at least five grand.'

Ziggy stared at the money. 'I don't understand.'

'Take our car. Find the girl. What was her name?'

'Rasha.'

'Right. Take her and go somewhere far away. Don't turn around, and don't come back for a long time.'

'But how, I mean, where?' Ziggy looked at the money, then back at me.

'You'll think of something,' I told him. I hoped he would.

'I'm sorry,' he said, 'about hitting you on the head back there.'

'I'll survive. Now get moving. When you've got the girl don't stop for anything. Understood?'

Ziggy nodded. Karima stepped forward and held her arms out. Awkwardly, the two of them embraced.

'Take care,' I heard her whisper.

He stepped back. 'Maybe, when all this is over . . .'

'Sure.' She smiled. 'I'd like that.'

He looked at me one last time, then he turned and got into the Mondeo. We watched him drive out of the parking area, then the rear lights vanished, swallowed up by the stream of moving vehicles.

Karima turned to me. 'OK, so where does that leave us?'

'I don't know about you,' I said, 'but I'm beat.'

I made one call to Momo and then tossed the phone on to the seat of the BMW. When I made to pick up my holdall she beat me to it.

'For God's sake, let me do something. Your stitches will never hold otherwise.'

I held up my hands in mock surrender. 'Whatever you say.'

At the reception desk there was a moment when the woman behind the counter asked if we wanted a double room. I was about to say no when Karima spoke up.

'That's fine,' she said. I looked at her. 'It's fine,' she repeated. 'I think after all that we deserve a drink.'

'Is it safe for us to be here?'

'Momo will assume that we left the BMW here and went on our way. Nobody in their right minds would decide to actually stay here.'

'He might just walk in and ask if they've seen us.'

'He would ask about three people, not a couple. And besides, they got their merchandise. Now they can go back to work.'

The Lounge Bar was on the top floor, with a view over the airport and, more importantly, the car park below. It was quiet. The young Asian man behind the counter was fiddling with his phone, which seemed to be much more absorbing than his surroundings. Eventually he managed to put it aside and attend to us.

'What would you like?' I asked Karima.

'Vodka. Cold.'

'Ice and lemon, tonic water?'

Karima nodded.

'We'll take two of them, and can we order food?' I asked. He handed us a couple of menus.

We sat in a corner booth with a view over the car park. Blinking lights tracked aircraft rising into the night sky, taking people on their way to places far away. Karima decided to call Rinke and check he was all right. The barman brought our drinks over.

'Do you think he'll be all right?' Karima asked when she'd finished with Rinke.

'Ziggy? If he stays low he'll be fine. They'll be fine,' I added.

'It's so funny – I hardly know him.' She was staring at her glass. 'I've never really known how to approach him. Now, suddenly, I feel as though I'd like to.' Her eyes lifted. 'Isn't that strange?'

'It won't be easy.'

'I know. I just feel it's the moment for me to try.'

'Then I wish you all the luck.' I raised my glass in a toast.

'I should thank you.'

'What for?'

'You didn't have to do that, to help him, I mean.'

'Ahh,' I waved it off. 'When I came back from the war,' I began, 'I thought I would just go back to my old life, but I really had no idea what that was.' The memories resurfaced as I spoke, and images I had long since consigned to somewhere at the back of my mind came flooding in. 'I mean, I didn't really know what I had done with my life before the war. Everything seemed to fade into insignificance. It's hard to explain. I felt as though I had found myself. Coming back to normality just made no sense to me. What people did with their lives made no sense. Jobs, paying off mortgages, raising a family. None of it.'

Maybe it was the vodka talking, or maybe it was just the relief of having come through the last couple of days. It felt like we'd reached a watershed. I could hear myself speak but I had no idea where all of this was coming from. I hadn't talked about this to anyone for years, and back then it was other veterans, people who basically felt the same. Now, for some reason it was important for me to tell her. It wasn't everything, but it was most of it.

'It wasn't a popular war. People forget that. The government took us into it for their own reasons. They ignored the protests. Hell, they broke the law. They took us into something they didn't understand and expected us to sort it out.'

I fell silent as the waiter arrived with fresh drinks for both of us. I looked out of the window in time to see Momo's Mercedes appear. They circled the car park once before stopping by the BMW. They were cautious, as if expecting a trap. Finally, after inspecting the car carefully, they got in and both vehicles sped away with a screeching of tyres.

The food arrived and for a time we ate in silence.

'When I came back, I knew. I knew what we had done. It's hard to explain, but I felt as though everyone was judging me. I'd seen the damage, the violence we'd created. Car bombs in street markets. That's something that never leaves you. Limbs hanging from shop awnings. Someone's guts lying in the dust.'

The look on Karima's face brought me to a halt.

'I'm sorry,' I said. 'I don't know where all of that came from.'

'It's all right,' she said. 'You don't have to apologize.'

Then she reached across and placed her hand over mine.

'Let's go to bed.'

Neither of us spoke as we waited for the lift. We stood in silence as it hummed quietly through the building. The thick carpet lining the corridor dampened the sound of our feet as we walked towards the room. Inside, we both went through the motions, moving to occupy separate corners, making them our own, the way you do with a room, putting down bags, draping coats over chairs. It was big enough for us to avoid each other.

'I think I'll take a shower,' she said.

'Sure.' I nodded.

She disappeared and I sat down in a weirdly shaped armchair in a corner of the room, suddenly unsure what I was doing. I hadn't been involved with anyone for longer than I cared to remember. I thought about turning on the flat-screen television on the wall, but I didn't. There was silence. I could hear the hiss of the water in the bathroom. It seemed to go on for a long time.

Then she was there again, standing barefoot on the carpet, a towel wrapped around her, tucked under her arms. I looked

at her. She didn't move. Her hair was dripping wet. I watched
a drop fall to her shoulder, slide along her collarbone and
disappear between her breasts. I got to my feet and took two
paces towards her.

'I haven't . . .' I took another step. She held up her hand
to silence me.

'No words, OK?'

I nodded, but had to speak anyway. 'It's been a long time.'

'Me too.' She nodded. Then she stepped closer and suddenly
she was within reach and I realized I had wanted this for a
long time. I traced a finger along the line of her shoulder,
feeling the soft smoothness of her skin. She stretched up on
her tiptoes to kiss me. We stood like that for a long time. Then
she shrugged the towel off and let it fall to the floor. I struggled with my clothes for a few moments before giving up.

'It's OK,' she said. 'Let me.'

She led me to the bed. I lay down and she took charge,
peeling away the sweaty, bloodstained layers. When she was
ready she climbed on top of me. I held her gently, feeling the
tremors coursing through her body. We moved together, slowly
building pace. I wanted to make it last and for a time I felt
as though I would, but then I felt a shudder going through her
body and into mine and I could no longer control myself. We
struggled for a few moments and then she slumped over me
and we were both still.

We lay there in silence, catching our breath. I didn't want
to speak. I didn't want to move. I wanted to stay there with
her on me and me in her. I felt as though a word by either of
us might destroy the spell. I think she felt the same.

I must have fallen asleep. I'm not sure how long I was out,
but when I opened my eyes she was lying next to me. I could
hear the steady rise and fall of her breathing and knew that
she was asleep. I got up and walked naked to the window to
look out. I wondered what was happening to me.

The following morning I made enquiries at the front desk
and took a taxi to a nearby electronics store to pick up a couple
of items. A pay-as-you-go phone and a small laptop that suited
our purposes and was ready to go. I handed it over to Karima.
She started it up and plugged in the hard disk. I wanted to

know that everything had not been in vain. She scanned the contents quickly.

'Everything there?' I asked.

'It looks fine. It hasn't been damaged.'

'Can you see which files they accessed?'

'That should be easy.'

I watched as she worked through the various folders that Ziggy and his friends had been using. I studied her profile. There was something about the level of concentration that fascinated me. I was beginning to see her in a different light, wondering, even as I did so, what had really changed and why I had been unable to see her that way before.

'What?' she asked, looking up suddenly and catching me staring.

'Nothing. No. Just thinking.'

She held my gaze. I got up.

'I'd better check on our travel arrangements.'

'Yes,' she said. 'Considering where we're standing, how about flying?'

I'd thought about it. It was the quickest way and we were right next to the airport, but I've always felt the need to mix things up.

'Rule number whatever, never take the obvious route. Don't make yourself too predictable.'

'Meaning, no flying?' Karima asked, looking back at me. 'They don't know we left the country, right?'

'We can't be certain of that. I've worked with these people, I know how they think and it's best never to assume.'

'Fair enough.' She went back to tapping keys on the laptop again. There was something soothing about the sound and I watched her for a while. A part of me would have liked to stay here and never move, safe in this little cocoon. I knew that was never going to happen. Daydreaming is a sure-fire way to get yourself killed.

For the next few hours we stayed out of sight in our room while she worked on trying to find out what Ziggy had done with her hard disk.

While Karima worked, I sat by the window and looked out. I was hoping that we would soon be able to turn this game around and go on the offensive. For that to work we had to be sure of what we were doing. Any cracks or weaknesses in our plan and we would be handing ourselves to them on a platter.

I can't really explain why I said what I did next. Perhaps it was the sense of us having crossed some kind of bridge, or maybe it was the feeling that whatever had developed between us could not last. Either way, without a huge stroke of luck, we were on a course bound for oblivion. There was nothing to lose.

'I have a boat.'

Karima was sitting cross-legged on the bed, the laptop cradled on her knees. Her eyes lifted from the screen and she stared at me for a moment.

'I would never have tagged you as the nautical type.'

'I'm not. Not really, or at least not the way you're thinking.'

'Then why a boat?'

'It's my way out.'

'An escape tunnel?'

'I've always been drawn to the idea of being completely free, being able to go anywhere.'

She nodded. 'You're a romantic at heart.'

'Maybe,' I said. 'I don't know.'

'So what kind of boat are we talking about?'

'Well, it's not much to look at, but it's in good shape and seaworthy.'

Karima considered the implications of what I was telling her. 'Look, I mean . . .' She stared down at her hands. 'Last night. I mean, it was nice, but I . . .'

'That's not why I'm telling you this,' I said, a little too quickly.

'Then why?'

I shrugged. I couldn't exactly think of a reason.

'OK, I get it. You have a boat. An escape route. And where are you going to go in this wonderful craft?'

'Well, I . . . I haven't really thought about it.' I hesitated. 'Where would you go?'

'Me?' She laughed and pushed her hands up through her hair. Then she lay back and stared at the ceiling. 'I can go anywhere in the world?'

'Anywhere. It's a boat. *Whitehavens.*'

'*Whitehavens*?'

'That's her name,' I said. 'The boat.'

'*Whitehavens*,' she repeated softly to herself. The way she said it, it sounded like an imaginary place, like Xanadu or El Dorado. Then she sat up and pulled the laptop to her again. 'It's a nice idea, but it's never going to happen.'

'Why not?' I asked.

Karima looked at me for a long time without saying anything.

'I'm not your dream girl,' she said finally. 'We're not going to sail off into the sunset and everything will magically solve itself.'

'Right.'

We were both silent after that. In the end I cleared my throat.

'Any luck?' I said, pointing at the computer she was cradling.

'Not really. Ziggy and his friends were using the data on banks. They were looking for accounts, trying to plot them into some kind of software they were building. I have to say, I don't really understand it.'

'Can you work out which accounts they were targeting?'

'Yes, I think so. It takes time because they have rearranged everything into folders of their own. I'm not sure why.'

'All we are looking for right now is sensitive material that might have triggered a warning.'

'Sure,' Karima nodded her agreement. 'Like a transfer of funds.'

'Something like that could do it, right?'

'Sure, but these transfers can be rerouted through up to ten different banks.'

'Take your time,' I said.

I left her to it, found my memory card and slotted it into the phone. I scrolled through the list of names and numbers until I came to the one I was looking for. Rab Otley, an old friend who ran a fishing smack, the *Aurora Grey*, out of Grimsby Harbour.

I texted him and waited. I looked at my watch and decided he was probably still sleeping if he'd been putting out nets the night before. Who still makes a living as a fisherman, I wondered, as I sat there pondering the future. The seas are being trawled by huge factory ships that sweep up everything on the seabed and spew it out as debris. Yet there was something reassuring about clinging to a profession so old-fashioned it was almost extinct. There were days when it felt as though we were all being thrown under the wheels of progress.

I sighed and looked across at Karima, still busy, her fingers running swiftly over the keys. The screen formed a tiny letterbox of blue light reflected on her face. Maybe it was me, but it felt as though the times when you came across something worth fighting for, in among all the chaos and pain of the world, were increasingly rare. It was hard to believe in anything anymore, let alone something, or someone, worth living for. When that happened, the best thing you could do was grab a hold and cling to it as tightly as possible.

The telephone next to me beeped. We were in business. 'What do you need?' read the message. I told him.

'I may have something,' said Karima.

I went over to sit beside her on the bed, fighting the urge to put my arms around her.

'What am I looking at?'

Her finger ran down a list of names on an invoice sheet.

'These are shell companies. They are basically set up to pass money from one place to another. The law is fairly loose on the matter so it's easily done.'

'Did you set these up?'

'A legal firm did the actual legwork, but I was able to use them.' Karima tilted her head slightly to look sideways at me. 'Do I sense disapproval?'

'I'm not in a position to judge you, and even if I was . . . I wouldn't.'

She considered that for a moment before finally nodding and turning her attention back to the screen.

'The trick is to keep the funds moving slowly in reasonable quantities. Sudden movements of large amounts of cash draw attention. The Inland Revenue is one thing, but there is a host of other bodies, Interpol, the FBI, ATF, DEA, who take an interest in tracking financial movements.'

'So you just shift it back and forth around the world?'

'That's pretty much how it works.'

I looked at the sums involved and let out a low whistle. 'Donny must have trusted you to let you have access to all of this.'

'Trust is one way of putting it. But I always knew that any mistakes on my part would be fatal. So I was careful, very careful.' She glanced askance at me. 'Which is why I never expected to meet someone like you.'

'So, you were never tempted? I mean, to skim a little off?'

'That's the kind of mistake that gets people killed. There's a responsibility here, and a lot of people do get tempted, for sure. People always think they will be the one to get away with it, that they are just that little bit smarter.' Karima shook her head. 'They never are.'

'Are there any people you can think of who might be behind all this?'

'It occurred to me.'

'Any suggestions?'

Karima clicked through to another document. 'Derek Sylvan. Ever heard of him?'

I had heard the name as it happened. I remembered Sylvan from a couple of meetings with Donny. 'He used to be a regular fixture, but I thought he'd retired.'

'A couple of years ago now.' She nodded. 'Before that he was running a financial services company along with a solicitor by the name of Barnaby Nathanson.'

'The one who was killed?'

'Exactly.' She looked up at me. 'Did you do it?'

'Kill Nathanson? Why would you ask that?'

Karima shrugged. 'That's your job, right?'

My whole life I had been concerned with what was right in front of me. Problem-solving. Getting from A to B in one piece, taking out the opposition, getting rid of evidence. Being discreet. I lived for the here and now. Nothing beyond the horizon. I never cared about whether or not the planet was burning up. Why did I feel differently now?

I got up off the bed and walked over to the window. I could

already feel my mood shifting. I watched a huge airliner screeching into the sky at a steep angle. It looked insane, a preposterous idea that happens millions of times a day all over the world. The sheer size of it. The defiance of gravity. It looked like the perfect symbol of man's unlimited capacity for self-delusion.

I sat down in one of the chairs by the window. Karima shut the lid of her laptop and put it aside. I tried to remember what I knew of Derek Sylvan. He was an associate of Donny's from the old days, one of the London mob who had thrown in his lot with the new world. Derek's big thing was a number plate scam that he'd run for years, siphoning money off the government. Truth be told, he wasn't really cut out for a life of crime. He had no stomach for violence. But he liked the high life, loved dressing up for a day at the races, champagne and women. I knew him from back then, when he had a tendency to drink himself off his face and someone would have to drive him home and sometimes that was me. General dogsbody. The thing about people who are too drunk to know where they are is that they tend to talk. So I knew things about Derek and more importantly, he knew me. I had seen him when he was weak and I had helped him. When he decided he'd had enough of the business he dropped out. His heart was never in it. He had health problems and his third marriage was on the skids. He had enough to settle down comfortably and keep out of everyone's way. Which is exactly what he did.

'Do you think he will help us?' Karima asked, after I had told her everything I knew.

I looked out at the sky. Heavy clouds formed into banks like some kind of submarine structure. Little flurries of rain spat at the window. I watched the drops slide sideways across the glass. 'Whether he's willing to help us or not is hard to say. But if you think he's tied up in all this then he's definitely worth a visit.'

There was a slight uplift of the chin at that, but nothing more. Deep down Karima was an honest person. She didn't like being reminded that she had been forced to do a few unsavoury things to keep her head above water. She hadn't told me about the trouble she had been in but I had my own suspicions. It had been a dark time for her. We both had dark moments in our past.

'Sorry?' I realized she had been speaking to me. I turned to face her.

'If I'm right, then this might be what Ziggy and his friends were doing. They were manipulating Sylvan's accounts. He got wind of it and alerted Donny.'

I nodded my agreement. 'We still need to find him.'

'I already have.' She threw her glasses aside and stretched her back, lifting her arms above her head. Then, aware I was staring at her she cocked her head. 'What's that look for?'

'Nothing,' I said. 'I was just thinking.'

'We still have a few hours to kill,' she said.

'Yes.'

She stood up and held out her hand. 'Nothing nicer than a rainy day for an excuse to stay in bed, don't you think?'

I got to my feet and came back over to her.

TWENTY-EIGHT

Rab's friend was up the coast at a place called Den Helder. It was an hour's ride from Amsterdam by train, which was fine. A bit of a detour, but I hadn't convinced myself that Ramzan and Shelby would have given up yet, so there was no point taking risks as far as I could see.

Brendan Beaumont was six feet tall with grey hair and a straggly moustache that hung down around the corners of his drooping mouth. He wore a grey boiler suit that was more holes than cloth. He stuck his hands in his pockets as he looked us over.

'Rab's friend, you say?'

I knew nothing more about him than Rab had told me. A Scot who had married and settled locally. The two of them had met in prison in Tyneside. His wife was part of the crew, a stout woman with strong hands and a fierce scowl. She took Karima inside to kit her out. We were to dress like the crew and follow instructions. There were only occasional checks out at sea but Brendan wasn't taking chances.

Karima reappeared in a set of yellow oilskins and handed me a similar outfit.

'Very fetching,' I said. She thumped me on the arm. The rest of the crew consisted of two men who didn't speak, just grunted and gestured. I got the impression they didn't like the situation much.

The ship was a small vessel with a mast either end on which to haul in the nets. As we puttered out of the harbour the sun was tipping towards the horizon. Ahead of us lay the dark sea. For the next few hours nothing much happened. We stayed out of sight where we could do the least damage while they did whatever they had to. Down below there was a main galley where Karima and I sat drinking coffee and trying to ignore the heaving of the boat.

'I'm not sure I was born with sea legs,' she said.

'It just takes time for your body to adjust,' I told her. 'Your balance system learns to act in a different way.'

'That must be it. I've never had much of a sense of balance.' She was smiling as she spoke. 'This boat of yours, what did you say its name was?'

'I told you already.' I laughed. 'Why don't you tell me what's on your mind?'

She looked down at her hands resting on the table. 'It's not that I don't want to run away with you. I just think we should take it one step at a time.'

'That's all I'm asking for.'

'Good. Then we understand each other.'

There was an awkward moment. I reached up to pull the hood of her oilskins up. 'Yellow suits you,' I said.

'Get lost!'

We both laughed. I couldn't explain it, but something inside me had come unstuck. It was a feeling of recklessness that I couldn't remember having experienced for a very long time. I grew serious for a moment.

'The boat is not registered in my name. Nobody knows about it except me, and now you.'

'I'm honoured.' She gave a mock bow and then squeezed my hand. 'I mean it. It's not every day that a woman gets invited to run away to sea.' There was another long silence. Then, 'I've been alone for so long, I think I'm out of practice.'

'You and me both.'

I'd spent years taking care of myself, keeping people at bay. I'd had women, but nothing serious. Brief encounters that were easy enough to back out of. Most figured out pretty quickly that I wasn't relationship material. I'd thought all of that was behind me. I tried to turn the conversation to more practical things.

'When we arrive we'll need to arrange transport.'

'What are we going to do when we see Sylvan?'

'If he's mixed up in all of this maybe he can explain what's going on.'

'You think if we tell him that it wasn't me trying to hack his accounts he'll understand?'

'It's worth a try,' I said. Truth be told, I wasn't sure Derek Sylvan was likely to cooperate, but it was the logical next step on the ladder. I looked at Karima. With her chin raised she looked proud, elegant and beautiful. 'What is it?'

'I don't know,' she smiled. 'It feels like an adventure. Sitting in a fishing boat like this.'

'I thought I was supposed to be the romantic.'

'You know what I mean.'

Pull yourself together Brodie, I thought to myself. What did I know about her, after all? She had saved my life. I knew that. Also that she was basically a good person. And I knew that I was grateful that for once I had failed in my work.

I left her there in the galley. We both needed time to think and being together seemed to produce the opposite effect.

Before we left the hotel in Amsterdam, I had taken a little walk and found a quiet spot where I'd tossed the broken down pieces of the weapons into a canal. The shotgun was nothing special, but the Browning had been with me for a long time. Still, that's the nature of tools. You use them and replace them. I had no choice. Crossing the Channel with a gun in tow was too risky. I didn't like the idea of coming to Sylvan with my

hands empty, but I knew that getting in touch with any of my
contacts would potentially set off an alarm alerting Donny to
our whereabouts.

Up on deck I was met by a blast of sea spray against my
face. I closed my eyes for a second to allow them to adjust
to the darkness. In the aft of the boat the two men were playing
out a net through a squeaky cable winch. It was going to be
a long night. In the wheelhouse I found the taciturn Brendan
squinting at the green glow of a sonar device.

'You have much experience at sea?' he asked.

'Fair weather sailor, I'm afraid.'

His face split in a grin. 'This is nothing. A gentle breeze.
You should go below, try to get some sleep.'

'Thanks, maybe later.'

It was just after midnight when I went below to wake
Karima. She was sleeping on one of the narrow bunks behind
the galley.

'We're there,' I said. 'Time to move. We're just off the
Norfolk Banks. They're getting ready for the transfer.'

She sat up and rubbed her eyes. As I helped her on with
her jacket she looked up at me. 'Are you sure about this?'

'It'll be fine,' I said, although I was already wondering at
the wisdom of the plan. Up on deck we squeezed into the
wheelhouse alongside the skipper and his wife. She looked us
up and down and said something I couldn't understand before
pushing her way out into the wind again.

'She doesn't like this kind of thing,' Brendan explained.
'The boat belongs to her father and she thinks if there is any
trouble we could lose it.'

'What do you think?'

He looked over at me. 'I think there are less and less fish
in the sea and we need to do what's necessary to pay the bills.'

On that note I handed him an envelope full of cash which
he stuffed inside his jacket. 'Just don't drop us in the drink.'

He threw his head back and laughed. 'Why? Are you going
to sue me?'

I exchanged looks with Karima. Not exactly the kind of
encouraging words you wanted to hear. The skipper pointed
ahead of us.

'There they are.'

I couldn't see anything, but a few moments later the door to the wheelhouse opened and one of the two men appeared.

'Off you go!' shouted the skipper. 'Happy landings!'

His laughter followed us out into the dark, wet night where a rope ladder led down over the side of the hull. Down below I could see the slick black rubber of an inflatable. Sitting in the stern was someone I had never seen before. Karima eyed the flimsy ladder flapping about and her face was a picture of terror, which I understood. It looked tricky even in good weather. The crewman gestured for her to step up to him where he was balanced on the gunwales.

'It's easy. Just don't look down.'

She climbed down the rope ladder and managed to get into the dinghy. When it came to my turn I discovered just how difficult it was to climb down a wet and slippery rope ladder in the dark. I landed without much elegance or dignity, but at least we had both made it safely this far. I sat opposite her as the man in the helm gave a thumbs up to the men on deck, then he twisted the throttle and we sped off towards the fishing smack that was bobbing gently less than a hundred metres away. It took another ten minutes to get us aboard. Altogether the whole operation had taken less than half an hour.

The *Aurora Grey* was a smaller vessel than the one we had just come from. It was also run in a more informal fashion. Rab was in the wheelhouse. The kid who had brought us across came in when he had finished his work and took over the helm.

'Let's go below,' said Rab. 'I have hot chocolate.'

The galley was more rudimentary than the one we had just left behind but it was warm and dry and that counted for a lot.

'Thanks for this, Rab. I owe you one.'

'Well, you were there for me when I was shot, remember? This is the least I can do.'

'You two served together?' Karima was curious.

'He was second in command of my platoon.' Rab poured two thick, steaming mugs of hot chocolate from a thermos flask and handed them over. Here everyone had to crouch down on facing bunks and there was no room for a table.

'We just need to be set ashore, and then you can forget us.'

'Well, I took the liberty of finding you a car. It's not much, but it belongs to a friend, so, if you can return it in one piece when you're done with it . . .'

'Much appreciated,' I said.

Rab stared down at the thermos he was still holding. 'I'm not going to ask any questions and of course you were never here. But it would ease my conscience a tad to know that you're not in serious trouble.'

'Since when did you grow a conscience, Rab?'

He laughed at that and then dismissed his own question. Rab never asked for anything, but he was willing to give everything he had to his friends.

'Forget I asked,' he said. 'I'd better get up top before Davey runs us ashore. Wouldn't be much help if we went down out here.'

When he had gone, I leaned back against the panelling behind me.

'Was this all really necessary?' Karima asked. 'Seems a bit dramatic.'

'I know. I'm sorry about that. Old habits. I've always preferred taking the long way around just to be safe.'

She nodded towards the upper deck. 'And you trust him? He sounded concerned.'

'Rab? Don't be fooled. He's up to his own tricks. Dig through the boxes of fish in the hold and you're liable to find a few surprises. He runs a nifty sideline in Class A drugs.'

'Doesn't show,' she said, looking around at the state of the ship.

'All part of the disguise, but he's also a messy bastard by nature.'

An hour or so later found us making our way up the road from the port to where a rusty old Saab 99 was parked.

'Is it just me?' I asked. 'Or is our transport gradually becoming more decrepit?'

'You're just feeling your age,' laughed Karima.

'That must be it.'

It felt strange to be back in England. A part of me wished we could have stayed on the other side of the water, out of sight and out of reach. Another part of me knew that until we finished this there would be nowhere that was safe for either of us.

TWENTY-NINE

Derek Sylvan had built himself a mansion on a hill. From the road you could just glimpse the top of the house nestling among the trees, the stone walls glowing in the late afternoon light. It was a picture of tranquillity.

We were parked in a lay-by on the A59. It was a fairly busy road with traffic between Bolton and Harrogate.

'Kind of idyllic round here,' said Karima, speaking my thoughts aloud.

'Well, it's a far cry from the East End of London where he grew up, which I think is the idea.'

'So, what's the plan?'

I didn't have one, to tell the truth, but I wasn't sure about the wisdom of sharing the fact at this point. We didn't have any weapons and no idea how much protection Sylvan had up there on the hill.

'We have the element of surprise,' I said. 'But that's about all that's in our favour.'

'But you've done this kind of thing before, right?'

'Plenty of times.' The rusty door gave a loud squeak as I cracked it open. I felt the same way, stiff from having been in the car for so long. After the drive over from Grimsby we had been sitting there for over an hour waiting for the daylight to fade. High on the hill, the trees cast their long shadows across the landscape. In less than half an hour it would be dark. I wanted to get up close to the house with enough light to be able to spot any sentries or trip wires, but little enough to give me some cover.

'It's best you wait for me here,' I said. Karima disagreed.

'No way,' she said, shaking her head. 'If you think I'm

going to sit here and let you go up there alone you've got another think coming. And besides, if this guy is the reason you were sent to kill me, I think I have a right to look him in the eye.'

There was no point arguing. In the short time we had spent together I had come to realize that Karima was not the kind of woman who was easily swayed. Once she had made up her mind about something you'd better get used to it, because it was liable to stay that way, come what may.

'OK,' I said. 'But you have to promise me to stay back until I am sure it's safe.'

She looked at me and folded her arms. 'I'm not sure what kind of women you've known in your life, but I'm betting they were nothing like me.'

'No argument there. I don't think I've ever met a woman like you.' I started to get out of the car. 'Have it your way, but don't say I didn't warn you.'

We left the car where it was and crossed over to walk up the road. I found a spot where we could climb over a low fence that gave us access to the land next to Sylvan's. The line we followed up the hill kept us below the ridge and hidden from the big house. When we reached the top I found a way through over the fence. It didn't look as though Sylvan was too worried about his safety. Or maybe he thought that putting signs about security along the front with a couple of cameras would be enough to deter people. And maybe it was, nine times out of ten. This wasn't one of them. The bottom of the main driveway was barred by an electrical gate. On this side, so far I had seen nothing.

'This is what comes from scrimping on security costs.'

Once over the fence we made our way through high grass as we circled around the house. If there were more cameras they would be on the driveway. He was betting that anyone who came out this far would arrive by car and drive through the front gate.

The front of the house maintained the appearance of old heritage, a monument to all that is dead and worthy of worship. On the other side, however, Derek Sylvan had gone to work.

The rear of the house had been enlarged by an ugly modern extension tacked on to the back of the old stone walls. Spread across the whole width of the building was an elaborate construction made of glass and steel. A set of arches rose up to meet in the middle where they formed a vaulted roof. It looked like some kind of Japanese pagoda. A huge, multifaceted, glass-walled conservatory. A split-level interior featured low sofas around a circular fireplace. On one side was a long swimming pool, fenced in by another glass wall. Running along the back was a bar and kitchen area with a glass dining table and high, leather-backed chairs. The fittings looked as though they had been selected by someone with money to burn but little style or taste.

'Must have cost a few bob,' Karima muttered.

'Los Angeles in the Pennines.'

We edged forward until we reached the limits of the trees. I told Karima to stay put while I took a closer look.

'Please, trust me on this.'

She didn't like it, but she consented with a brief nod. I bent low and moved across the stretch of lawn to the house. The light from the south was cut off by the main building, which meant that I had more shadows to cover me. When I reached the nearest corner, I stopped to peer round the side of the black iron post. I could smell the chlorine in the pool and could see that the sliding doors were at least partially open. I couldn't see anyone about. I was halfway towards the door when I realized my mistake.

There was someone in the pool.

Steam rose from the surface of the heated water. The swimmer was moving with slow, steady strokes towards the far end. I reached the cover of the doorframe and stopped, dropping to one knee. I watched as the swimmer climbed out of the water. It was a woman. Hard to tell much about her except she was blonde and not in the habit of wearing a bathing suit. The advantages of having a pool of your own and the privacy to use it. She slipped on a robe and walked towards the main house, stopping at the high counter that ran along the rear of the extension area.

She didn't hear me as I came up alongside the pool and

through the doors to the main living area. She had her back to me, standing by the bar.

'Hello there.'

She turned to face me. In one hand she held what looked like a cocktail glass containing a reddish liquid. She was around forty. She hadn't bothered to fasten the front of the robe and seemed in no hurry to do so.

'Well, hello,' she said, taking a sip from her drink. 'Where did you spring from?'

I gestured over my shoulder with a thumb. 'Overland. The scenic route.'

'Do I need to be alarmed?'

'That depends.' I studied her eyes, wondering how much of this she was getting. 'I was hoping to speak to Derek.'

'Oh.' Her face fell. 'And there was me thinking it was my lucky day.'

The glazed look told me that she was on something, a sedative, a strong one. She looked like she could barely walk, let alone swim. People drowned that way all the time. She took a step towards me, stumbled and recovered.

'I'm honoured. Would you like a drink?'

She fished the straw out of her glass and held it up. A drop of liquid fell and ran down between her breasts. I followed it down as far as was decent. I saw her gaze shift slowly to a spot over my shoulder. I turned to see Karima walking up along the side of the pool.

'This is getting more interesting,' said the woman.

'I was wondering where you'd got to,' Karima said, looking the woman up and down.

'Don't worry yourself, love,' the woman said, as she drew the sides of her robe together and tied the sash. 'He's been the perfect gentleman.'

'Who's a perfect gentleman?'

Derek Sylvan was older than I remembered. He wore a heavy set of spectacles but the grey hair was still thick and straight. It flopped down over his right eye. His face was tanned, as if he spent a lot of time in sunnier climes. He was wearing a bathrobe that stopped just short of his knees. He looked us over. His eyes were sharp.

'How the hell did you get in here?'

'They just appeared out of nowhere,' the woman explained, taking a sip from her drink.

'Is that so?' Sylvan was smiling as he went behind the counter. He was still smiling when his hand came up to reveal a neat little automatic. A Sig Sauer P226. A nice weapon. Not cheap and not a toy. Standard issue for Special Forces, Navy SEALs and all the other bad boys, ditto a collector's item for men who wanted something fancy to wave about.

'So, let's hear it,' he said. 'What's this all about?'

'You don't remember me?' I asked.

'Should I?' Sylvan frowned.

'My name's Brodie. I work for Donny Apostolis, or used to.'

'Donny, eh?' The frown deepened as his memory started to do its work. 'You used to do his heavy work.'

'Sometimes.'

'Sure, I remember.' He nodded slowly. 'So what brings you here? Or do you just like spying on Natasha?'

'That wasn't intentional.'

'I'll bet it wasn't. Who's your friend?'

'She used to be Donny's accountant.'

'Did she now?' Sylvan looked Karima over as he placed the gun down on the marble counter and dropped ice cubes into a glass before drowning them in Scotch. If he remembered her, he gave no indication of it. Taking a sip, he said, 'I still don't hear an explanation of what you are doing on my property.'

'We think there's been a misunderstanding,' I began. 'We're here to try and clear it up.'

'A misunderstanding?' Sylvan frowned. 'Sounds to me like you're here to ask for a favour, and I don't do favours for anyone.'

'At least give us a chance to explain,' I said.

Sylvan shrugged. 'You've got five minutes. I've already pressed the alarm button. The security firm have a car on the way.'

'OK.' I looked sideways at Karima. 'Donny took out a hit on Karima here. I think you're the reason he did so.'

'What makes you think that?' Derek Sylvan swirled the whisky round his glass and took another sip.

Karima stepped in. 'I've looked over your accounts. I can see that someone has been tampering with your overseas holdings. You concluded that it was an inside job, which is a reasonable assumption. Nobody else had access to those accounts. So you went to Donny and complained. He said he'd take care of it.' She glanced at me. 'And that was the start of it.'

'Interesting.' Sylvan's eyes flicked between the two of us. 'I mean, you two lovebirds came up with this all by yourselves?' The Sig Sauer was back in his hand and he waved it to move us over to his left. 'I know a shakedown when I see it.'

'It's not a shakedown,' I said.

'And we're not lovebirds,' added Karima. Natasha suppressed a smile at that.

'You should listen to what she has to say,' I said. 'She knows what she's talking about.'

'I don't doubt it. What I'd like to know is what you thought to gain by coming here.'

'We have a death sentence hanging over us,' Karima said. 'We just want to clear things up.'

Sylvan considered this in silence for a moment, then he gestured with the gun barrel towards the glass dining table. 'Sit down and we'll wait for security to arrive.' Karima and I took seats on one side and Sylvan sat at the head of the table. For a moment there was silence. Sylvan lifted his glass to sip his drink.

'All right,' he said. 'Let's hear it.'

'Your money was funnelled into several shell companies. One of them was Knox Mediatic.'

'You're an accountant, right? So you know.' Sylvan shrugged. 'My money is spread out across dozens of companies. It's hard to keep track of what's where.'

Karima looked at me. I knew what she was thinking. If Sylvan was bluffing he was doing a good job of it. I looked over at Natasha who was perched on a bar stool sipping her drink. She made a show of crossing her legs, which forced the robe open again. It was a distraction, perhaps intended.

'Donny took out a hit on her, you say?' Sylvan was

addressing me again. 'That's what you used to do for him, right?'

'That's right.'

Sylvan chuckled. 'So let me see if I've got this right. You go down to kill her and she spins you a yarn about me being behind the whole thing. She tells you there's a way to make some good money out of this and she's going to share it all with you. Oh, and she probably fucked your brains out while she was telling you. How am I doing?'

'Very droll,' I said. 'But nothing to do with the facts.'

'Really? You're saying you didn't shag her? I would, in a heartbeat.'

Natasha smiled again, as if the idea amused her.

'I'm saying that she can show you what happened to your money,' I told him.

'Right.' Sylvan was smiling. 'You came here to persuade me that someone has been tampering with my finances. And you're the only person who can fix it, right? All I have to do is call Donny off. Is that how it plays?'

Neither Karima nor I said a word. There didn't seem to be any need. But Sylvan was having second thoughts.

'Natasha, put your legs together and bring me my phone, will you.'

She did as she was told, slipping off the stool and strolling over, pausing only to pick the phone off the counter. He took it from her.

Now I thought I remembered her, from the old days, a hostess at one of Donny's clubs, a fancy place in the West End that he had inherited from Goran Malevich. I realized that Sylvan was studying me as he tapped his phone. He held it to his ear.

'Derek Sylvan here. Yes, I think there's been a false alarm. No need for your team. Yes, I'm sure of it. Absolutely. Just some old friends dropping by unannounced. Thank you.' Sylvan was on his feet now. He faced me across the table. 'I remember you now. You're ex-army. You used to work for Goran. When he died you went to Donny.'

'I'm surprised you remember.'

'I have an eye for detail. I store it all up here.' He tapped his right temple with the barrel of the gun. 'Most of the time it just sits there, but every now and then something pops up and suddenly it all makes sense.'

'I'll take your word for it,' I said.

'The question I'm asking myself is why would someone like you turn against Donny? You're the faithful attack dog. You never turn on your master. So is this all for her sake, or is there something else going on?' Sylvan was circling the table now, walking behind us. 'Maybe it's the other way around.'

He waited for my reaction. When he decided none was coming he turned to Karima. 'All right,' he said. 'Explain to me exactly what it is you know about my money.'

With a glance at me, Karima started her pitch. 'Novo Elysium was set up as a property investment firm, an umbrella company that was used by a number of clients, some of them legit, others not. Hundreds of millions passed through their books. Money went out of the country, to Dubai, Doha, and a number of tax havens in the Caribbean. Some of it came back and was funnelled into properties, mostly in the London area. You couldn't track this money easily, which was the point.'

Sylvan sniffed and waved his empty glass in the air. Natasha sashayed over to the bar to fetch him a refill. Karima went on.

'Knox Mediatic was actually a real company. They ran a couple of local radio stations in Brixton. They had an address in Kingston, Jamaica.'

'I know all of this,' said Sylvan impatiently, clearly familiar with all the details.

'What you don't know is that a few months ago a group of hackers got access to certain information. Account numbers, transfer codes, passwords.'

'Now how would they do that?'

Karima folded her arms. 'One of them is my son.'

'Ah,' Sylvan nodded as he took his fresh drink. 'Now we're getting somewhere. Your son is a hacker. What did he and his friends want, to help themselves to my money?'

'No,' Karima shook her head. 'They have some idea of breaking down the banking system, saving the planet.'

'Right,' nodded Sylvan. 'They want to change the world.'

'Something like that.' Karima paused. 'The point is, the damage has been repaired. The holes have been patched up and I have their word they won't do it again.'

'Their word?' Sylvan laughed. 'What kind of make-believe world do you live in? Nobody's word counts for anything nowadays.'

'I know my son.'

'Yeah? Then why didn't you know that he'd accessed your files?'

'It's the truth,' I said. I wouldn't have shared as much information with him as Karima had done, but now it was out there, maybe it wasn't so bad. 'You can tell Donny to call off the contract.'

Sylvan's eyes swerved back to me. 'You really don't get this, do you?'

I said nothing. Waited for him to go on.

Sylvan was smiling. His eyes glittered. He was enjoying this.

'I keep waiting for the penny to drop,' he said. 'But it looks like that's not going to happen, so let me lay this out for you both.' Sylvan leaned over the table towards me. 'This isn't about her. She was never the target. You were.'

THIRTY

There was a long silence after that. I could hear birds chirping somewhere out there behind us in the trees. It was almost dark. Lights came on inside the pool, filling the area with a blue glow.

'You used to work for Goran in the old days,' Sylvan began.

'We've already established that fact,' I said. 'Where are you going with this?'

'I'm just trying to get things straight, so that we're all clear, all on the same page.' Sylvan was smiling. He twirled the ice around his glass. 'Maybe you'd like a drink now?'

'I'm fine,' I said.

Karima shook her head in answer to the same question. For some reason I had the feeling Sylvan was playing for time. Everything was being slowed down. Natasha disappeared, presumably to put some clothes on.

'Why don't you just get to the point?'

'We're getting there,' Sylvan said. 'You went to work for Donny right after Goran was killed, right?'

'Like I said, we know all of this.'

'Sure we do, but I'm curious. What made you switch sides and go over to Donny? He was Goran's arch enemy.'

I leaned back. 'I go where the work takes me.'

'Would you say you're a loyal person, Brodie?'

'Is that what we're talking about, loyalty?'

Sylvan got to his feet again and began to stroll, gun hanging by his side, drink in the other hand. He went over to the counter. A row of lights came on automatically as he approached. They hung from what looked like a zinc drain-pipe. Expensive, like everything else, in a tasteless kind of way.

'There's nothing wrong with switching sides when it suits you.'

I glanced over at Karima, who was frowning at me as if to ask where all this was coming from. I didn't have anything to tell her. Sylvan carried on. He seemed to like the sound of his own voice.

'You moved on to Donny quickly, right around the time Goran was shot to pieces in a car park in Brighton.' He was behind the bar again. The automatic rested on top of the counter, the dark barrel pointing towards me. 'There was a woman. Zelda was her name. Remember her?'

I nodded. I remembered Zelda. She had worked in one of Goran's clubs.

'She was about to turn star witness against him. She was going to lay Goran's business out on a platter and send him to prison for a very long time.'

I was aware of Karima watching me as Sylvan went on.

'What was Goran doing in Brighton, do you suppose?' he asked. I said nothing. 'What would take him all the way down there, do you think?' He returned to his seat at the table, placing the gun on the glass in front of him. 'Maybe he felt like breathing some of that sea air, or maybe, just maybe, someone told him they'd found his girl and he wanted to have a word with her in person.'

'If you've got a point, why don't you make it?'

'Goran is gunned down and the girl disappears. Suddenly everyone is out of the picture. A clean sweep.'

Sylvan sat back and studied me for a moment.

'That was strange. I mean, nobody misses Goran. He was a nasty piece of work.' He raised a finger. 'But it's the loose ends that worry me. And this girl, she's a loose end.'

'How so?' Karima asked. She was curious now. Sylvan liked that. He smiled at her. It wasn't a nice smile. It was the smile of someone who likes to break things.

'Let me explain. The girl has the dirt on Goran, so why kill her when Goran's gone? Makes no sense, right? So she had to have something else. Something on someone else. Someone who had been close to Goran. Someone who was planning a big move. Is it making any sense now?'

'I can't say it is,' she replied.

Sylvan laughed. He was talking to Karima now. I was forgotten.

'I've been in this business a long time. A small player, biding my time, hedging my bets. I'm not ambitious and once people know that I'm not planning to fuck them over they relax. They trust me because I'm not a threat.' He leaned his elbows on the table. 'That's when you start to hear the interesting stuff. People take you into their confidence. That's why I know all about Sal Ziyade.'

'Ziyade?' echoed Karima. She turned to me, but I wasn't playing. I started to get to my feet.

'This is a waste of time. We should be going.'

'What has this got to do with Sal Ziyade?' Karima asked. She was looking back and forth between the two of us but she wanted me to answer. Derek Sylvan took this as his cue to continue. He looked at Karima.

'You know who Sal Ziyade is, right?'

I put my hand out to Karima. 'We have to leave.'

'Relax, champ, can't you see? She's interested.' He smiled at her. 'You see, this Sal, he's a real piece of work.' He tapped a forefinger to his temple. 'I mean, up here. Confused, you might call it. Complicated background. He changed his name at one point. Did you know that?' He wasn't expecting an answer from anyone. 'Nobody knew what he was up to. Hard to keep track of someone when they're operating under another name.' His gaze swivelled to me. 'I forget, of course, you must know all of this, because this was around the time you killed that woman.'

'Zelda? You're saying I killed Zelda?' I could feel Karima's eyes on me.

'Did you?' she asked.

I ignored the question, addressing myself to Sylvan. 'What does this have to do with anything? It was years ago.'

'Nearly five years, if I remember correctly,' Sylvan said. 'The fact that you killed her is not important. It's what you do, right? That's how the two of you met, remember?'

'Why is this relevant?' Karima asked.

'Because it's the reason why you're in the mess you're in right now, sweetheart.' Sylvan smiled. I turned my head to see Natasha returning. Her hair was pinned up and she was dressed in a long black evening dress slashed down the front. She looked more alert, as if she had taken a line of coke to liven herself up. She went behind the bar to fix herself another drink.

'Bring us some white wine will you, darling,' Sylvan called, raising an eyebrow at Karima. 'I think our guests would like a drink now.' Karima said nothing. She was eager to hear more.

'That makes no sense,' she said. 'If Brodie was the real target why bring me into it?'

'Just bear with me for a moment, please,' Sylvan said calmly. 'I assume that he wasn't alone. He had someone with him? Another gunman?'

Karima nodded. 'A young man.'

'Donny's nephew, Zephyr,' I supplied. 'He was just a kid. No experience. Donny wouldn't send someone like that after me.'

Sylvan disagreed. 'That's exactly who he'd send, the last person you'd expect. You'd never see it coming.'

There was some logic to that. As Natasha brought over the wine and started pouring glasses for everyone, I thought back to the start of all this. I remembered how cocky Zef had been. Was that because Donny had promised him a shot at the big time? That sounded like Donny's idea of fun, pitting us against one another, springing a surprise on me. I'd always had the feeling Donny resented that about me, the fact that I had survived for so long, that I had more experience than him.

'Maybe you're overestimating Donny's opinion of you,' Sylvan said, interrupting my thoughts. 'Maybe he thought the kid could handle you without too much trouble.'

'What you're saying makes no sense,' I said. 'Donny called me when we were there, told me a long story about how Zef had been disloyal. He'd gone over to the Ziyades, according to Donny.'

'And you didn't find that odd?' Sylvan chuckled. 'That he would ask you to kill his own nephew?'

'Everyone knows how unpredictable Donny can be.'

'And everyone knows how important family is to Donny, right?' Sylvan leaned over to refill Karima's glass. She was going at it hard.

'I trusted him,' I said quietly. Even as I spoke the words I realized that I was confessing my mistake. Trusting Donny was a fool's game, no matter how long you've known him.

'You trusted him.' Sylvan nodded. 'Just like he trusted you back then, with this girl, Zelda.'

'You're twisting things around,' I said.

'Am I?' Sylvan was watching us both. I could see what he was doing, but Karima was swallowing a lot of it. 'Didn't you think it was odd that he should accuse his nephew of working for Ziyade?'

I looked at him. 'How is it you know so much about all this?'

'Now that is a good question. The fact is that Ziyade had already approached me. He is planning a takeover. I told him to go to hell. Donny and I have had our differences over the years, but loyalty still counts for something.'

'Nice to know,' I muttered.

I took a moment to check on Natasha. She was back at her high stool beside the bar with an ice bucket in which she had placed the bottle of white wine. She pulled the hem of her dress up as she crossed her legs, revealing flashy red shoes. I was thinking about Sylvan's gun and how fast a man his age could move. Then Karima got to her feet. She reached for the bottle to refill her glass to the rim and then wandered away. I didn't like where this was heading. Now would be a good time to move. Sylvan's attention was divided between me and Karima who was across the other side of the room. Sylvan was watching her. I would still have to move quickly if I wanted to get hold of the Sig Sauer before he had a chance to pick it up and shoot me.

'I understand what you're trying to do,' I began. 'You're trying to flip this to make it look as though I was a part of something that I wasn't.'

'Really, that's your best defence?'

'The way I see it, Donny is covering his tracks. He was worried about Karima, thanks to you. He suspected she was up to something devious with his onshore accounts. He also wanted his nephew out of the way. I was the useful idiot who would take care of both things. That left him with one loose end. Me.'

I glanced over at Karima. She looked worried.

'The rest of it is pure speculation on your part.'

'Speculation?' Sylvan guffawed theatrically. 'I've got an idea. Why don't we call Donny and ask him?' He reached for his phone with his left hand.

'Donny?' I echoed. I was getting a bad feeling about all this. So far Sylvan had given us nothing except his elaborate theatricals. He was good at that and he had us all eating out of the palm of his hand.

'Of course. He knows you're here, after all.'

It took a moment for that to sink in. Sylvan had pulled a fast one. He'd been playing for time. That's what all of this had been about.

'Nice one,' I said slowly. 'There was no alarm sent to the security company. You were calling Donny.'

'Attaboy! Now you're thinking.' Sylvan clapped his hands.

Across the room, I heard Karima swear. 'What the hell is going on?'

I turned to her. 'This was a mistake. We have to go. Now!' I started to get to my feet.

Sylvan raised the automatic. 'I don't think so. Sit.' He tapped the screen of his phone. 'It won't be long now.'

Even as he spoke we heard the sound of a buzzer coming from somewhere. Sylvan snapped his fingers.

'Natasha, dear, would you do the honours?'

With a smile, she slid off her stool and strolled over to the wall where there was an intercom. I got up and walked over to join her. On the little grey screen I could see a car at the outer gate. There were two men in it. I didn't have to look too closely. I already knew who they were.

Shelby and Ramzan.

THIRTY-ONE

I went over to Karima and grabbed her by the arm. She shook me off.

'Leave me alone,' she said. She went straight past me, heading for the bar. This time she went around the side and started dropping ice cubes into a glass. 'This whole thing is insane!'

'Now is not the time,' I said urgently.

'Really? And when is the time exactly?' She pulled up a bottle of vodka from under the counter and poured it liberally over the ice. 'I don't think I know you any more,' she said, her eyes cold. 'I'm not sure I ever really knew you.'

'This is his game, Karima. He's been playing for time.'

'Well, maybe I've just given up caring?'

She walked round the counter and straight past me without

looking. I could see it was pointless trying to change her mind. Sylvan had sown enough doubt there to ensure that she had lost whatever trust she ever had in me.

'Sit down, Brodie.' Derek Sylvan wagged the gun in the direction of the chair I had just vacated. 'You're not going anywhere for the minute.'

I sat. I was angry enough to go for him, but I knew that this wasn't the moment. Between the two of us I reckoned I stood a chance of getting the gun off him before he managed to shoot me. I would have said the odds were even on that score. But I wasn't alone and Karima had become an unknown factor. I should have been ready to leave her behind, but something was stopping me from doing that right now. I could feel the window of opportunity sliding rapidly closed over me, like the lid of a coffin.

A few moments later I saw the darkness behind the house broken by a set of car headlights raking the night sky, bouncing between the glass angles around us as a powerful vehicle swept up the hill and into the driveway. We all turned to watch as the two figures approached. One of them, Shelby, pressed his face against the glass, shielding his eyes from the light to peer inside. Sylvan motioned for them to go round to the pool door. The two men strolled up, taking their time.

Shelby was wearing a crumpled brown suit and a tie pulled away from his unbuttoned shirt collar. His face was covered in greying stubble that matched the short hair that remained on his head. Ramzan was the taller of the two. He wore a tight-fitting leather jacket and dark jeans. He nodded towards me.

'Brodie.'

'Raz.'

Shelby was busy eyeing up Natasha. He sniffed and rubbed his chin as he approached the bar, before digging his fingers into a silver bowl of peanuts and throwing a handful into his mouth.

'Not a bad place you have here. Not bad at all.' He winked at Natasha who did not respond.

'Come on in, boys,' said Sylvan. 'Make yourselves at home. Would you like a drink?'

Shelby seemed to like the idea, while Ramzan ignored the question. He wasn't here on a social visit. He came over to the table and sat down at the far end with his back to the wall, where he could cover everyone in the room.

'You're a hard man to find,' he said to me.

'You know how it is.' I shrugged. 'Always better to keep moving.'

'Sure.' Ramzan nodded.

'Lucky you two were in the area,' said Sylvan. It was his house and he didn't seem to like the fact that nobody was paying him much attention.

'We've been chasing our tails looking for these two,' said Shelby, while pouring himself a glass of Sylvan's expensive Scotch. He held up the bottle to examine the label and nodded his approval like a seasoned connoisseur. 'Nice.'

Sylvan got up and went over to put the whisky back under the counter. 'It should be at four hundred quid a bottle.'

'You hear that, Raz?' Shelby let out a laugh like a drainpipe. 'We're in the wrong business, mate. Look at this place.' He strolled off around the room, running a hand over the leather chairs. 'Plush fittings, pool, and a tasty bit of talent.' He brushed the backs of his fingers down Natasha's arm. 'I'll bet this one's not even wearing knickers. They're like that.'

'Watch your mouth,' said Derek Sylvan.

Shelby got the cue he'd been waiting for. He spun round on him.

'Careful, old man,' he snarled. 'You called us, remember? And we don't work for you. We work for Donny and he's not too happy about this situation.' He wagged a finger in the air. 'That much I can tell you.'

'What situation?' Sylvan sounded mystified.

'Well, it's obvious, innit? For starters, what are these two doing here? I mean, why did they come here?'

'What are you talking about?' Sylvan demanded. 'I called Donny to let him know.'

'Well, that's your story.' Shelby nodded. 'All I'm saying is that to some people it could look like you got cold feet and decided to bail.'

'Bail on what?'

'Hey, I'm just the messenger, right?' Shelby was circling back to the bar, leaning over Natasha's shoulder, lifting her hair, sniffing.

'Stop that,' ordered Sylvan.

'Or what?' Shelby stepped back and looked over to him.

I glanced over at Ramzan. His face was expressionless. There wasn't a smile or even the remotest sign of curiosity. He noticed me looking at him and held my eye. It was clear who was in charge. Shelby was the attack dog. He would let him have just enough leash to get us all hot and bothered. This wasn't the first time they had done this sort of thing. Shelby was just playing his part.

'I'm not putting up with this,' said Sylvan. 'I'm calling Donny. You owe me respect.'

Bad move. Anyone could have seen that. Still, gamely he went for his phone. Shelby put out a hand, grabbed hold of the bathrobe, jerked him back and slammed him against the bar. We all heard the crack as Sylvan's head hit the marble counter. He went sprawling, his robe coming undone.

'You're showing a little too much there,' said Shelby as he stepped over him. 'You ought to cover yourself up, especially in the company of ladies.' With that he slammed a vicious kick into the man's ribs. Sylvan cried out. Natasha screamed. Shelby kicked him again and then a third time. It was Karima who stepped in. She put a hand on Shelby's arm. I tensed up, preparing to intervene. But instead of lashing out, Shelby turned to her and smiled, as if surprised to see her there.

'It's all right,' he said. 'I'm not going to hurt him.' He leaned over Sylvan, picked up the Sig Sauer and slipped it into his jacket pocket. 'Just loosening him up a little bit.'

'Perhaps it's time for us to leave.' Ramzan nodded to me and got to his feet.

THIRTY-TWO

We drove in two cars, with me and Ramzan in their Audi A5 Sportback and Shelby following behind with Karima in the Saab.

'He's going to keep his greasy paws off her, right?'

'Don't worry about him,' Ramzan murmured, glancing in the mirror. 'His bark is worse than his bite. He gets carried away sometimes.'

'I hope so, for his sake.'

That brought a chuckle. 'Still the tough guy, huh, Brodie?' He was silent for a moment. 'So she's what this is all about?'

'How do you mean?'

'How do I mean? How do you think I mean?' Ramzan looked over at me. 'You fucked up big time, Brodie.'

'What can I tell you?' I looked out of the window. 'I've seen worse.'

'I'll bet you have,' he said, shifting in his seat. 'When I came up you were a legend. The gold standard that everyone aspired to.'

'That was a long time ago.'

'Not that long.' Ramzan shook his head. 'For what it's worth, I don't think you deserve this. Whatever happened between you and Ziyade, you've shown your loyalty to Donny for years.'

'There's nothing between me and Ziyade. It's bullshit, Raz, and you know it.'

'I just do what I'm told, Brodie. You know me.'

'This is all Donny's play.'

'I hear that, but I still don't get it. You wasted his nephew. How did you think it was going to work out?'

'What choice did I have? He asked me to do it, Raz.'

'And you didn't think about maybe giving this one a miss?'

'I work for him, same as you do.' I was watching his face

as I spoke and thought I detected a hint of sympathy. I went on. 'There wasn't time. In the end, the kid tried to take me out. Where I was standing I didn't have a lot of options.'

'He was a kid, still couldn't blow his own nose.'

'I know that.'

It still sat badly with me. I wished there had been another way out, but wishing never changed anything, except in fairy tales.

'Why would he even ask you to do that? I mean, what reason did he give?'

'According to Donny, it was the kid who was selling him out to Ziyade.'

Ramzan stared at me. 'Are you serious?'

'That's the story he sold me. He's related to them, or he was. His mother.'

'Right.' Ramzan's head tipped slowly.

'I should have worked it out there and then,' I said quietly. 'Donny could never let word get out that he'd taken out his own nephew.' I took a deep breath, inhaling the smell of the car. I was willing to bet that the moment Donny finished talking to me he would have been on the phone to these two, Ramzan and Shelby. I wondered what the plan was and where we were going and how long it would take to get there.

'So tell me about the woman,' said Ramzan.

'Karima? She was doing Donny's accounts. She's retired, out of the game.'

'You know the rules, Brodie.' Ramzan heaved a sigh. 'You're a soldier, like me. We just do what we're told.'

'That's how it's meant to be. Sometimes it doesn't work out that way.'

'How involved are you with her?'

'I don't know,' I said. 'Honestly. A few hours ago I might have said there was something there, but I have a feeling I just blew it.'

'Even if what you're telling me is true, an old dog like you ought to know better.'

'It was a set-up. I'm willing to bet that the minute Donny finished telling me to do the kid he was on the phone to you. What did he tell you?'

'He told us you'd gone off the deep end. The woman, the mark, had turned your head and you'd killed Zef and taken off with the woman and some money she took from him.'

'And you believed him?'

'Never a good idea to get involved,' Ramzan went on, shaking his head like some old Buddhist sage, rubbing it in. 'You were sent up to take care of her.'

'That's right. Take care of her, and then the kid. It didn't work out that way.'

'You can say that again.' He gave a low whistle.

In the glow of the dashboard I could just make out his features. I couldn't read the expression on his face. I was getting the sense that he was trying to get me to talk, maybe because he didn't want to think about how this was going to end. 'I've got to say, I'm a little surprised you fell for it, Brodie.'

'You know how it is when you're in the middle of something. You have to make choices quickly. So that's what I did.'

'You didn't like the kid, though, did you?' I could make out his smile now. 'Admit it. Nobody liked that little shit. Always acting like royalty because he was family, like none of us had earned that right. Hell, I would've whacked the little fucker myself.'

'We've all been young, Raz. We've all done things we regret.'

'I hear you.' Ramzan chuckled, shaking his head. 'Little shit!'

When I tilted my head I could see the Saab behind us in the side mirror. They must have left the interior light on. It looked as though Karima and Shelby were having a conversation. I wondered what they were talking about. My thoughts took me back to that afternoon, back to when I was standing in her garden, watching her and Zef through the kitchen window. It was a smart move of her to talk him into a deal. That was what I'd thought at the time. Now I wondered. What exactly had she told him?

As if he was reading my thoughts, Ramzan said, 'You know why she got out, right?'

'Sure. She told me she was tired of the whole thing. Wanted to make a fresh start.'

'Well, there could be some truth to that, but it was around the time her old man bought it.'

'Her old man?' I turned to him again. I didn't need any more surprises.

Ramzan shrugged. 'I don't think they were actually married.'

'What happened?'

He stared at me. 'You don't know who her old man was?'

'I wouldn't be asking if I did.'

'It was Pete Singh. You remember Pete, right?'

I remembered Pete Singh. Small-time club owner and all-round loose cannon. He ran a couple of strip clubs and poker rooms and got in over his head on a cocaine deal with a real cowboy outfit of Ukrainians. He then made the unwise decision of trying to bluff Donny, telling him the matter was taken care of when it wasn't. One thing Donny hates is people who think they can fool him. On that subject, he was always unforgiving.

I shifted uncomfortably in my seat. 'He topped himself, didn't he?'

'Taped a tube from the exhaust pipe into his car window and drank himself into oblivion.' Ramzan shot me a glance. 'But you don't need me to tell you that, right?'

I didn't need him to tell me. I'd have liked to forget all about Pete Singh, now more than ever, but that's not how it works.

'Where did you hear about that?'

'Donny told me,' said Ramzan quietly.

'Right.' I wondered what else Donny might have told him.

I peered into the darkness ahead. We were way out of town now. I could see the lights of a village somewhere down to our left, but we were driving north, north-west as far as I could tell.

'Where are we going?'

'You'll see.' Ramzan was silent for a time, staring into the hollow tunnel of our headlights boring through the blackness. 'You must have known this was coming,' he murmured.

'Sooner or later,' I said. 'Yes, I guess I knew.' I took a deep breath. 'We all know it's going to come someday.'

'I hear you.' Ramzan nodded.

'I suppose the long and the short of it was I didn't care. You get to a point where it no longer matters. You make a decision, you have to be willing to take the consequences, whichever way the cards fall.'

'Sounds like a death wish to me.'

'I don't know if I'd put it like that,' I said. But I wasn't sure he was too far off the mark. Maybe it was something that had been building up inside me. That recklessness of spirit that comes when we have given up and all we want is for it to end. Some of that old darkness that I had brought back with me from the war. I thought I'd shaken it off, but maybe it had just been there all this time, lying dormant within. I could explain most things, but this felt different, as if there had been a moment there, that afternoon, when I realized I had stopped caring what happened to me. I knew I would be caught out. A part of me was even looking forward to it.

'You know it's not personal, right?'

'It's funny how often I've used that same expression.' I looked out of the side window. 'Feels different when you're on this end of it.'

I squinted at the side mirror again. The interior light had been switched off and you could only see the outlines of the two people inside. It felt as though I was being tailed by ghosts, as though the past was following me. Maybe it had been all this time and I just never noticed it.

'She doesn't know, does she?' Ramzan was shaking his head. 'Some mess you got yourself into, bro.'

'Is it much further?' I asked. I was growing tired of this conversation. It was personal and I wasn't sure I wanted to share it with the man who was about to put a bullet in my head.

'Don't worry, we'll be there soon.'

'You know that you can just let us go,' I said.

'Oh, yeah, and how does that work, then?'

'We just disappear. Nobody ever sees us again.'

'You know I can't do that,' he said. 'Disappear how?'

'Just go,' I said. 'Simple. Keep going and never come back.'

'It's never going to happen, bro.'

We drove in silence for another thirty minutes or so. It was raining lightly as we slowed and turned off the road on to a wide track that led up into the trees. Ramzan waited to make sure the Saab was behind us before nudging the Audi gently forward. We proceeded slowly upwards for about a mile until we reached a wooden boom blocking the way for vehicles and came to a halt. I heard the squeak of the brakes behind us and turned to watch Shelby climbing out of the car. In the brief flare of light in the interior I could see Karima had her head to one side and her eyes closed as if she was sleeping. Ramzan pushed a button and the boot of the Audi opened. Shelby disappeared from sight and then emerged holding a large pair of bolt cutters. He walked right past us. In the glow of the headlights we watched him cut through the chain and push the barrier out of the way.

'Shit!' said Ramzan. I saw he was looking in the mirror and turned in time to see a shadow breaking away from the Saab. Karima was making a run for it. Shelby saw it at the same time. He dropped the bolt cutters and went after her. I opened the side door and stepped out of the car before Ramzan could say anything. I watched Karima try to run up a steep embankment, grabbing hold of branches, saplings, her feet sliding in the soft, muddy earth.

Shelby caught up with her. It wasn't difficult. He grabbed an ankle and pulled her face down on to the leafy ground, then he grabbed a handful of her hair and hauled her to her feet. Karima let out a scream.

'Tell him to go easy on her,' I snarled. Ramzan yelled to Shelby, who swore back in return. Karima was shoved into the car, then Shelby ran round to the driver's side.

'She's all right.' Ramzan called for me to get back in the car. I wanted to go over and check, but Karima was staring off to the side and wouldn't look at me. 'Forget it, Brodie. Get in the car.'

I got back in and we drove past the barrier and up into the woodland.

'It's nice here this time of year,' said Ramzan. 'Forest of Bowland.'

'You're in the wrong line of business,' I said. 'You should have been a tour guide.'

'A holy man once explained to me that life is just a slice of eternity.'

I looked at him. 'A holy man? You're joking.'

Ramzan shook his head in earnest. 'I take that shit seriously.'

The cone of fierce white light drilled into the darkness around us, turning the world a weird monochrome out of which little flashes of colour emerged. Autumn trees resplendent in fiery orange and gold. It made the journey feel like some mystical voyage into the unknown, except that I knew what lay at the end of this track, and it wasn't good.

THIRTY-THREE

We left the cars and began to walk, Shelby at the front, tugging a struggling Karima along with him while Ramzan and I followed at an easier pace. She kept glancing over her shoulder at me as if wanting to know if I was in on this, if I had made a deal. Maybe she thought I was going to be spared and this was just the end of the job I had come to do when we had first met. I wondered how much Shelby had told her on the drive up here. It had looked to me like they had had quite a conversation back there in the car. It would have been just like him to start needling her that way.

'She's not a part of this,' I said.

'You're kidding, right?' Ramzan came to a halt. He shook his head. 'She must have got her claws into you good.'

'I'm just saying, you can let her go. I'm the one you want. Donny would understand.'

'Are you really willing to take that chance, cut her loose when she knows what she knows? She saw you whack the kid, remember?'

'What difference would that make to me?' I shrugged. 'I'd be out of it.'

Ramzan mulled that one over. If I was dead, what could Karima say about me that could harm me? He thought about it, but you could have staked a solid bet on him coming to the conclusion he did.

'I can't bend the rules,' he said finally. 'You know that. Donny would not be happy. Nobody likes loose ends, especially him. I would be painting a sign on my back, and it would come one day when I was least expecting it. Kind of like you,' he added.

'You're right,' I said. And he was. I never saw it. I never thought Donny would put some kid up to it. Last thing I expected.

'Yeah.' Ramzan nodded. 'Well, you can see the logic of it, right? Has a certain poetry to it.'

'Poetry?'

He looked at me. 'Yeah, man, everything has poetry if it's done right.'

'Right.' We walked a few more paces. I said, 'I'm guessing this is not the first time you've been out this way.'

'Actually, this was Shelby's idea. Me, I'm not interested in getting that far away from the car. But he likes his nature, this boy.'

'Well, good for him. I mean,' I looked up at the trees and took a long, deep breath, 'it's not a bad place to end.'

'I can think of worse. Remember that job in Belfast?'

'I'd forgotten you were there,' I said. 'That was a while back.'

'I was just a kid. I just remember the god awful weather and that used car dump where we took care of the guy.'

'That was a miserable fucking place to die.' I still remembered the stink of the mud.

'Too right. We were staying in some absolute dive.'

'A guesthouse. Smelt like a rat had died under the floorboards.'

'I remember that.' He laughed. 'The food messed up my stomach something wicked.' Up ahead, Shelby turned to look back at us. He was getting jumpy. 'Good times,' said Ramzan quietly.

'Yeah,' I agreed. 'Good times.' I nodded ahead of us. 'What about him?'

'Shelby? He's all right. Lacks focus, easily distracted. Thinks with his dick. You saw him back there with Sylvan's woman. Money and women. He would drop anything for a hint of either.'

Ramzan drew to a halt and turned to me. 'That's what I always appreciated about you, Brodie. There was always clarity with you.' He sniffed, pausing for a beat. 'Makes this a little easier.'

We walked on.

'Why do I feel I'm talking myself into a shallow grave?' I asked.

'You know how this works, Brodie.'

'I know the drill.'

'Right.'

We came to a halt at a wide clearing in the track. The ground was carpeted with a thick layer of leaves. All sound and movement seemed to stop in that space. A steep embankment rose up on the left and the hill fell away into darkness and shadows on the right. The track narrowed as it continued up ahead.

Karima let out a sharp cry as Shelby gave her a shove, sending her sprawling. She lay where she fell on the ground for a moment before lifting herself up on to her hands and knees. Shelby looked back at Ramzan and grinned.

'Not sure I'm going to be able to resist having a taste of this one,' he said.

'Knock yourself out,' said Ramzan. 'But first we have business to take care of.'

He gestured for me to move over towards the edge of the clearing. I stood with my back to the drop.

'You want to do it?' Ramzan asked.

'No, it's OK.' Shelby was stroking his chin, still thinking about Karima. He was half turned away from her. Ramzan was right, he was easily distracted.

'Any last requests?' Ramzan asked.

'Next time you see Donny, tell him I said to go fuck himself.'

Ramzan lifted his chin. 'Not sure I will use those exact words but I'll give him the gist of it.' He pulled out a Glock and started screwing a dampener on to the barrel. We were miles from anywhere and nobody was going to hear anything, but he didn't like to take chances.

Over his shoulder I could see Karima moving her hands around under the cover of the leaves. I did my best not to look. If she was going to do something she would have to hurry up or it was going to be too late for both of us.

Ramzan pulled back the slide to put one in the breech. He stepped back and raised his arm.

'So long, Brodie,' he said.

'See you on the other side,' I said. Over his shoulder I saw Karima swing the heavy branch into the back of Shelby's left knee. He never saw it coming and let out a scream as it dug itself in. There must have been something sharp there. He went down as she rose up. She swung again, this time aiming for his head. I felt that one.

'Hey!' Ramzan yelled, turning to aim the gun at her.

I covered the distance between us in one leap and hit him hard in the right kidney. I felt it dig in, despite the coat he was wearing which softened the blow. His arm jerked up and I heard the shot. His left hand went instinctively to his back as I hit him again, this time with the heel of my hand just behind his ear. He went down and stayed down. Shelby was moaning and groaning, trying to get to his feet. I grabbed Karima's hand and pulled her up.

'Run!' I yelled.

We ran.

THIRTY-FOUR

I had no idea where we were. I didn't know the area or the landscape; all I knew was that we had to put as much distance as possible between us and them. I would have liked to have picked up the Glock, but it had vanished beneath the leaves and there wasn't time to stop and search for it.

We ran up the track a way as it was the obvious route out of the clearing. When we reached a sharp corner, I tugged Karima off the path to the right and we plunged straight down a steep hillside into the darkness. I had no idea what was down there. I lost count of the number of trees I crashed into. I felt branches ramming into me, some of them snapping against my face. I heard Karima crying out. My jacket caught on something and I felt the stitches ripping, then I came to a halt.

I was lying sprawled on the ground, facing down. I picked myself up and looked around. Karima had come to a stop a little further up. I crawled back towards her on my hands and knees. I couldn't see much. It was pitch dark.

'Are you all right?' I whispered. 'Nothing broken?'

'I don't think so.'

'OK, good. We have to keep moving.'

I helped her up and we moved together, sliding down from tree to tree, catching and holding one another up. I made no conscious decision which direction to take; what mattered was to keep moving. The ground became muddy and soft as the angle levelled off. There was running water somewhere to our left. I headed towards it.

The stream was narrow and bright with moonlight, a silver tongue licking through the gully. It was going to be impossible to avoid getting wet, so I waded straight in and reached up to help Karima down. She pushed my hand aside and struggled in by herself. Luckily, the water wasn't that deep and the current was not too fast. We scrambled out on the other side and fought our way through thin saplings and bushes. We followed the hillside around and the sound of the water faded into the distance. The going became easier as the ground hardened under foot. I was cold now, soaked from the waist down, and I imagined Karima was the same. It was important to keep moving to stay warm. She wanted to stop and rest, but I urged her on.

'Not yet,' I said. 'Further on.'

Steam rose from our clothes as we walked. I felt exhausted and would have liked nothing better than to have curled up on the ground to rest, but we were high up and the nights were still cold. Out here in the open that could have meant certain death.

The trees thinned and fell away behind us until we were looking over an open landscape that stretched away under the stars. I could make out a soft line of hills rising and falling. I turned to Karima.

'How are you doing?' I asked.

'I'm tired and cold,' she said. 'But I'm OK.'

'It's not safe to stay here. We need to keep moving.'

'I'll be all right. Don't worry about me.' She was staring at the ground as she spoke. 'I mean it, I just don't want to go back.'

I put out a hand and lifted her chin. 'We walk until we find a place to shelter. That way our clothes will dry off.'

'Whatever,' she shrugged 'It's easier to keep walking.'

'It'll be OK,' I said, trying to sound reassuring.

She turned on me. 'You know you don't have to take care of me, right? I've been managing fine all these years by myself.'

'Good to know,' I said, before moving past her.

The ground was rough and uneven, difficult to see in the dark. We were both tired. It was like stumbling along blind, our feet dipping suddenly into holes and crashing into grassy mounds. The wind was picking up and I wondered if the weather was turning. It would be bad to be caught out in the rain. I could see clouds gathering in the west. I hoped we would be lucky.

We walked for another two hours before calling a halt. We were on the slopes of one of the hills and it was starting to rain. I headed for what looked like a large rocky outcrop. It was a natural shelter beneath a large boulder that was big enough for us to sit under. It was a good spot with a wide view of the landscape. It would keep us dry and hidden and perhaps we would be warm enough to get some sleep.

I looked back again over the way we had come. In the distance I could see the forest. I couldn't see any lights following us. That was good, but a part of me still wondered if they had some way of tracking us.

We huddled together on the cold rock. I took off my jacket and wrapped it around both of us so that we could share our warmth. The night was dark and silent but for the sound of rain falling on thick grass all around us.

'I thought I was going to die,' Karima said quietly.

'I thought so too. You saved us both.'

'It was a mistake going to Sylvan's house.'

'In a way, yes,' I agreed. 'But at least we now know that Donny wasn't trying to kill just you.'

'I find it hard to believe,' she said, shaking her head. 'After all, he trusted you. It makes no sense.'

'These things rarely do,' I said.

'What happens next?'

I'd been thinking about that one for a while now. There was no easy way to put it.

'We're both loose ends. We may have got away from them this time, but if not Ramzan and Shelby they'll send someone else.'

'So we have to keep moving. Where do we go?' she asked.

'Good question. Donny won't want any of this coming out.'

Karima looked me in the eye. 'Whichever way you turn it, he'll want us dead.'

'I'm afraid so.'

There was silence after that for a time. The rain fell. The wind blew. I tightened my arm around her shoulders to draw her closer. Karima leaned her head against mine.

'You know,' she said, 'it's strange, but back there I really felt I didn't know you.'

'I have a past. It's not perfect, but it's what it is.'

'I know. I suppose we both have histories.' Her eyes met mine and lingered. It felt like a warning. This could be a big mistake. Whatever *this* was. 'What I'm trying to say is that I'm glad we're still together, despite everything else.'

'I'm glad too.'

We fell silent again. It seemed strange to be talking like this when we were out in the middle of nowhere in the middle of the night with two very dangerous men trying to kill us, but at the same time it made perfect sense.

'I'm still not completely clear,' Karima said, after a time. 'Back at the house Sylvan was talking about Goran Malevich. What does he have to do with anything?'

'It's a long story.' I sighed.

'I'm not going anywhere and there's nothing else for us to do out here.'

I thought about it for a moment and realized that this was something that wasn't going to go away. I let my mind roll back.

'It was a difficult time. There was a lot of turbulence in London, a lot of people vying for control of certain sections of the business.'

'I remember the name, Goran.'

'Well, Goran Malevich was one of the heavyweights. He ran a Serbian mob. They were in direct competition with Donny, but there were those who thought Goran was getting too big for his own boots.'

'And the woman – who was she?'

'Zelda. That was her stage name. She started out as a dancer at one of Goran's clubs.'

'By dancer, you mean stripper,' Karima said quickly. It wasn't a question.

'They give them different names, but yes, that's what it boils down to. Anyway, I knew that Zelda was about to grass on Goran.'

'How did you know that?'

I paused as it came back. 'I was friends with an undercover cop who was grooming her. A detective inspector with the Met by the name of Cal Drake.'

'So you decided to use this information to switch sides and work for Donny?'

I listened to the rain falling on thick grass. 'It was a little more complicated than that.'

'Isn't it always?'

'New players were coming in,' I said. 'Trying to squeeze the old guard out. Donny had made a lot of enemies over the years.' I stared out at the dark landscape as the memory of that time came back. 'That's how you survive – knowing when to cut loose and move on.'

'Did you kill her?' Karima looked at me. I could only see shadows where her eyes were.

'No, in the end I didn't,' I said, letting the air slowly out of my lungs. 'I went there to get hold of a notebook she had. It contained names, dates. Enough to take Goran and others down.'

As a distinction it was small, almost non-existent.

'I might as well have killed her. I led them to her.'

'So who killed her?'

'A nasty piece of work by the name of Khan. A heavy for a certain Hamid Balushi who ran the scummy end of operations for Goran. Basically a slum landlord who ran prostitutes and all kinds of shit out of his properties.' I took a deep breath. 'He cut off her head.'

'How could someone do that?'

'Khan could do a lot of things.' I listened to the rain for a time. 'Balushi wanted to keep the head as some kind of collateral to use as leverage at a later date.'

'What a sick world you live in.'

'Lived in. Past tense,' I said.

'What happened to the cop? Did he at least arrest them?'

'He tried. But he was taken off the case. It wasn't easy.'

'It never is, right?' She was staring at my face in the darkness. I looked away.

'All of this has happened for a reason.'

She gave a cold laugh. 'Do you really believe that?'

'I'm not going back to that life, Karima. No matter what happens.'

'Well, maybe,' she said.

'I need you to believe me.'

'Why? What difference does it make what I believe?'

'I need someone to believe me and you're the nearest I've got to that.'

'Touching.'

'We're going to get out of this mess.'

'This is you trying to reassure me again. I warned you about that.'

'I know it's hard, but you just have to trust me.'

Karima looked out at the dark, wet landscape and was silent.

'Try to get some sleep,' I said.

THIRTY-FIVE

Neither of us could really get any rest. It was too cold and uncomfortable for that. At some point, though, I felt Karima's body relax and the sound of her breathing told me she was asleep.

I must have closed my eyes too for a time. When I opened them again I saw a thin band of light on the horizon cracking the darkness. It was like a shell opening. The rain had stopped and birds were singing, hopping over the moorlands. A light mist hung over the valley below us. My limbs felt stiff and cold. Karima stirred and woke up. She straightened up with a sigh.

'God, I'm freezing.' She shuddered.

'We should get moving. We'll warm up that way.'

I had an idea that we should keep walking in a north-westerly direction. I didn't know the area but I knew that we had left Shelby and Ramzan behind us in the southeast and that it was best to keep moving the other way.

Being able to see was an advantage. In daylight, the landscape was less menacing and more manageable. It certainly made it easier to walk and within a short while we hit a path that wound its way along the bottom of the valley and took us in a northerly direction. For a time the sun came out, breaking through the cloud cover and dissolving the mist. The rounded peaks emerged as if from a dream.

We walked for several hours. The sun started to dry things out and the air felt warm. We stopped by a stream to drink water. There was something idyllic about the whole day, despite the fact that we hadn't eaten anything and both of us were tired and hungry.

By early afternoon we had reached a col between two ridges. Below us we could see the stone walls that marked the edge of the national park. Beyond that a tarmac road curved away and in the distance smoke could be seen rising from a grove of trees.

It took another hour to reach the road and forty minutes or so to climb the gentle rise. A thin plume of smoke announced a cottage set behind some trees. Karima rested on a low wall.

'I'm not sure I can go on.' She raised a hand and let it drop. 'I mean, how much further do we have to walk?'

'Maybe not that far.' I looked up at the house. 'Let's ask. Maybe we can buy something here.'

'Wait a second. Do you have any money?'

'I have some cash,' I said, pulling up a money belt I carried around my waist. 'Along with a couple of credit cards in different names.'

'That should do it,' she said.

We were in luck. A woman in her sixties came to the door. She had grey hair and a cheerful-looking Labrador at her heels. As we stood there I spotted a plaque in the window that read Vacancies. I pointed at it.

'Yes, of course, come in.' She stepped aside. 'I had to take the sign in for repair.' She saw the blank looks. 'Bed and Breakfast? I have a post by the gate but it was blown down in the storm, smashed to pieces. Walkers, are you?' She was looking at our clothes in a way that suggested we were somewhat lacking in that respect. We didn't quite fit the bill of seasoned ramblers. I was wearing a waxed jacket, better suited for riding a motorcycle, along with jeans and sturdy boots. Karima's denim jacket and disintegrating pumps were less than convincing. But who knows, nowadays people venture out without much of a clue about anything.

'Yes,' I said, trying to sound a confident note. 'We came over the hill this morning.'

'Well, you're in luck, I've just finished making some fresh scones. How does that sound?'

Karima looked as though she might faint. It felt absurd to be sitting in a well-furnished living room complete with overstuffed sofas and porcelain dogs on the mantelpiece, but there you go. Over tea and scones, Mrs Barton told us her life story, or as good as. We listened and tried not to eat as if we hadn't seen food in twenty-four hours, but she noticed all the same. When we were finally in our room, laid out on the bed, incapable of moving, Karima said, 'She's on to us.'

I tried to play it down. 'She thinks something is awry. We just don't look like your average hill walkers.'

'I've always hated that look. The plastic mac and the heavy boots.' Karima looked around her and started to giggle. 'Doesn't it feel ridiculous to be here in this room? After last night, I mean. It's all so quaint.'

She was right. There were cushions on the bed and prints of cats on the walls. I got up and went over to the window. Looking out, I could see the hillside where we had sheltered the night before.

'We can't stay here for long,' I said. 'Sooner or later they will come around this side and start looking for us here.'

'What do you suggest?' There was a note of despair in her voice. 'It seems so hopeless. I mean, we can't just keep running.'

'I know. I've been thinking about that.'

'And . . .?' She got up off the bed and came over to stand facing me. 'What is it you're not telling me? Don't you trust me anymore?'

'It's not that,' I began. 'I just got the impression that, you know, after last night, with everything that was said . . .'

Karima was shaking her head. 'I thought I was going to die last night. Don't you get that?'

I was still thinking about how to answer when she spun round and walked away.

'I'm going to take a bath,' she said over her shoulder. She left the door ajar and a moment later I heard the water running. She was in there for about fifteen minutes before she began to speak.

'All my life men have been telling me what to do. Go here, go there. Do this, do that.' She fell silent. I didn't say anything. I had the feeling she wasn't finished. 'We just go along, trying to avoid trouble, violence, pain.'

I went over to lean in the doorway. I couldn't see her round the door, but I had the feeling I was hearing a confession.

'Men never stop to think that maybe there's another way. They just carry on doing the same – pushing, pushing. They think we women are incapable of doing anything better than them.'

She fell silent again. I waited for her to go on. Her voice sounded distant, as if she were addressing someone who was far away.

'I took my time. I moved a little here, a little there. Small amounts that I knew he would never miss. Donny's empire is so big even he doesn't understand what is moving where. He watches his men, his partners. The slightest move and he's on them, sorting it out, sending in the hard men. Men like you, who do his dirty work.'

'But he doesn't watch the numbers,' I said. 'That's what you're saying?'

'I'm saying he never looks beyond the bottom line. He wants to see that everything is square, that the numbers line up.' She broke off and then laughed softly. 'I had a friend. She used to smuggle diamonds. I always used to laugh. She said it was safer than heroin. The little bags can tear and you die on the plane. So she did diamonds. Nobody talks about it, but everyone loves diamonds. Their value stays constant. Everyone wants to avoid paying tax and so on. So it's a good thing to invest in.'

'And that's what you did?'

'The thing about diamonds, they are small – tiny, in fact. You can carry them in your pocket, sewn into the lining of your coat, or inside a tampon. One place you can guarantee a man won't be interested in looking.'

'They have women to do those checks.'

'Yes, but it never really happens, does it?'

'So what are you saying?'

'I'm saying that once you've seen how easy it is for large sums of money to come and go in the click of a mouse, you start to yearn for things to be way more concrete, stuff you can hold in your hand.'

'Like diamonds.'

'Exactly.' I couldn't see her, but I heard her give a long sigh. 'I really thought I was going to die up there on that hill. I can't believe we made it.'

'Amen to that,' I murmured.

The next morning we asked Mrs Barton to order us a taxi to take us to the nearest station.

'Had enough of walking, have you?' she asked, with a look at our footwear.

'I think next time we'll come better prepared,' I said. That seemed to satisfy her.

We bought bus tickets heading to Lancaster. Then we switched to another bus on to Carlisle. From there we took a train across country, zig-zagging back and forth, taking the first available service in whichever direction.

'Is all of this necessary?' Karima asked that afternoon as we sat on an uncomfortable bench and waited for yet another train.

'I told you, there are two rules. The first is to run as fast as you can.'

'I know,' she said. 'And the second is never run in a straight line.'

'Atta girl. You're learning.'

'I have a good teacher,' she said.

We spent a night in Newcastle, then another in Berwick. We chose simple places with no demands and paid cash every time, leaving no trace of having been there.

Slowly, we made our way north. Sitting on another bus leaving Fort William, Karima tucked her arm through mine.

'This mystery place of yours had better be something really special.'

'It is,' I said.

THIRTY-SIX

We walked down through the little town towards the sea. A fresh wind was blowing. The sun was shining and the bay stretched out to the north-west, a long, slick tongue of blue water that widened as it reached towards the horizon. The marina was south of the village. We walked along the low shoreline for about ten minutes, past the post office and the harbour master's office to a small natural inlet. Alongside a high quay about a dozen large fishing boats were moored. Protected by this was a much lower landing that stretched out into the water. On both sides of this wooden jetty smaller craft were tied up. These ranged from little two-man fishing smacks to open launches and elegantly varnished yachts. I led the way until I found what I was looking for. Karima came up and stood beside me.

It wasn't much to look at. A forty-foot Catalina ketch. It was robust and simple. More importantly, it had been sitting on that row of vessels for years, since long before I bought it. It didn't stand out or draw attention to itself.

'Whitehavens,' Karima read the name on the stern. 'It's bigger than I imagined,' she said, turning to me. 'So what do we do now?'

'We need to get a few things – supplies, fuel.'

'And how do we do that?'

While she was speaking my attention was distracted by the high-pitched whine of an engine. I looked over towards the road where a quad bike was coming to a stop at the end of the quay. The rider had long white hair and a beard to match. He brought the bike to a halt and hopped out of the saddle, unbuckling his helmet to hang it over one of the handlebars.

'Can I help you?' he called as he started towards us.

'Now what?' Karima was suddenly alarmed.

'Don't worry,' I said, 'I've got this.' I stepped past her and started down the jetty to meet him.

The man was halfway along before he stopped. Pushing the windblown strands of hair out of his eyes, he swore under his breath.

'No! I don't believe it. Is that you?'

'It's me, Henny.'

He let out a wild screech of laughter that sent the gulls scrambling for the sky. Coming forward, he threw his arms around me and lifted me in a bear hug until my feet left the ground. Henrik Heimdal was in his seventies but had spent most of his life outdoors and still had the body to show for it.

'Why didn't you tell me you were coming up?'

'It wasn't planned exactly. Spur of the moment thing.' I noticed him looking Karima over. 'This is Henrik,' I said. 'Henrik, meet Karima.'

'Well, charmed, I'm sure.' Henny's blue eyes twinkled as he grinned at her. 'So you've come to see the old girl? Still in perfect shape. I take her out on the water every week or so, just so she doesn't lose her feel for it.'

'She looks great,' I said, turning to look at the ketch.

'She is. You're coming up to the house, aren't you? Mary would never forgive me if you didn't. Have you got a place to stay? Are you in a car?'

I shook my head. 'All we've got is what we're wearing.'

'OK, well, that's no problem. We can fix you up no bother.' Henny nodded towards the shore. 'I've only got the bike with me now. If you hang on here, I can nip up and fetch the car.'

'We can start walking slowly that way.'

With that he waved and walked back to hop up on to the bike and speed away. Karima laughed as we started back along the shore.

'What a character! Old army buddy, I suppose?'

'Actually, Henrik is one of the few people I know who pre-dates my army days.' I stopped to fill my lungs with fresh air and take in the landscape. Henrik and Mary lived in a small farmhouse perched on the flank of the soft hillside overlooking the bay. We hadn't managed to get back to the town and were still walking north along the road when Henrik returned driving an old navy blue Land Rover. We both squeezed into the front seat and once he'd managed to turn it around the car thundered through the small town and out round Strath Bay before clanking and thumping its way up the narrow track towards the house.

It was years since I had been here. I had first come to this part of the world when I was a teenager. I was on the run, on the road, trying to decide what to do with my life, not wanting to go back to anything I knew. I'd decided to travel as far as I could and luck led me here. It was luck too that had given me a lift in a car driven by Henrik, who talked nonstop for the hour or so it took to get from the Inverness road out here, and in that space of time he had told me his life story and offered me a place to stay for as long as I liked. And there was work to be had, helping out with the livestock and on the fishing boats. The summer I spent here was one of the best of my life, and since then I had returned again and again.

Henrik's wife Mary was a round-faced, robust woman, her hands rough from years of manual labour, her cheeks red from the wind. She was hanging laundry out on a line behind the house when we arrived, the cotton sheets whipping in the wind like sails. It was hard to imagine two people better matched, to each other and to this life. They didn't have much, but what they had they were always willing to share.

Inside the house with a fierce fire burning we drank tea laced with Henrik's whisky and ate freshly baked rolls with butter. Mary and Henrik talked about local matters. Who was doing what, how the weather was changing, which was all fine for us. They seemed to sense that we didn't really want to talk about what it was that had led us here. Eventually, as the light was draining from the sky and we had eaten a simple meal of soup and bread, Henrik and I retired to the living room while Karima and Mary chatted in the kitchen.

'So,' he said, raising his eyebrows. 'Unexpected trip, eh? Any idea where you are headed?'

'No,' I confessed. 'Truth be told, we're in a little trouble, Henrik.'

'That much I had managed to work out.' He fetched the whisky and filled two glasses before settling back into his armchair by the window. 'She's seems like a fine woman,' he nodded, studying his glass.

'Yes, she is.' I couldn't really say much more. I wouldn't have known where to start. 'The thing is, once we leave here there's no knowing when we might be able to come back.'

Henrik nodded philosophically. 'I'm seventy-seven years old. I don't know from one day to the next if I'll see another sunset.' He lifted his glass in salute. 'Life is for living in the present.'

'I wish I could tell you more, but I don't want to put you in any danger, and that's why we will be leaving tomorrow.'

'So soon?'

'It's too risky to stay on.'

'I understand.' He looked into the fire. 'I've never asked what you get up to when you're not here. I've always been clear about that.'

'Yes, you have, and I've always appreciated it.'

'I've always trusted you, son, and that means more than all the rest of it. It's a rare thing, being able to put your life in someone else's hands, but those are the people that count. The rest, as they say, is just noise.'

That night I woke up to see Karima standing naked by the window. The glow of the moon illuminated her body so that for a minute I wondered what I was seeing.

'Come back to bed,' I said, 'before you catch cold.'

'It's so beautiful out there, the sea, I mean, in this light. It looks as if it contains all kinds of magical creatures.'

'In the summer you can see Minke whales and dolphins. They're pretty magical.'

I lifted the side of the duvet as she came back to lie in my arms. I stroked her hair as her head rested on my chest.

'They're quite a special couple,' she said. 'Why all the Norwegian flags?'

'His father came from there during the war. He was in the resistance and managed to escape from the Nazis and come over here. Henrik still speaks some of the language.'

'He really likes you.'

'I feel closer to him than any family I've ever had, certainly more than my own father, though that's not saying much.'

Karima raised herself up to study my eyes. 'Are you sure about this? I mean, about taking me with you?'

'As sure as I've ever been about anything.'

She kissed me sweetly at first and then with more passion, then she slid on top of me and we made love once more before falling asleep.

The next morning was spent checking the boat and restocking it with food and fuel. Henrik had been true to his word and kept an eye on her, and the *Whitehavens* was in good shape. Still, I ran the motor until I was satisfied it sounded smooth and untroubled. I put up the sails and made sure the compass and navigation instruments were working and all the batteries were charged.

After that we regrouped up at the house for a big lunch Mary had prepared.

'Are you really sure you have to leave so soon?' she asked me as I was helping her in the kitchen.

I set down the plates I was carrying. 'I wish we didn't have to,' I said. 'You know how much I love it here.'

'Well, I'm sure you know best.' She rested a hand on my arm and sighed. 'He's not getting any younger, you know, and just seeing you makes him feel better.'

I pressed her hand. 'I'll be back. I promise. When things have settled down. But right now is not a good time.'

Mary nodded as if she understood. After we had eaten I

walked up to the barn at the back of the house. In one corner there was a stack of hay bales. I moved them one by one and then swept the dry straw aside to reveal a trapdoor in the floor. I put my hand through the hole in the wood and lifted it.

Henrik's father, old man Heimdal, had built this as a safe room for his family. In the Norway of his youth he had seen how society could turn on you and he wanted to be prepared. So he had dug out a space large enough for his wife and children to hide in. It wasn't that he thought the Nazis would overrun Scotland, but he didn't want to be caught out if they did. It didn't seem all that crazy an idea, even today.

But right now it was empty. I climbed down the short set of steps and dragged what I was looking for into the light and then bumped it up the stairs. The last time I was here, three years ago, I had packed a few essentials into a large military locker. It was made of toughened plastic and was pretty much indestructible. I unlocked it, undid the fastenings and opened the lid. Inside was my old army rucksack along with some carefully sealed packets of cash wrapped in plastic. Dollars, euros and pounds. Another packet contained several identity cards and driving licences, all with my face on them but with different names. There were two passports, one Swiss and the other Venezuelan. There were also a couple of guns. A Ruger snub-nosed hammerless .357 revolver and a 9mm Beretta along with spare clips and two boxes of ammunition. I carried everything up and set it by the door of the barn, then I went back down the steps to put things back in place. I bent over to close the trapdoor. When I straightened up and turned around I found Karima pointing the Ruger at me.

THIRTY-SEVEN

'You should be careful with that,' I said. 'It has a very light trigger.'

The gun didn't waver. She was clearly nervous, pushing a hand through her hair.

'What's this about, Karima?'

'You know what it's about,' she said.

'Let's just put down the gun and talk things over.'

Karima shook her head. 'Pete. You killed Pete.'

'Shelby told you,' I said. I remembered wondering what he was telling her. Now I knew. 'In the car. That's what this is about?'

'I just want to know.'

'I thought we were good. I thought, last night . . .'

'Last night was just . . .' She searched for the words and, not finding them, gave a shrug. 'We shared a moment. It's nothing more than that.'

'I don't believe you,' I said. I waited.

'What is all this?' she asked, gesturing at the trunk. 'Another of Brodie's little stashes?'

'My escape hatch. Money and a new identity.' Again, I waited and again she said nothing. 'It's a new start. Just the two of us. Like we agreed. We can go anywhere in the world.'

'I don't think so,' she said. I was worried about the Ruger. She was holding the gun with both hands, she was trembling so much. 'Did you kill him? Did you kill Pete?'

'Karima, listen to me. Shelby told you that because he was trying to mess with your head. He wanted this to happen. Don't you see?'

'It doesn't matter what he wanted,' Karima insisted. 'All of this.' She gestured at the bag. 'Us. I mean, I can't just forget it. Pete meant something to me.'

'I understand that.'

'Do you?' She looked me in the eye. 'I wonder if you can understand anything at all about how I feel.'

'I understand you're upset.'

'Then you need to tell me whether or not you killed him.'

'Think what you're doing, please.' I held up both my hands. 'Whatever happened in the past, none of that matters. We're here, together, in this moment. This is *our* chance.'

'What are you talking about?' Her face crumpled, screwing itself up in pain. 'What can we build on this? Lies, more lies?' She was shaking her head. 'Death. That's what holds us together.'

'That's not true, and you know it.'

She wasn't hearing me. 'You can't build anything on a lie,' she said. The gun was still pointed at my heart. I wanted to say something, I just didn't know where to start.

'Look, I don't know very much about this sort of thing,' I started. I saw the blank look on her face. 'I mean, relationships. I've never been good at them, and to be honest, I haven't had a lot of practice.' I paused. I still couldn't tell if I was having any impact. 'The point is I think we have something here. I believe that.'

'What are you trying to say?'

'I'm saying I don't know the words. I don't know how this is supposed to go, but I know what I feel. This. Us. It's real.'

'How can I trust you?' She wasn't letting me off that easily. 'I'm pointing a gun at you. You'll say anything.'

'That's not true and you know it. Last night you felt it. What's changed?'

'I realized that I can't go through with this, with you, without knowing the truth.' Her chest was heaving as she struggled to get the words out.

'Pete's gone,' I said quietly. 'And truth be told, nobody misses him.'

'I loved him,' she said, her voice breaking.

'Maybe you did. And maybe for a time back then you needed him.'

'How can you say that?' She scowled. 'You don't know me. You didn't know me back then.'

'No, I didn't, but I knew him, a little bit. He wasn't a good person, Karima. He hurt people. You know why they wanted him taken out? Because he was a liability. He was out of control, and sooner or later he was going to bring the whole house down on top of him.'

'You think that excuses what you did?'

'I'm not trying to justify it. It was a job. In this game saying no to an order is as good as signing your own death warrant.'

'I see.' A half smile appeared on her face. 'That's how you deal with it, is it? Telling yourself little lies that make it easier to live with what you've done?'

'I don't need to tell myself lies. I accept what I've done. I take full responsibility.' I shifted my weight from one foot to the other. 'If you're going to shoot me then hurry up and get it over with. And please, do it right. I don't want to spend the rest of my life in a wheelchair.'

She levelled the gun at my chest and I shook my head.

'Closer,' I said. 'You should stand closer.'

She hesitated. 'I . . .' she began.

I saw something in her eyes that I hoped was doubt, but whatever she might have been about to say was lost in the whine of Henrik's quad coming up the hill. The high-pitched intensity of the engine told me that trouble was coming. To cast aside any possible doubt, he was pressing the horn over and over in long bursts.

'Something's wrong,' I said. The look on Karima's face told me she had the same feeling. She stepped back and lowered the Ruger. As I went by her I picked up the Beretta from the trunk and checked it was loaded. We ran round to the front of the house to see Henrik skidding as he came up the last fifty metres from the road.

'What's going on?' Karima asked.

Henrik had spotted us and was waving frantically, standing up in the saddle. Then, without warning, he suddenly twisted and tumbled sideways. The bike carried on a few metres before coming slowly to a halt.

The crack of a high-powered rifle echoed from the distance, rolling across the hillside.

'Get inside!' I yelled. Karima stared at me but didn't move. 'Go on!' I waved her back.

As I ran down towards Henrik, I had the image of her expression impressed on my brain. I was trying to analyse it even as I was taking in what was in front of me.

Henrik lay on his back. The hole in his chest was big enough to put your fist into. His eyes were open. The only thing you could say was that he probably hadn't even felt it. He'd been killed instantly.

The next bullet passed close to my head, so close I felt it before I heard it. I threw myself to the ground and started crawling back over towards the house. Rule number one: you can't fight a rifle with a handgun.

I reached Karima who was crouched down on one knee and

pulled her to me. She seemed to be in shock, paralyzed, unable to move. I grasped her shoulders and shook her.

'Listen to me. Stay low. Don't lift your head.'

I could feel her trembling. 'Where are they?'

From the angle of the bullet that had killed Henrik, my guess was the scrappy line of trees off to our east, but I wasn't going to spend time investigating.

'We have to get out of here.'

I looked past Karima and saw Mary standing in the doorway of the house. I waved for her to get inside.

'Get down on the floor!'

'Where's Henny?' she cried.

I couldn't bring myself to tell her. 'Just get inside and stay down!' I yelled. Taking Karima's hand, I dragged her with me. I still wasn't too sure she wouldn't shoot me herself. We raced around the side of the house where we at least had some protection. In the barn, I started loading the rucksack with packages of money, documents and ammunition. 'Do you still have the revolver?'

She showed it to me. 'Keep it with you,' I said. 'Shooting me is going to have to wait.'

Pulling the rucksack on to my back, I took her hand again and led the way through to the other side of the barn. I paused to look down over the hillside. There was a good chance that someone was waiting for us on the other side.

'Who is it?' she asked.

'Don't you know?'

'What?'

'My money is on Shelby and Ramzan,' I said, still looking out.

'But how?' she asked. 'How could they find us?'

I'd like to have known the answer to that one myself, although it was academic as far as resolving our current problem went. I surveyed the open ground below the house. I could see heather and clumps of long grass blowing in the wind, rocks that appeared one moment and disappeared the next. I waited as long as I could before deciding that it was safe.

'OK, let's go. Stay low.'

We bent double as we ran, keeping the house between us and the shooter as we went up the hillside towards the top of the ridge. I listened for the sound of a shot. If they were accurate they would hit us before we heard anything, but all the same. When no more shots came, I assumed that they were waiting to be sure it was safe to advance on the house.

The ground grew more rocky and open. We reached the ridge and slipped over. It felt safer on the other side and I took a moment to assess our position. To our left the land tapered off towards the sea. I could see the distant surge of spume where it broke over the rocks. A rough track led off north-east in the direction of the coastal road. Ahead of us was a scrubby patch of rocks and heather with the odd clump of Scotch pine. It was fairly open ground, but we were ahead of them and the light was fading. Soon it would be difficult for them to pick us out in that mixed terrain.

From time to time I looked back over my shoulder as we ran, the heavy rucksack thumping hard against my back. From here we could only see the roof of the farmhouse, the top edges of the stone walls stark against the waning light. More importantly, I didn't hear any more shots.

When we reached the next ridge we came to a halt and collapsed on the ground, gasping for breath. I shrugged the rucksack off. Karima was crying in soft, gentle sobs.

'That poor man,' she whispered. 'We killed him.'

I looked at her and said nothing. She was right, of course. I would never forget the image of Henrik lying on the ground, his eyes staring sightlessly at the sky. It was lodged in my memory forever. He was the kindest man I had ever known. This was the last safe spot in the world for me, and now that too was ruined.

'How could they find us?' I asked, clenching my fists.

'What?' Karima sniffed and wiped her nose.

'Nobody knew about this place. Nobody.' I waited for the words to sink in. 'Except you. I told you about *Whitehavens* . . . and you told Shelby.'

'No!' Karima put her hand over her mouth. 'No, I swear. I never told him.'

'When you were in the car alone with him. He told you about

Pete Singh. He told you I was the one who killed him. So you told him about the boat. They could have traced it to here.'

'No!' She stretched out a hand towards me. 'I wouldn't betray you.'

I brushed her off. 'What is it with you?' I asked. I was angry. I could feel the bitterness pouring out of me. 'One minute you want to kill me and the next you want me to believe you weren't planning to hurt me? At least have the decency to admit it. Shelby told you about Pete Singh. You were shocked and upset and wanted to hurt me, so you told him.'

'No, it's not true.' She was shaking her head. 'Yes, he told me, but I knew what he was playing at. I knew he was trying to turn me against you.'

'You wanted to get back at me,' I said. 'Why not, it makes perfect sense. You loved Pete. You told me so yourself.'

'No, it wasn't like that. No matter how angry I was, I wanted to hear your side.' She lowered her head for a moment and sobbed quietly to herself. Then, in a low voice, she asked, 'Do you think they've killed her too . . . Mary?'

I looked back across towards the farmhouse. We hadn't heard any more shots, but that didn't mean anything. There were plenty of other ways of killing someone. And of course they would have to kill her. It made no sense to leave her there. She was a witness. It was always better to get rid of witnesses. First, they would ask her what she knew, where we were going. Then they would kill her. I could see her lying on the kitchen floor in a pool of blood. I closed my eyes and squeezed them tightly to try and make it go away, but the image stayed.

'What do we do now?' Karima asked.

'It'll be dark soon. They'll be waiting up there for us to come back, or they'll split up and one of them will go down to the harbour to wait.'

'Why didn't they come after us?'

'It's risky,' I said, looking at the hill. 'Coming down there they would have been exposed. They don't know what kind of weapons we might have. They're being cautious.'

To the left I could still make out a rough track and in the distance a small loch. There were lots of little inlets and lakes around here. It was like a maze. That was one thing in our favour – I knew the landscape from having walked it often over the years, alone or with Henrik. We'd had lots of great talks out here, about the universe and life. Henrik never ceased to view the world with wonder.

I knew that if we made our way on from here then just north of us we would eventually reach the road. If we were lucky we could catch a lift and then just keep moving. A part of me said that was the logical plan. Another part of me wanted to turn around right now and face them, just finish it once and for all.

I looked back over the ground we had just covered. We could wait here for them and pick them off as they came. But they were too smart for that. What would I do in their shoes? They could have decided to circle round the hill, one of them on foot, the other bringing the car. I couldn't see anything, but that didn't mean much. Shelby and Ramzan were good. You didn't see their type generally until it was too late.

'So what do we do?' Karima was still sniffing softly to herself. 'I mean, how do we get away from them?'

I didn't have anything to say. We had been so close. The boat was stocked and ready to depart. Just a couple of hours more and we would have been gone.

'Is there still a chance?' Karima asked, her eyes searching mine.

I wasn't prepared to give up on the *Whitehavens*, I realized. Not yet. I'd come too far and paid too much for that. Shelby and Ramzan would probably be able to work that out for themselves too. They would be waiting.

THIRTY-EIGHT

We made ourselves as comfortable as possible, each of us sitting with our backs to a large boulder. The ground was sandy and soft. I put my head back and closed my eyes. The Beretta was in my hand, resting in my lap. I could hear the branches creaking overhead, swaying back and forth. There was something ancient and reassuring about that sound, and for a time it brought me some calm. I was thinking about Mary, about leaving her behind. I tried telling myself that that was what she would have wanted. I wasn't doing a good job of convincing myself.

'I'm sorry,' Karima said. 'For pointing the gun at you earlier.'

I opened my eyes and looked at her.

'I wasn't going to shoot you,' she said.

'Well, you'd probably have been justified in doing it.'

'No.' She shook her head. 'I don't believe in that – an eye for an eye. All of that nonsense. Killing you wouldn't bring Pete back.' She looked down at her hands. 'I just saw the gun lying there and I had to do it. I had to try. I just needed to know if I could.'

'I get it.' I shifted my position. 'Whatever happens to us, you're always free to go.'

'I know.' She was sitting with her legs straight out in front of her. Now she brought her knees up and wrapped her arms around them, hugging herself.

'Pete wasn't a good person, I know that. But you're right. At the time, I needed him. I convinced myself that I loved him, but the truth is that he was cruel to me and to others. He used to tell me I would never become anything, that I was a stupid mongrel bitch who was only good for one thing.'

'Why didn't you leave him?'

Her shoulders lifted and fell. 'I don't know. I was finally clean, for the first time in years. I wasn't doing drugs. Pete was also clean, and that was a good thing. I had a job, doing what I had trained to do. I was good at it. It kept me sane.'

'Kept you sane?'

'Numbers. To me, it's almost therapeutic, the beauty of numbers. You can't cheat them. Yes, you can fiddle the books. That I could do. You move things from where they should be to somewhere else, or change the original figures when they are entered. But once they are in there, they have to add up.'

'So, how did you fiddle the books?'

'I just did what they told me. If Donny said I want this much to invest here, or that much to be in my account in Djakarta, then I could do it.' She allowed herself a smile. 'I was good at that. So good that nobody really knew where anything was except me.'

'And Donny trusted you with all of this?'

Karima nodded quickly. 'He said he trusted me more than any of the others. That used to annoy Pete.'

I took a moment to turn and look back out across the hill in the direction we had come from. I could make out the lighter colour of the sandy track leading down to the road. I still saw nothing moving. Night was coming down quickly. The shadows were growing longer and a chill was creeping into the air. Satisfied that nothing and nobody was out there, I turned back to Karima.

'So what did Donny say when you told him you were quitting?'

'He understood. He wasn't happy, but he knew that Pete's death had hit me hard.'

That sounded like classic Donny. It's only after he's ordered the hit that he realizes it will cost him his accountant.

Her features seemed to dissolve in the shadows. How well did I really know her? Was I blind because I was afraid of losing her? As I was staring at her a thought occurred to me.

'Do you still have your phone?'

'It's here.' She reached into her pocket. 'It's not on though. I've kept it off all this time.'

I took it from her and undid the back to remove the battery but found nothing. It could still be an app. I didn't want to switch the phone on. I placed it on a rock, picked up another one and smashed it to pieces. I should have done that a long time ago. I was slipping.

'Is that it?' Karima asked.

'I hope so. It could also be a GPS tracker. Go through your pockets, see if there's something there that you don't recognize.'

She did that and found nothing. 'How about your purse?'

Karima held out a small leather wallet. I went through it. It had a little pocket for change. I pulled out a small silver disc, the size of a coin.

'That's why they aren't coming after us,' I said, holding it up. 'They don't need to, they know exactly where we are.'

Karima held my gaze firmly. 'So, you believe me now?' she asked.

'I believe you. Shelby must have slipped it into your purse when you were in the car with him.'

'My jacket was on the back seat. I fell asleep for a time.'

I was kicking myself for not having been more thorough. I'd made a mistake and Henny and Mary had paid the price. It meant that all of our manoeuvres had been in vain. They'd known exactly where we were all the time. Even now, they could just track us to a convenient point where they would be ready for us.

It also meant there was a chance they didn't know about the boat. I reached into the rucksack and pulled out my survival knife. I held it up so she could see the compass fixed on the hilt.

'I've walked in this area a lot. If we head in a north-easterly direction we should be able to circle around and strike the main road north of the town.'

'You can find your way in the dark?'

'I think so. There are plenty of paths and it's a clear night.'

'What's your plan?'

I looked her in the eye. 'We're still leaving here on that boat. If you want to, that is.'

She hesitated for only a moment before nodding.

'Then let's get a move on. We'll leave this here.' I placed the tracker on the top of a flat rock. 'They'll think we're going to sit out the night before moving. Ready?'

Karima nodded. I led the way. It was slow going, moving over uneven ground in the dark without tripping or banging into something, but I slowed the pace so that we could move steadily and find a rhythm. As our eyes got used to the light it got easier. We came to a clearing. I pointed.

'There's a lake over there. We'll circle around the south side.'

'OK.'

We set off across the open ground. I was still cautious. I didn't actually know how close Shelby and Ramzan were. They might have been out there somewhere on high ground with a night vision sight, in which case they could pick us off at leisure. The only way to find out was to move.

It took us an hour to reach the road, moving carefully over what turned out to be difficult terrain to navigate in the dark. I had a torch in my rucksack, but I didn't want to risk giving our position away.

We were almost on the road before we saw them. Headlights coming steadily along from the direction of Gairloch. We dropped down behind a stone wall and waited for the car to pass.

'How safe is it, walking along the road?' Karima asked.

'It's the fastest route.' I shrugged. 'We just have to be ready to get out of the way if anything comes along.'

I was trying to work out what Shelby and Ramzan's game plan would be. Would they wait until morning before closing in on the location of the tracker, or would they decide to come for us in the early hours when we were most likely to be asleep?

Second-guessing the enemy was a mug's game, and in this case was made more complicated by the fact that Shelby and Ramzan were different. Ramzan was more cautious. It would have been him on the rifle. He liked to cover all the angles, leave nothing to chance. Shelby was the more headstrong of the two, which made him the unpredictable element. If he got an idea into his head he might just go for it, regardless of the consequences, to himself or others.

We walked along the road in silence.

'It's beautiful,' said Karima, breaking into my thoughts. We stopped for a moment to look up. The sky was so thick with stars it was impossible to estimate their number. 'Do you think we'll get out of here alive?' she asked quietly.

'Of course,' I said. I started to walk on but Karima grasped my arm. She turned and kissed me. It was long and passionate, and for a time it distracted me from the feeling that we were in a very exposed place. Then I pulled back. 'I'm sorry,' I said. 'I'm really not sure where I stand on this.'

'I understand,' she said. 'I just want you to know that I'm sorry for doubting you. Whatever happened in the past, we have to put it behind us.'

'So you're not planning on shooting me?'

She shook her head.

'Let's just take it one step at a time, shall we?'

'That makes sense. For what it's worth, I'm sorry about your friends. They were nice people.'

'Yes, they were.'

We walked on. The road was quiet and we encountered only one more vehicle before we reached the town. A local farmer in an old van that rattled and thumped its way towards us, which gave us plenty of time to duck down out of sight.

The town was quiet. A weekday evening. Everyone was home getting ready for an early night. The glow of television sets flickered behind the curtains of a few windows. Others were dark. We passed a pub that was already closed. When we got down to the harbour master's office the parking area was deserted except for a couple who were sitting in a car smoking.

We held back. I motioned for Karima to step off the road into the shadows. I could make out the bow of the *Whitehavens*. The febrile snap of steel cables against masts echoed across the water. Somewhere the discordant ring of a bell tolled. Other than that, it was quiet. Nothing was moving.

'You think they're here?' Karima whispered. I couldn't answer. There was no way of knowing. I motioned for her to stay back while I went forward. The couple in the car saw me as I drew level with them. They started up the car and drove quietly away.

I had reached the start of the jetty when a voice came out of the darkness.

'Stay perfectly still.'

Shelby stepped out from behind a row of hawthorns holding a pistol. He looked cold, as if he'd been waiting a long time. He waved the gun.

'On your knees.'

I did as I was told.

'Lose the rucksack.'

I slipped it off my shoulders and let it slide to the ground. Shelby pushed it to one side with his foot.

'The problem with you, Brodie, is that you're old-school. When you have a plan, you stick with it come what may.'

I looked up at him. 'You didn't have to kill Henrik.'

'The old man? Well, sorry, pal, but that was your call. If

you hadn't dragged him into your sorry mess, him and the old lady would still be alive.' He circled around me and then leaned over to bring his mouth close to my ear. 'How does that make you feel, knowing you caused their deaths?'

'You didn't have to kill them,' I repeated.

'That's not how it works and you know it. Loose ends. We all hate loose ends, right?'

He reached round to pat under my jacket, making sure to keep the pistol pressed against the back of my head. He found the Beretta and brought it out, tucking it into his pocket.

'This whole thing could have been ended back there in the forest, but no, you had to go running off with your girlfriend. Speaking of which, where is the foxy babe?'

I didn't answer. The thing that really got under Shelby's skin was not being obeyed. He was holding the gun after all. He thought that meant he was in charge. He stepped back and kicked me squarely in the back. I fell forward, managing to bring my arms down in time to break my fall. He leaned over me again.

'You must be getting deaf in your old age. I asked you a question.'

The answer came from behind him.

'I'm here,' said Karima.

Shelby straightened up to face her. I lifted myself back up on to my knees. Karima stood a few feet away.

'Ah, the lady in question,' he said. He eyed her up. 'You disappointed me back there. I thought we had something going.'

'Can't be helped,' she shrugged.

'I have to say, it's a mystery to me what you're doing with this loser.' He gestured at me with the gun he was holding.

'Maybe you're right.'

'OK.' Shelby turned that over in his head. He looked at me. 'Are you saying you're having second thoughts?'

'Maybe.' She shrugged again. 'I'm not sure I'm cut out for a life at sea.'

'Yeah, I hear that. Ahoy matey!' Shelby sniggered at his own wit. 'Still, all due respect. I mean, you're a fine-looking woman but I would need some more incentive.'

'How about half a million in diamonds?'

Shelby cocked his head to one side. He winked down at me.

'She's quick on the draw, eh?'

'I'm good for it,' said Karima. 'Why do you think Donny wanted me taken care of?'

'We've been through all that. It's nothing to do with you. It's him Donny wanted.'

'I know, I heard. I mean, why would he send you after me and tell you I have five million of his?'

'Five?' Shelby licked his lips. 'You said half.'

'That's all I have on me,' she said. 'Besides, I'm not giving you all of it. I earned it.'

'Well, to be clear, it actually belongs to Donny.' He paused for a second. 'No, I don't believe it. You couldn't have taken that much without him noticing.'

'Why not? I'm very good at what I do. He didn't even know it was missing. You know Donny. Numbers aren't his thing. He deals with people, people like you.'

Shelby gave a loud sniff. He wasn't sure if she was dissing him or not, but he wanted to hear more.

Karima obliged. 'Donny likes to spend cash. He has no real idea how much is being put where. Only I did.'

'So he found out as soon as you left?'

'Not exactly.' She smiled.

It was rather a foxy smile, even I had to admit that.

'I siphoned the money into so many different accounts, he had no idea where it was or how much it was. I told you,' she said. She had her hands in the pockets of her jacket. She stepped towards him. 'I'm good at what I do.'

Shelby was licking his lips. She had him eating out of her hand. What I couldn't see was how she was going to convert this into an opportunity for us to get round him. Or maybe 'us' wasn't a part of this plan.

'You crafty bastard!' Shelby said with a laugh, looking back at me. 'This is why you let her go? You wanted all that money for yourself.'

I shrugged. 'You can't blame me.'

'No, damn right. I'd have done the same myself.' He turned

back to Karima. 'I'd have done a lot more to her and all. So where is this half a million?'

Karima lifted up her handbag. 'Right here,' she said.

Shelby smelled a rat. He shook his head. 'I went through that. There's no half a million in there.'

'You know all about me, right?'

'Uh huh,' mumbled Shelby. He glanced at me. He didn't see where this was going. Karima was unzipping her bag.

'You know I used to live in Amsterdam.' She waited for Shelby to nod. 'What's Amsterdam famous for?' She was holding up a packet of tampons.

'Tampons?' Shelby frowned.

'Diamonds,' corrected Karima. She opened the box and extracted one. She held the little tube up. 'The thing about uncut diamonds is that they are virtually untraceable. They can be traded almost anywhere in the world, and they don't take up much space.'

'Jesus,' muttered Shelby. 'You've been keeping them up your snatch?'

Karima was moving as she spoke. She lifted her arm high.

'What are you doing?' he asked.

'How do I know I can trust you?'

'What do you need to know?' Shelby asked. 'We dump this loser and head off into the wild blue yonder. You and me and the five million.'

She was shaking her head. 'I'm not sure I want to share it with you. I'm not sure I want to share it with anyone.'

'Hey.' Shelby grinned, holding his arms wide. 'Don't be like that.'

By now Karima had reached the edge of the quay. The water was just below her. She raised her hand again.

'Hey, wait a second!' Shelby shouted, beginning to panic. 'Don't do anything stupid.'

'How do I know I can trust you? What about your partner, where is he?'

'You don't need to worry about him,' Shelby reassured her. 'I can take care of him.' He took another step towards her, stretching out his hand. 'This is about us, darling.'

Karima swung her arm back and tossed the tampon high over her head and into the water.

Shelby rushed forward. He was swearing and stamping his feet. He didn't hear me at all. He didn't hear anything, not even when I sliced through his hamstring with the survival knife. While he was occupied with Karima I had managed to reach into the rucksack pocket and grab the knife.

He let out a scream as he sank down on to one knee, clutching the back of his leg. I stuck the knife into his side. I knew where to put it. It came in low and went up under his ribs and straight into his heart. But I must have been out of practice because my aim was off. He began to struggle. I levered myself on to him, holding him down with my weight, my left hand clamped over his mouth, my right hand twisting the hilt of the knife. Shelby was strong and he was fighting back. The blood was warm, flooding over my hand, making it hard to hold on to the slippery hilt. For a few moments I thought we were done for. Then, just as suddenly, it was over. Shelby stopped fighting. He gave a deep sigh and lay still. I waited for a few moments, not daring to release my grip until I was sure. Then I sat up and pushed him off me. I dragged the knife out of his ribcage and wiped the blade on his clothes. When I looked up I saw Karima watching me with horror.

'It was either him or us,' I said.

She nodded silently. I looked up at her. She was scared. I was afraid she was going to scream.

'You were good, though,' I said. 'I have to say, I was almost convinced myself.'

'How do you know I wasn't telling the truth?' she asked.

I straightened up. 'I don't. But I think you're too smart to throw a fortune in diamonds away like that.' I gestured at Shelby. 'Let me finish dealing with this.'

'Right.'

I dragged the body across the quay and back through the bushes where Shelby had been hiding. There was a shallow escarpment and I rolled him down it. I left him there and staggered over to the shoreline. I knelt down and felt the cool water running over my hands. I thought I was going to be sick and I stayed there, head down, waiting for the nausea to pass. Eventually I walked back up the narrow little pebble beach and climbed the escarpment.

When I reached Karima she was sitting down, staring at the ground. She seemed surprised to see me when she looked up. She saw the blood on my clothes.

'Are you hurt?' she asked.

'No,' I said. 'I'm fine.' I knelt beside her and put my hands on her shoulders. She was shaking, going into shock.

'I can't deal with all this . . .' she said, her voice breaking. 'This death.'

'We're almost done.'

She had tears in her eyes. She wiped them away from her cheeks and sniffed. 'What about the other one?'

'I don't see him and I don't see the car. I'm assuming he's looking for us somewhere else.'

'OK.' She nodded. 'So what do we do?'

'We get on the boat and leave, just like we planned.'

She looked doubtful. 'Can we really do that?'

'We have to.' I stood up and stretched out my hand to her. 'Come on, it's not much further.'

After a moment she nodded her agreement and took my hand. We had to move quickly now. Ramzan could be back at any moment.

I slung the rucksack over one shoulder and grabbed Karima by the elbow. I wanted to steady her and at the same time reassure her. Whatever happened in the long run, we had to get through this together. We walked the last few metres to the jetty and then made our way along it. I stopped from time to time to look back, but I saw nothing. A solitary car went by on the road. Not Ramzan's Audi. It sped off along the coast, the headlights scything through the black night as they rose with the hill.

The boat was almost at the end of the jetty. It was moored just as it should be. I studied it for signs of change. The tarp was still in place over the cockpit. I stepped aboard, undid the rubber fastenings and rolled it clear. I switched on the ignition and checked the electrical circuits were working. I motioned for Karima to come aboard.

'Stay low,' I said. I pressed the button to engage the starter. The engine came to life, filling the air with a gentle rumble that sounded as loud as thunder to my ears. I moved swiftly, untying the moorings before hopping back aboard and stepping into the cockpit to grab the wheel. As we puttered slowly free of the jetty I kept an eye on the shore. We weren't out of trouble yet. If Ramzan pulled up now with that high-powered rifle he could still do a lot of damage.

'Down below you'll find a couple of life jackets,' I said. 'Here,' I went to undo the hatch door, but she beat me to it, waved me back.

'I can do that. You focus on getting us out of here in one piece.'

She disappeared down the steps into the cabin. I steered gently round the end of the jetty. Once we were on the other side of the big pier we would be shielded from the shore by the fishing boats moored alongside it.

The water was black and silky. I could see lights along the shore. Ahead of us to the south the ridge of the Cuillins of Skye was visible. To my right the hillside came into view. I didn't have to look hard to pinpoint Henrik and Mary's place. It stuck out of the dark like a beacon. They had set it on fire. I could see the flames rising up into the night sky, glowing embers breaking loose and flying up in little flurries. There was a set of flashing blue lights up there already and another set moving along the road. A fire engine. I watched it slow as it turned on to the track to go up to the house. I remembered walking down that hill this afternoon. It felt like a lifetime ago.

By now we were free of the harbour, still moving slowly, with the bay opening up on either side. The engine was still low so as not to draw attention. I was sailing without navigation lights. It was dangerous but I couldn't take the chance of being spotted.

My eyes were adjusting to the darkness. I knew these waters fairly well, even though it was a while since I'd been out, especially in the dark. I remembered the last time I'd been here with Henrik for a day's fishing. We'd been trailed by dolphins for over an hour that afternoon. That was already getting on for three years ago. I had sworn to myself, as we came in with the sun setting behind us, that I would find a way of spending more time here. There was just something magical about the place. There always would be, but now I knew that a chapter in my life had ended. This place would always be a reminder of Henrik and Mary. I took a long last look at the blaze on the hillside and turned my attention to the sea ahead. As I reached over to flip on the GPS chart I realized that something was wrong.

Somewhere at the back of my mind I must have already registered it. I knew it instinctively when Karima reached for the hatch to go down below. It should have been locked. It wasn't. I'd had other things on my mind – and there was always the possibility that I had forgotten to lock it when we had come on board to store the provisions – but I had logged it anyway. I reached behind me for the Beretta that was tucked into the back of my waistband.

'Karima?'

There was no reply. I pushed the throttle back to a quarter speed and set the wheel for open waters. I quietly checked there was a bullet in the breech, then I ducked and stepped slowly down through the hatch.

'Hello, Brodie,' said Ramzan.

THIRTY-NINE

He was standing in the middle of the floor with Karima clasped tightly to him, his right forearm locked around her throat. Ramzan was left-handed. In that hand he was holding what looked like Derek Sylvan's fancy Sig Sauer.

'Throw the gun on to the bunk over there.' He nodded. 'Gently.'

I did so. I could see the terror in Karima's eyes, but there was nothing I could do about that. She had a gun barrel pressed to her temple. That was enough to put the fear of God into most people.

'I'm curious,' I said. 'Just as a matter of interest, how did you find out about the boat?'

'Actually it was Shelby. He said this is the ends of the earth. Why the fuck would anyone come to such a godforsaken place? It was a good question. I knew you well enough to know that if you were coming here it had to be for a reason. Either you were planning to lay low or you had a means of transport. So I called Donny. He sends his regards, by the way. Anyway, according to him, he was curious about how you used to just take off and disappear for days on end. This was a few years ago. One time he decided to send someone to follow you.' Ramzan gave a shrug. 'Donny hates the idea of people having secrets. So that's how he knew about this place.'

'He never told me,' I said.

'Why would he? This way he always has you at a disadvantage.' He paused. 'What happened to Shelby?'

'He lost focus.'

Ramzan nodded. 'That was always his problem. If I told him once, I told him a thousand times.'

'Some people never listen,' I said. I looked at Karima. 'How are we going to resolve this?'

'Well, the way I see it,' Ramzan said, 'we don't have much choice. We are heading out to open sea, I take it?'

I nodded.

'Good,' he said. 'Then we may as well get comfortable for a while.'

'Do you mind if I go back up top? I don't want us to run aground by accident.'

'That would be a shame,' agreed Ramzan. 'Go ahead. But no tricks.' He dragged Karima down on to the bunk with him and sat there, his left arm around her neck, the gun barrel to her temple. Then he reached into his pocket for a zip tie and strapped her right hand to the frame of the bunk.

I went up the steps to the aft deck and stepped into the cockpit. I took hold of the wheel and swung it. We were still moving slowly. I was trying to buy some time. I needed to think. I considered all the options, including running the yacht on to the rocks. There was no guarantee that would work. It would certainly destroy the *Whitehavens*.

My army rucksack was lying on the deck. It contained the survival knife. To reach the bag I had to step across the deck. Ramzan would be able to see me through the hatch. I could feel the swell beginning to rise as the water beneath us got deeper. The deck shuddered as a heavy wave hit the bow. If I turned hard west that would get worse. Perhaps there was some way of destabilizing the vessel and then jumping Ramzan.

Before I could develop my plan any further, Ramzan appeared in the hatchway. He came up the steps and leaned against the side of the companionway, holding on to the grab rail for support.

'So, how are conditions up here?'

'You know anything about boats?' I asked, my eyes on the water.

Ramzan laughed. 'Me, I'm a city boy. But hey, how difficult can it be?'

'Wise words,' I said. 'How far out are we going?'

He looked over his shoulder. 'A little further, not much. There must be tides out here.'

'Tides? Is that what you're looking for?'

'I'll be frank with you, Brodie,' he said. 'I don't like this any more than you do, but it has to be done. I can't go home empty-handed now.'

'What difference does it make?' I asked. 'You let us go, nobody sees us ever again. We could make it worth your while.'

'Sure, I've heard it all before, remember? Cut the engine,' he said. 'This is far enough.'

'If I cut the engine we'll start to drift.'

Ramzan thought about that for a minute. He didn't look too comfortable. He glanced back towards the shore. I could see him calculating how easy it would be to get back there.

'Turn her around,' he said. 'And go slow. This'll have to do.'

'Look, I understand this is about me, but you should be able to let her go for five million, right?'

'Five million what? Fish?' Ramzan laughed at his own joke.

'Dollars, euros, whatever you want. In diamonds, right here.'

'Is that what you tried on Shelby?' Ramzan asked. 'Even if it was true, why shouldn't I just take them anyway?'

'Because,' I said, 'we're men of our word, you and I. Honour has to count for something. You let her go and you get the diamonds. Nobody else knows about them.'

He thought about that for a time. The hull was rocking back and forth in the swell. He didn't want to be out here a moment longer than was necessary.

'Where are they, these diamonds?' Ramzan asked slowly.

'Right there, in the bag.' I nodded at the rucksack. He looked at it, and then back to me. He was still holding the Sig Sauer.

'You'd better not be trying it on with me, Brodie, or I'll skin her alive in front of you.'

'We're soldiers, Raz, remember? We do what we have to do. That's all we have.'

I let the words hang there. I knew he'd take the bait. He had nothing to lose and everything to gain. He leaned over and pulled the bag towards him.

'Side pocket,' I said. 'Down at the bottom.'

He unzipped the pocket and thrust his hand in. To do this Ramzan had to let go of the grab rail. He was off balance. As he dug around, I spun the wheel. The boat swung round. A heavy wave hit us side on. Ramzan was thrown towards the gunwale. He put out a hand to stop himself going over the side.

I was already on top of him. I had a length of mooring rope in my hands and twisted it around his neck. We rolled until I was underneath him with my legs around him from behind. His arms were still free and flailing about as I tightened the rope around his neck, cutting off the supply of blood to his brain. In a few seconds he would pass out. I felt him scrabbling around for the gun. He managed to get it and let off two quick shots before the Sig Sauer tumbled from his hand. I kept the pressure up until I was sure that he was dead. I felt the life go out of him and he slumped back over me. I pushed him aside and scrambled out from underneath him.

It took a moment to realize that he was actually dead. I picked up the pistol anyway and threw it overboard. I went through his pockets and found the Beretta, which I tucked back into the rucksack. Then I got up and corrected our course.

The deck settled down as we headed out again. I looked down at Ramzan. His head lolled from side to side.

'Karima,' I called out. 'It's OK. It's all over.'

There was no reply. I suddenly wondered if Ramzan had decided to take care of her before he came up from below. Quickly, I fixed the wheel and then went down through the hatch.

She was still sitting on the floor next to the bunk, her hand tethered to the frame. She was slumped over to one side. I knew something was very wrong.

'Karima?' I knelt down in front of her. She lifted her head and looked at me, her eyes unfocussed. I found a knife and cut the zip tie that fastened her wrist to the bunk frame. 'Karima?'

She lifted her head and opened her eyes. 'I think I've been shot.'

'You have to stay awake. You hear me?'

She murmured something that I couldn't catch. I took her hand gently away from her midriff. One of Ramzan's wild shots must have hit her. The front of her jersey was soaked with blood. I lifted it slowly to take a look. I'd seen stomach wounds before and this was not good. She started to push me away.

'No. No,' she moaned.

'Wait, wait!' I scrabbled around to try and find a first aid kit.

She put out a hand. 'Stop, please. Just . . .' She tried to smile. 'Just sit with me.'

I slipped on to the floor alongside her. 'Listen, you just hold on. I'll swing around. We can be ashore again in twenty minutes. We have to get you to the hospital.'

'No,' she whispered. 'Don't go anywhere. Stay here. Just hold me.'

I put my arms around her shoulders and drew her to me. She leaned into me with a sigh.

'Oh, that's good,' she said. 'I just want to stay like this for a time.' She was silent for a moment. 'Can you feel it?' she whispered. 'It's like we're floating off into the future. And everything is possible. Isn't that amazing.'

'Yes,' I said, my voice hoarse. 'It's amazing.'

'We can go where we like. We can be who we want to be.' She gave a little laugh. 'We're free.'

I held her to me. I could feel the breath fluttering unevenly through her body, beating like tiny wings trapped inside her.

'Can you see the stars?' she said.

'Yes,' I said. It was almost true. I could see a narrow sliver of sky through the hatch, but no stars.

'I'm so happy,' she said, 'I feel like crying.'

I don't know how long I held her like that. After a time I could feel that it was over. I shifted my weight and let her down slowly. I drew a blanket down to cover her. I stood there for a moment, swaying in the dark. I hardly knew where I was. I felt numb and alone.

I stumbled back up the steps to the aft deck and rolled Ramzan's body over the side. There was a brief splash and then he was gone. I had no idea which way the tide would carry him. I didn't much care. Then I stepped down into the cockpit and took hold of the wheel. I corrected the course slightly, then, feeling the wind on my back, I moved forward, untied the main sail and hauled it up. The wind took hold of it and I felt the deck tilt slightly. I went back to the wheel. We were headed straight out into the open sea. All around me the water was slick and black and shiny, like the skin of some great forgotten creature. Ahead of me the sky was now truly filled with stars. A vast canopy of glittering lights. I blinked to clear my eyes. I had to smile. I had no idea where I was headed. It didn't seem to matter all that much anymore.